An Ohnita Harbor Mystery

The Secrets of

STILL

WATERS

CHASM

From New York Times Bestselling Author

PATRICIA CRISAFULLI

The Secrets of

STILL
WATERS
CHASM

PATRICIA CRISAFULLI

woodhall press
Woodhall Press | Norwalk, CT

Woodhall Press, 81 Old Saugatuck Road, Norwalk, CT 06855
WoodhallPress.com

Cover design: Jessica Dionne
Layout artist: L.J. Mucci

Library of Congress Cataloging-in-Publication Data available
ISBN 978-1-954907-64-5   (paper: alk paper)
ISBN 978-1-954907-65-2   (electronic)

First Edition
Distributed by Independent Publishers Group
(800) 888-4741

Printed in the United States of America

This is a work of fiction. Names, characters, businesses, events and incidents are the products of the author's imagination. Any resemblance
to actual persons, living or dead, or actual events is purely coincidental.

AUTHOR'S NOTE

Still Waters Chasm won't be found on any map of New York State, but some of the places that inspired this fictional spot can be: Ausable Chasm, "the Grand Canyon of the Adirondacks"; the Salmon River Reservoir at the outer edge of Oswego County; and the Finger Lakes in the western part of New York State that do, indeed, go down to more than 600 feet in depth. I combined them all into one place, and any geological anomalies that result are the fault of my overactive imagination.

A special thanks to Loren Fleckenstein, good friend and sailing enthusiast, who helped me channel the inventiveness of Robert Fulton into a fictional last experiment with the Nautilus. I also consulted Cynthia Owen Philip's extensive biography of Fulton.

Sincere thanks to Ivy Gocker in her previous role as library director at The Adirondack Experience, The Museum on Blue Mountain Lake, for sharing so many details with me—from the moose head to the "secret" door.

I am forever grateful for authors Ava Green, Nicole Apelian, Claude Davis and Arin Murphy-Hiscock for their wonderful books I consulted regarding the plants in this book. Most of all, the generous conversations with clinical herbalist and apothecary Heather Nic an Fhleisdeir, in her apothecary Mrs. Thompson's Herbs, Gifts & Folklore in Eugene, Oregon, guided me in building Lucinda's garden around the story and true-to-life conversations about herbs. Any errors I may have inadvertently introduced are mine alone.

To my husband, Joe Tulacz, with all my love—
Partner, Best Friend, North Star

The woods are lovely, dark and deep,
But I have promises to keep . . .

—Robert Frost

CHAPTER
ONE

Gabriela ran the palm of her hand over the feathery ferns, smiling at the tickle against her skin. All around them the woods closed in, except for this tiny oasis where the conifers had thinned and an oak tree had fallen some time ago. She sat on the ground, smelling the loamy scent of decay and new growth, and Daniel stretched out beside her, eyes closed. They had followed a narrow path off the main trail, just to see where it led, and had stopped here for water and a snack. Now it looked like Daniel was planning to take a nap.

She studied the ground for a moment, then flopped down beside him. Something sharp poked her in the side through her sweatshirt and long-sleeved top, and Gabriela reached under her ribs to remove a stick. Relaxing, she rested her head on Daniel's shoulder and watched tiny spotlights of sunshine dance across the ground. Her sigh became a deep hum.

Rolling onto her back, Gabriela gazed straight through a gap in the leafy canopy and into a patch of September sky. She felt the heat Daniel radiated, one of the dozen small things she'd delighted in learning about him over the past two and a half months of their relationship. He turned and kissed her deeply. When he pulled back, Gabriela opened her eyes and scanned every line and angle of his face.

"There's nobody else around," he said.

Gabriela propped herself on her elbow. "Except the next hiker to come up this trail."

Daniel leaned over, gave her a quick kiss, then sat up. "You're right." He winced slightly as he rotated his shoulder. "And I keep forgetting I'm pushing fifty. This ground isn't easy on the back."

"Forty-eight isn't fifty," Gabriela said. Six months ago, she had turned forty. She liked that Daniel had a few years on her, but not too many. Sitting up, she tossed aside another piece of tree branch. "I keep getting jabbed with these."

Daniel extended his long legs and stretched. "Hey, I thought you were the outdoorsy type, or have you been leading me on all this time? You're probably going to tell me you're afraid of bears." A laugh caressed his words.

"Uh-huh." Gabriela picked two leaves out of Daniel's straight gray hair, which fell nearly to his shoulders.

He gathered a ponytail at the nape of his neck and tied it with a leather cord. "I'm serious. There are bears up here."

"And lions and tigers." Gabriela got to her feet.

"I've seen black bears up here. And they've spotted a few wolves in the Adirondacks."

As she hoisted her backpack, Gabriela imagined yellow eyes peering out of the woods and her thoughts soured. Would those animals slink away from them, not wanting to be seen, or would they sense the vulnerability of two humans alone? Suddenly she felt certain something really was watching them.

Her chest tightened and her breath quickened. They had not seen another person since leaving Daniel's SUV in a shallow turnoff at the side of the road—a long way away. Her ears strained to detect any sound other than the wind swishing the branches. A twig snapped and the clearing seemed to darken, as if thick clouds blotted out the sky. Her throat constricted, and she fingered the one-inch scar on her throat from a knife that, just three months ago, had flirted with her carotid artery.

Breathe! Gabriela pulled her mind back from an abyss of panic. She inhaled to a count of five, her lungs filling to the maximum, then exhaled to the same rhythm. The fist around her gut loosened; her galloping heart slowed. With each deep breath her vision improved, and Gabriela knew that meant her adrenaline levels had dropped. Glancing over, she saw Daniel adjusting the laces of his hiking boots as if nothing had happened. *Because nothing did*, she scolded herself.

Everything seemed to trigger her these days. Gabriela thought back to a week before, when her mother had dropped a handful of silverware on the kitchen counter and the metallic clatter had made tears spring to her eyes. She hated these episodes of feeling out of control, even though the therapist she'd seen a few times had assured her that such reactions were normal after a major trauma. No, Gabriela told herself, panic attacks and irrational fears had to be faced and purged. She'd found an article in *Psychology Today* about exposure therapy, in which patients confronted their phobias instead of avoiding them. While that treatment normally happened in a safe environment controlled by a therapist, Gabriela told herself she didn't have that luxury. She'd deal with her traumas head-on, whenever and wherever they arose, and she'd do it on her own.

"So," Gabriela began, forcing cheerfulness into her voice, "how far to the lake?"

"Well, this little detour probably added a mile to our trek." Daniel said. "Once we get back to the main trail, it's another mile and a half. You tired?"

Gabriela took in another deep breath. "Good to go."

She pulled a red bandana out of the side pocket of her backpack and rolled it into a headband to tie back her shoulder-length dark curly hair that proclaimed her Italian-American heritage as much as her name: Gabriela Annunciata Domenici. As she adjusted the knot and tucked in the ends, Gabriela watched Daniel put on a dark blue billed cap embroidered with DRD—his company name and his initials for Daniel Red Deer. She fondly recalled the day, just five months ago, she'd picked DRD Roofing out of an online listing because half a tree had fallen on her house. How much her life had changed since then. Three months ago, she added solemnly to herself, her life had almost ended.

Gabriela yanked her head to her left, as if looking away from a gruesome scene even though it remained in her mind. She focused her attention on the carpet of leaves and pine needles and named the colors she saw underfoot: green, brown, gray, and the yellow-orange of one leaf. Calmness returned. The trick she'd read about—deliberately noticing the smallest details to immerse herself in the here and now—had worked.

"My sunglasses." Daniel patted his pockets.

Gabriela blinked rapidly as she fully rejoined the moment and helped him search the ground.

"Found them!" Daniel called out.

Gabriela continued scanning the clearing and noticed a faint indentation in the undergrowth on the far side. It lay in the opposite direction of the narrow path that had led them off the main trail to this place. She walked toward it.

"This way." Daniel pointed in the other direction.

She beckoned him over. "Let's see where this goes."

Daniel pushed back the bill of his cap. "Okay, but you're adding time and distance to our hike."

"Yes—I know. I promise we won't go that far."

The path soon faded into the forest floor and seemed to scramble in a dozen possible directions. Gabriela looked behind at their footprints pressed into the damp earth. Assured that they could retrace their steps and not get lost, she continued a few more yards, then stopped. Rugged tread stamped the ground. Kicking away old leaves, Gabriela studied the mark. "Somebody walked here—and probably not that long ago."

Daniel tipped his head back and blew out his breath. "You want to keep going?"

She felt his impatience—they were supposed to be hiking to the lake—but couldn't quell her curiosity. "Just a little farther."

The boot prints became more visible, and Gabriela followed them until she could see bright daylight ahead. She and Daniel pushed through a thicket of bramble bushes and emerged into a sun-bleached space—a hundred feet across, Gabriela estimated, maybe more. Within it, every tree had been cut down and the undergrowth bulldozed to bare earth. It looked like a wound, exposing desiccated earth.

"Shit," Daniel hissed.

In the center of the clearing sat a heavy-duty truck with a reinforced cab. It carried what looked like a compressor enclosed in a wire mesh cage; below it, a thick slab of metal fitted flat against the ground, connected to the truck by hydraulic arms.

Gabriela walked around the truck, not certain of what she hoped to find, other than some clue as to why someone had parked this equipment here. When she completed her circumnavigation, she met Daniel, who stood at the back of the truck. He laced his fingers through the weave of the wire mesh. "This isn't for logging, that's for damn sure," he said.

"Why cut down every tree just to park this monstrosity?" Gabriela examined the doors of the cab a second time, looking for a name or logo, but found only shiny black paint. At five-foot-two, she couldn't make the first step onto the running board to look inside, but Daniel could.

"The bastards left the keys in the ignition. I'd like to throw them into the woods," he said.

Gabriela angled her gaze upward through the window on the driver's side. A blue neon light danced around the rearview mirror—a sensor of some sort, she guessed. "We'd better go."

Daniel kept walking across the clearing. He stopped, and Gabriela caught up with him in five steps. The land dipped precipitously. Below the rim rested a bulldozer and two more black-cabbed trucks, though much smaller than the massive one behind them. A dirt road snaked through the trees.

"What the hell are they building up here?" Gabriela asked. "This can't be for somebody's cabin."

Daniel took off his hat and swiped his arm across his forehead. "Could be another access road. Or maybe the Forest Service wants a new fire tower, though you'd think they'd put it higher on the ridge."

The longer she looked at this site, the more dread plucked at her nerves. She gulped to get enough oxygen into her lungs. "Let's go." She took Daniel's arm and pulled him toward the path.

As they trudged over large clods of dirt, she saw the remains of a small rabbit, its body flattened in the track made by some piece of machinery—life literally squeezed out of it. She pressed her eyes shut, blocking the constriction in her own body.

———

As they retraced their steps, Gabriela told herself she'd just been triggered. There was no logical reason to fear a truck at a construction site. When Daniel started listing possible reasons for what they'd seen,

Gabriela named every idea she could come up with—a valuable stand of timber, a remote vacation home, a cluster of cabins—but with each suggestion they came back to two incongruities: clear-cutting such a large area and a gigantic truck that was obviously not for construction.

When they finally reached the main trail, their pace quickened. Gabriela felt her spirits lift as they walked among maples just starting to show the blush of their fall colors, rustling oaks that rained down acorns, smooth-barked beeches, and hemlocks with graceful boughs. The scarred, bulldozed earth seemed as far away as a half-forgotten nightmare.

The September sun rose above the trees and stood nearly at its apex. Gabriela paused to retrieve her water bottle from her backpack and took four long swallows. She offered it to Daniel, who drank deeply. When they'd had their fill, she replaced the bottle and reached for his hand to continue walking. She recited what she'd read the night before about this part of northern New York State: how during the most recent ice age great glaciers had carved deep lakes and chasms and piled debris and earth into tall foothills. Just thirty miles from where they hiked rose the Adirondack Mountains, which contained some of the oldest rocks in the United States—more than one billion years old. "Who knows? Maybe some of these stones too," she said, kicking one with the toe of her hiking shoes.

"Always the librarian," Daniel replied.

Gabriela caught the deepening smile lines around his eyes. "Guilty. But I like knowing stuff."

"And I like hearing it."

The trail curved to the right, the trees parted, and Gabriela gasped at her first glimpse of the rocky walls of Still Waters Chasm. Taking slow steps toward the edge, Gabriela peered over, expecting a sheer drop-off. Instead, the chasm walls sloped downward to the long, thin Still Waters Lake, nearly a hundred feet below. On the other side, rocks lay in horizontal bands like the layers of a cake, except where they had heaved up, in some places nearly vertically.

Gabriela scanned the rugged land stretching in all directions. Not one human-made structure could be seen. "I can see why you love it here."

Daniel came up beside her and placed his hand gently on her back. "It's one of my favorite places. We used to come here two or three times during the summer and fall."

We, Gabriela registered. Daniel and his late wife, Vicki. It only made sense that every one of his favorite places would be tied up in memories of her. Aiming a big smile in Daniel's direction, Gabriela thanked him for bringing her there. "I've been looking forward to seeing it since you first told me about this place."

"Me, too."

They walked hand in hand as the forest transitioned from oaks and hemlocks to shrubs. Then the trail flattened out, and they stepped onto the stony shoreline of Still Waters Lake. Crouched at the edge, where tiny waves beat a light rhythm, Gabriela dipped her fingers into the water. Yelping, she withdrew her hand. "My God, that's cold."

"Never warms up." Daniel explained that the lake plunged to more than six hundred feet deep in the middle.

"Wait. You're kidding, right? Six hundred feet?" Gabriela interrupted.

"Carved out by the glaciers, remember?" Daniel nudged her gently. "So I get to teach you something."

Gabriela listened intently to his explanation of a river that had flowed here some fifty thousand years ago, carving out a valley. Then the glaciers descended, gouging out the earth and making this chasm deeper and wider. The melting glaciers formed the lake, now fed by snow runoff from the higher elevations and springs that bubbled out of the ground and flowed through Still Waters Lake and into the Little Rocky River. He pointed to the right, beyond their line of sight. "Canoeists come up Little Rocky to the lake. I've done it once or twice, myself."

Canoeing would be strenuous, and the thought of tipping over into that icy water scared her, but Gabriela pushed past those reservations. "Let's try it sometime. I've gone kayaking, so canoeing can't be that hard."

Daniel palpated her bicep. "I'd say you're strong enough for it."

Gabriela pumped her arms in the air. "Lifting all those books every day."

They followed the curve of the lake, skirting a small marsh studded with cattails. Up ahead, the bleached hulk of a tree trunk rested on the shoreline and, beside it, an upturned canoe, its deep green finish glistening in the sun. Gabriela looked behind them, wondering if they should walk in the other direction to preserve the illusion of being the only people here, but Daniel continued forward. On the other side of the tree trunk, hidden from sight until they reached the canoe, a man stretched out, faceup, on the rocks.

For an instant, Gabriela recalled Daniel reclining on the ground and wondered if this man might be sleeping. Then a faint gurgling noise grabbed her full attention. She dropped her backpack and rushed over to him. He looked to be about thirty, dressed in jeans and a plaid shirt with a gray quilted vest. His body trembled stiffly, his legs and arms rigid against stones along the shoreline. "Help me roll him on his side," she ordered.

Daniel grabbed the man by the shoulders, lifted him away from a puddle of vomit around his head. The man's body shuddered, then went limp.

CHAPTER
TWO

Gabriela began to detach, as if floating above the scene and watching herself attending to the man while Daniel waved his cell phone in the air and complained about getting no signal. *Focus*, she commanded herself, and recalled the first-aid training she had received years ago and the refresher courses she took periodically. Pressing her fingers into the man's neck, she felt for a pulse. *Nothing*—or perhaps just very faint.

Her vision dimmed, narrowing to a tunnel. To stop it, Gabriela swept her gaze over the water, across the beach, and the woods behind them. She saw another person there, lying on the ground where the stony shoreline met the trees. Her consciousness slammed back into her body, and Gabriela took off, stumbling over rocks to reach a woman. At the sight of the gray face and half-open eyes, Gabriela's perception blurred again, and she shook her head vigorously to clear her brain. Vomit, she noticed, rimmed the woman's mouth and streaked her neatly plaited brown hair. She took note of the woman's jeans and a red quilted vest over a long-sleeved T-shirt.

11

Gabriela tried to detect a pulse but felt only cold flesh. The woman had been dead long enough for her body to cool.

Turning back toward the beach, she saw Daniel splashing the man's face with water. "Come on, wake up!" he yelled.

Piercing the swirl of fear, one thought whipped Gabriela into action: She had to save this man. Rushing over, she knelt beside his body and began rapid chest compressions to a count of thirty, then breathed twice into his mouth. "Go get help," she told Daniel between breaths.

"I'm not leaving you here," he said.

"And I'm not leaving him."

"Then we're both staying."

Gabriela kept up the cycle of compressions and rescue breaths until her muscles began to ache. She then placed Daniel's hands on the man's chest and showed him how to do the compressions while she kept forcing air into the man's lungs. They continued, keeping blood and oxygen flowing to his brain and internal organs. Pains shot down her legs from kneeling on the rocks, and her back ached, but Gabriela didn't stop. "Come on, breathe," she begged.

The man's face grayed to the same pallor as the woman's and his body cooled. Daniel stopped. "He's gone."

Gabriela sank into a seated position on the rocks and pulled her legs into her body, her forehead resting on her knees. Three months ago, other people had saved her. Why couldn't she do the same for this man?

Daniel held up his phone again, then stuffed it into his pocket. "We need to go back up the trail to get a signal."

Gabriela thought of emergency defibrillators, the possibility that trained EMTs could shock the man back to life. "I'll stay and keep up the compressions."

"No, he's dead, and I'm not leaving you here—not after what you've been through."

Tears flooded her eyes and spilled down her cheeks. "Then you stay, and I'll go."

Daniel shook his head. "We'll both go. As soon as we can call, we'll come back."

Gabriela tried another round of compressions and rescue breaths on the man, and Daniel took several photos of both bodies and the shoreline with the bleached tree trunk as a visual map they could text to the EMTs. Before leaving the beach, Gabriela pressed her fingers against the man's neck again but felt nothing except cold, inanimate flesh.

As hard as they pushed themselves, it took twenty-five minutes to reach a spot where they could get cell phone service. Gabriela saw the signal on her phone first and dialed. When the emergency operator answered, her words tumbled out: two people, vomiting, seizure, one dead—the other unresponsive. "We have pictures. We can send them." When the dispatcher asked for their location, Gabriela tried to remember, but her mind blanked and refused to give up the details. She handed the phone to Daniel.

Shaking from exertion, Gabriela lowered herself slowly to the ground. When Daniel ended the call, he reached for her hand. She accepted the help to her feet, then started running back down the trail toward the beach, thinking of only one thing: The man could not die; the paramedics would save him.

"This way," Daniel called out and veered off the trail. Gabriela followed, grabbing at tree trunks to brace herself as they descended directly to the lake. The extreme exertion spent her adrenaline rush, and Gabriela felt calmer but exhausted by the time they reached the lake. Only then did she feel the sting on the backs of her hands and see the bloody scratches from branches and thorns. They'd been gone a total of forty-two minutes.

At the water's edge, smaller stones made better footing as they ran. Chilly water seeped into Gabriela's hiking shoes, giving her mind a point of concentration. Up ahead, the bleached tree trunk lay on the shore. But no canoe, no bodies.

Gabriela and Daniel walked the beach in both directions, calling out every few minutes, but heard only their echoing words bouncing off the chasm walls. After another half hour, a uniformed man emerged through the trees. Sweat darkened the back and sides of his light gray shirt. Over his shoulder, he carried a portable defibrillator.

State trooper Douglas Morrison introduced himself and explained that the paramedics would arrive within fifteen minutes. Gabriela exchanged a look with Daniel, and they both started speaking, her words spilling over his in a disjointed explanation.

The state trooper leaned over, hands braced against his thighs, and breathed through his mouth. "I thought you said one was dead and one was unresponsive."

"That's true. But when we came back from making the call up the trail, they weren't here anymore," Gabriela explained.

Daniel showed the photos on his phone. "The woman's body was cold." He swiped the screen to another photo. "The man was having a seizure, then stopped breathing. Gabriela did CPR and showed me how to do chest compressions, but he never came around."

Trooper Morrison gave them both a hard look. "And now they've disappeared."

"We didn't make this up," Gabriela said.

"It would be a crime if you did."

Gabriela pointed to a thin crust of dried vomit on one of the rocks. "Here—this is where we found him." She ran over to where the woman's body had been and insisted the state trooper see the small patch of vomit there.

Trooper Morrison studied the photos on Daniel's phone again and asked them to describe exactly what they had seen and done when they arrived at the site. They repeated the story, word for word. The state trooper's radio crackled; the paramedics had arrived. He told them that whoever had been on the beach must have recovered sufficiently to leave on their own.

Gabriela spoke up. "Officer, we are professional people. Daniel owns DRD Roofing, and I'm the executive director of the Ohnita Harbor Public Library. We know what we saw."

"You work at the old library that looks like a castle?" the state trooper asked.

"I'm the executive director," she repeated.

"You folks had some serious trouble there a few months ago. Bunch of art thefts and a couple of murders."

Gabriela nodded, not wanting to discuss the scandal and how close she'd come to being murder victim number three at the hands of the president of the library's board of trustees. Instinctively, she put her fingers to her neck and felt the scar.

When Trooper Morrison suggested they look farther down the beach, they walked the shoreline together, scanning for any signs of two people and their canoe. The longer they walked, the more Gabriela knew they would find nothing.

The state trooper planted his hands on his hips and looked across the lake. "Maybe your campers had too much to drink. After they puked and passed out, they felt better. They came to while you were gone."

Gabriela shook her head. "That just doesn't seem possible. The woman was completely unresponsive."

"Maybe your CPR worked on the man, and he carried her out of here. Who knows?"

The thought cheered her a little. At least the people hadn't died. No matter how implausible it seemed, at least one, maybe both, of the campers must have regained consciousness, packed up their stuff, and left. Then a sickening realization came to her. She and Daniel had left their backpacks on the beach when they ran up the trail to get help. Now their gear was missing too. Her forehead furrowed. "They took our stuff. So much for being good Samaritans."

"What are you missing?" Trooper Morrison asked.

"Food, water, extra socks," Daniel said. "Good thing I have my keys on me. My wallet's in the car."

"Same here." Gabriela recalled how she'd tried to stuff her purse into her backpack, then hid it under the front seat instead. Otherwise, her driver's license, credit cards, and everything else would be gone.

As they headed back to the road, Daniel talked with Trooper Morrison, but Gabriela purposefully lagged behind them. She knew what she'd seen: the man's body tensing in a seizure and the woman completely lifeless with no pulse. How could they suddenly feel better, clean themselves up, pack their stuff, and paddle away in a canoe? It was impossible, she told herself, except that was what appeared to have happened.

"What will you do now?" Daniel asked Trooper Morrison when they finally reached the road.

"Check to see if anybody shows up at the emergency room. But given what we found here, I doubt it."

As the state trooper got into the cruiser, Gabriela stopped him. "You do believe us, don't you?" She waited for him to respond.

16

"You came across two people. Your photos show that pretty clearly. But it's obvious they're not dead. We have to assume they're okay, which is a good thing. You folks drive carefully."

The cruiser pulled off the shoulder and back onto the road.

Gabriela's mind alternated between relief that the two campers hadn't died and disgust that they'd simply left and taken her backpack and Daniel's. Maybe they'd been disoriented when they came to and grabbed everything while packing up their canoe. She thought of the ID tags on their backpacks. The campers might phone to return their things. Then they could find out how these two people had recovered so quickly.

CHAPTER

THREE

Every time her cell phone rang, Gabriela expected the call to be from the state police with an update on the two campers. She imagined scenarios: The man and the woman had been hospitalized; they had been treated and released; they had recovered on their own; they had returned her backpack and Daniel's. After three days, Gabriela told herself to let it go. She had enough to occupy her time as the newly appointed executive director of the Ohnita Harbor Public Library, a 160-year-old institution with a gaping budget deficit and too small a staff to run the place.

Built to resemble a Norman castle, the library and its surrounding grounds occupied an entire city block. A month ago, a developer had approached the city with an offer to convert the library into senior residences. The proceeds would more than pay for a smaller, more efficient facility. The new city administration hated the idea—they all loved The Castle, as they affectionately called the library. But increasingly, Gabriela had to admit, it seemed like the solution to all their problems.

Gabriela spent much of the day in her office, working through reports, scheduling staff, parsing out meager resources, and collaborating with City Hall on a grant proposal. But she devoted at least an hour a day to the circulation desk, to spell off the two women who worked there and assure herself that she remained close to the library patrons.

"I can't decide." An elderly woman set two thick volumes on the circulation desk.

On the book spines, Gabriela saw the "921" tag of biographies. One cover promised to reveal the vision of mega-entrepreneur Elon Musk; the other claimed to share the untold story of Elizabeth Taylor, although Gabriela couldn't imagine many unexamined tidbits of Liz's life remained unearthed. "What drew you to these particular books?" she asked.

The woman pursed her lips at Elon Musk. "Well, this young man seems to be everywhere, so I figure I better find out what he's all about." Her mouth relaxed into a smile at the other book. "And who doesn't love Liz?"

"You answered your own question. Read about Elon first, then treat yourself to Liz." Gabriela scanned the woman's card. "And you have thirty days to return them, so you can check both out now."

When the library patron left, Gabriela felt something brush past her ankles. Reaching down, she touched the thick fur on Nathaniel's back, and when she scratched him, his purring amplified. A stray cat, Nathaniel alternated between the library, the police station, and City Hall. With his sleek black coat and white-tipped tail, Nathaniel could be seen napping on the comfortable chairs in the reading nook, and whenever he got into something he shouldn't—like stealing power cords and headsets—the cat streaked out of sight.

Gabriela gave the cat one last scratch. "I have to get back upstairs, but you can come visit me for a treat." Nathaniel blinked his yellow-green eyes at her.

In the late afternoon, Gabriela looked up from her desk at the sound of her son's voice as he said hello to Delmina Duro, who occupied the executive assistant post in the outer administration office. Overhearing his one- and two-word responses to Delmina's questions about school, Gabriela smiled. Having just turned eleven, Ben was still shy, but at least he could converse with adults.

He flopped into the chair opposite her desk. "Can we go?"

"Soon," Gabriela told him as she finished typing an email.

Ben groaned. "Soon means an hour. Can I go back to the park? The other kids are still there."

Gabriela kept typing, then hit the Send button. She had so much more to do but could log on at home that evening. "Done for now. I'll drive you back to the park, but we can only stay half an hour."

The boy scrambled out of the chair and headed for the stairs. Gabriela trailed behind him. "See you tomorrow, Delmina. I'll finish up the board report at home tonight."

"You better catch Ben first." Delmina pointed out the doorway, and they both laughed.

At the park, Ben joined a game of tag with kids his age. As Gabriela walked the perimeter for exercise, she noticed that two of the children in the group were girls who ran just as fast and played just as hard as the boys. She smiled and quickened her step. After thirty minutes, Gabriela raised her arm over her head to signal Ben, but he didn't stop. She stood off to the side, watching her son weave in and out, trying to evade capture until someone got tagged and became "it." Hearing Ben's laughter above the other voices, Gabriela gladly waited for the next break in the action to wave him over. This time he complied and came running, sweaty and dirt-streaked, and looking so happy it made her heart soar.

⁓

At her desk at home that night and all the next day at the library, Gabriela dove into the busyness and heavy workload, finding both solace and distraction from the anxiety that scratched at her nerves. A month ago she had blamed the stress of the job, the crush of mounting responsibilities, and the scandal of murders, thefts, and corruption that had rocked Ohnita Harbor. But since finding the two campers at Still Waters, her fears had escalated, and at times an overwhelming dread enveloped her.

Early on Thursday morning she dropped her keys three times on the front steps of the library before she finally managed to open the heavy wooden doors. Standing there—throat constricted, heart racing, palms dripping sweat—she finally admitted the problem. Every time she entered the Ohnita Harbor Public Library, she returned to the scene of the crime against her. As quickly as she registered the thought, Gabriela tried to dismiss it. But climbing the stairs toward her office, she replayed the scene: She had come to work very early one morning in late June and found her office door ajar. Pushing it open slowly, she'd confronted Don Andreesen, a respected attorney and president of the library's board of trustees, as he rummaged through her desk. She could still see the cold determination in his eyes as he searched for keys to open a cabinet so he could steal a small medieval cross that had been in the library's possession.

Her body stiffened at the memory of seeing the hunting knife in Don's hand—then the prick of the sharp point, the slice of the blade, and the warm stickiness of her own blood flowing down her neck.

She had fought back and stopped him, and now Don faced life in prison for two murders and the attempt on her life. But the ghost of that day still lurked behind every half-closed door and in every creak on the stairs or jagged shadow in the hallway. This place she had come to love she now feared.

"Get a grip," Gabriela hissed at herself as she unlocked the administration suite, passed Delmina's empty desk, and opened her office. She gave the door a shove, letting it bang against the metal waste can beside her desk: a warning shot to anyone—real or imagined—who might be lurking in the corner. She snapped on her office lights and got to work.

An hour later, the library came to life. Gabriela went downstairs to greet Mike, who brought in the book return cart from the outside receptacle, and Francine Clarke as she logged into the circulation system. Delmina bustled in, and Gabriela followed her upstairs to the administration offices, listening to updates, messages, and questions. Gabriela plowed through emails and reports until 9:45, when she met with Delmina to discuss the three Bs, as they jokingly called their constant worries: budget, bills, and building repairs. Too little of the first one, too much of other two. After gathering up her things, Gabriela reminded Delmina that she would return around two o'clock. Even as she considered the amount of work she left behind on her desk, Gabriela confirmed her resolve to complete her mission of the day.

Today's visit would take her to the furthest outreaches of Ohnita County and the tiny two-room library in the Town of Livery, which had closed six months earlier because of a lack of funding and patronage. Even without its library, Gabriela vowed that Livery wouldn't be forgotten. As head of the largest library in the North Country Library System, Gabriela made advocacy for the smaller communities a priority. She would bring a program to Livery at least once a month, even if she had to do it all herself.

At least today I have reinforcements, Gabriela thought with a laugh as she pulled up in front of her mother's house.

"Five minutes late," Agnese Domenici said. "Now we hurry." She pulled a rosary out of her purse.

"Is my driving that bad?" Gabriela teased.

Agnese raised the strand of light blue beads from her lap. "You drive, I pray. You see—we get there faster."

They passed houses spaced farther apart and fields that had once been pastures now growing wild with shrubs and small trees. Idyllic, but also a hard life of fierce winters and tough times as many of the factories, mills, and processing plants in the area had closed over the years. As she drove, Gabriela overheard her mother muttering prayers in Italian, the melodic words repeated like a chant. *Ave Maria, piena di grazia. . . .* The rhythmic sound became meditative, and Gabriela's thoughts drifted into the well-worn groove of worries about the library and the budget deficit that seemed unsolvable. Her mind hopscotched to the events at Still Waters Chasm: the woman who had appeared to be dead, the man taking his last breath.

"What you cook tonight?" Agnese asked. "Daniel's coming, *si?*"

Gabriela's thoughts broke off. "Oh, I made eggplant Parmesan last night. I have plenty left over. Ben can have pasta."

Agnese frowned. "He eats too much pasta."

"And—" Gabriela inhaled slowly not wanting to argue with her mother yet again over her son's picky eating. "I'll make a salad."

Agnese let the rosary collapse in her lap. "You make Daniel a steak. No leftovers."

"First of all, he loves eggplant Parmesan. And second, I have to work until five and get home before Ben does. He rode his bike to school and I told him he could go to the park afterwards."

"I cook for Daniel."

"You can come for dinner too, but I'm not changing the menu."

"I bring meatballs. You tell him you made them."

"No, you tell him *you* made them. This isn't 1950. 'The way to a man's heart is through his stomach' and all that."

"Who says that? It's true."

Gabriela felt the stare from her mother's dark eyes, the pupils nearly indistinguishable from the irises. "Go back to your prayers, Mama."

The rosary beads rattled as Agnese reengaged with them. "I pray to St. Anne. You know why?"

Gabriela pushed on the accelerator, edging past the speed limit.

"For you to get married. Maybe have another baby."

With no other cars in sight, Gabriela pressed harder on the gas pedal.

They reached the welcome sign for the Town of Livery at 11:09, which was cutting it close for a program that began at 11:30. Main Street consisted of a gas station–convenience store, a diner, four store-fronts—two occupied, two vacant—and a small church. A flashing yellow light dangled above the intersection near the volunteer fire department station; cars slowed down but did not stop.

Gabriela parked at the curb near a one-story brick building with peeling white trim. The front door opened, and a gray-haired man dressed in khakis and a button-down shirt stepped out. She greeted Todd Watson, a member of the county board of supervisors who lived out this way. He'd been so helpful when she'd asked him about using the Town of Livery Library for the outreach program.

"No trouble finding us, I trust." Todd shook Gabriela's hand and introduced himself to Agnese.

"None at all," Gabriela assured him.

Entering the tiny library, Gabriela saw that three men and a woman had already arrived. They milled in the back of the room, behind two rows of folding chairs. She called out a greeting, and they murmured in response.

The air felt stale, like an old attic. It took some effort, but Gabriela raised a window. A mild breeze blew through the room.

As Gabriela finished setting up, she gave her mother the job of arranging the refreshments. Agnese frowned at two packages of store-bought cookies. "Next time, I make homemade."

"Next time, I'll let you." Gabriela set a carton of lemonade and one of fruit punch, still cold from the cooler in her car, on the table along with a stack of paper cups.

A woman in a softly gathered skirt and a white top scattered with blue flowers stepped through the door. Her long silvery hair, gathered in combs at her temples, fell in waves down her back. Gabriela didn't recognize her but returned the broad smile the woman beamed in her direction.

"Lucinda Nanz," the woman replied after Gabriela introduced herself.

When Todd came over to greet her, Lucinda held up a small paper bag. "Brought you some more tea, just like you asked. Spearmint, peppermint, ginger, and meadowsweet."

Gabriela had never heard of meadowsweet, though the name sounded appealing. She leaned in to get a better look.

Lucinda held up a second bag. "This is for Marlene. I've marked it with her name, but you can clearly see it's different. It's got rose petals in it. Plus some borage, sage, rosemary, and lady's mantle. It should help her feel more comfortable at night."

26

Gabriela took another step forward. "Sounds amazing. Do you have a tea shop?"

Lucinda shook her head. "No. Just my gardens."

Gabriela waited to hear more, but Lucinda offered no further information. Another woman beckoned from across the room, and Lucinda excused herself to speak with her.

Todd whispered to Gabriela. "You have to ask her directly. Lucinda won't offer unless you do."

"Ask for—?"

"Tea. She'll make you a blend for what you need, but you have to ask."

Gabriela straightened one of the folding chairs, aligning it with the rest in the row. "Oh, I was just making conversation."

"You should ask her. Best tea you'll ever drink." Todd gave a quick nod, then left to greet two people coming in the door.

Gabriela slipped past them and stepped outside, scanning the street for the guest speaker. The local author had confirmed the day before that he would be there, but she saw no one. Her silenced cell phone revealed no missed calls or messages.

By 11:30, about a dozen people sat in the audience, which Gabriela considered a decent turnout for the first program. Most were retirees, but two women came with small children who left trails of crumbs from the tray of cookies on the refreshment table to back of the room, where their mothers kept them occupied. At 11:35 people seemed restless, so Gabriela went ahead without the speaker. Fortunately, she had a copy of his book, *North County Fishing: Lore, Lures, and Locations*, and read aloud a particularly descriptive passage. She asked if anyone in the audience had a fishing story to share. No one said anything; then Lucinda spoke up: "Our lakes, rivers, and streams have been fished for thousands of years, since the days of the first native peoples. We think of the Iroquois as hunters, but they fished as well.

And they gathered roots, berries, and nuts. They made maple syrup, and they knew which plants were good for medicine."

The crowd rustled a little bit, which Gabriela figured was a sign of impatience that the author still hadn't shown up. "Does anyone have a favorite fishing spot?" she asked.

"You're the one who saw them two campers you thought was dead," said a barrel-chested, gray-haired man in a plaid shirt crisscrossed by suspenders.

Gabriela took a step back. "Yes, yes—that was me. How did you hear about it?"

"We got scanners," the man continued. "State police said your name loud and clear."

So that's why they had showed up for the program, Gabriela thought. So much for trying to offer enrichment after the closure of the town library.

"Why'd you think they were dead?" he asked.

"Who's dead? What's he saying?" Agnese demanded.

"I was hiking with a friend," Gabriela explained to the audience. "We found two people by the lake. They were unresponsive."

"You told the police they were dead," the man insisted.

Lucinda spun around. "Jake, this nice woman has come all this way to give you something to listen to other than whatever nonsense goes on in your head."

The man squinted at her. "You gonna hex me?"

Hex him? Gabriela recoiled. What kind of misogynistic crap was that?

"You're already a toad, Jake," Lucinda said. "So I'd have to turn you into a prince." Everybody, including Jake, laughed.

What seemed offensive at first now struck Gabriela as teasing among people who had known one another for years. "Tough crowd," she said, smiling. The scowls and smirks she got in return told her the attempt at humor had missed the mark. "We were talking about—"

"You going again to Still Waters?" someone in the back called out.

Jake swiveled toward the voice. "Yeah, maybe she'll find some more not-dead people." Laughter rippled through the room, and a wave of heat rushed across Gabriela's cheeks.

"*Malocchio!*" Agnese forked her index finger and pinkie and aimed the counter-curse in Jake's direction. "You be nice to my daughter."

"Mama," Gabriela said, shaking her head. When she turned toward the audience, she saw Lucinda nodding in Agnese's direction.

A sound at the door broke the tension as the guest speaker entered, sputtering apologies and excuses about not finding the place. Gabriela hustled him to the front of the room, made a brief introduction, and asked the author to talk about his favorite fishing spots. When he mentioned a bridge over the Salmon River, Jake interrupted with a scowl. "That's fine if you want to stand there with a hundred other people who don't know what they're doing. You gotta go where nobody else does. There's a bend in the river, about two miles upstream from there. When the salmon are running, you can practically reach in and grab one."

Somebody else agreed with Jake, but two others disagreed, and now they had a full-fledged discussion. As long as nobody threw a punch or a chair, Gabriela would consider it a successful program. At 12:45 she led a weak round of applause for the author, handed him an envelope with a thank-you note and a twenty-dollar bill, and announced a drawing for her copy of the author's book, which he would sign for the winner.

As they left, several people told Gabriela how much they enjoyed the program. "We'll do it again, for sure," she told them.

One of the young mothers stopped on her way out the door. "Thanks for letting us bring the kids. It's good to get out, you know?"

The children had played so quietly throughout the program, Gabriela had hardly noticed them. "If we put on a story hour, would you come? Do you think other parents would?"

The woman shrugged. "Suppose so." Her toddler grabbed her wrist, planted his tiny sneakers against her leg, and climbed as if she were a jungle gym.

After the women left, Gabriela looked around for Agnese, who had been cleaning up the refreshment table the last time she checked. She spotted her in the far corner with Lucinda. Approaching them, Gabriela overheard her mother's comment: "*Va bene*. We come."

"Where are we going, Mama?" Gabriela inquired.

"Her house. I ask her about all this tea she gives to people. She says she grows, so I tell her I want to see."

"Agnese told me that back in Italy her mother grew herbs both for cooking and for healing," Lucinda added.

Gabriela hadn't heard that one before. "I have a little basil in my garden, does that count?"

Agnese took Lucinda's arm and started toward the front door. "We come, and you tell me what's in your tea, okay?"

"I'll do more than that," Lucinda said. "I'll introduce you to my flowers, and then I'll know what kind of tea to make for you."

As they left the building, Gabriela spoke to her mother in a low voice. "We can't stay long. I've got to get back to work." But as she opened the car door for her mother, Gabriela felt her curiosity stir at the thought of a woman who consulted her flowers when making tea for guests.

CHAPTER

FOUR

Lucinda lived about five miles out of town in a small stone house with black shutters. A profusion of tiger lilies blossomed where the gravel driveway met the pitted blacktop of the country road. Pulling in slowly, Gabriela admired the red geraniums and yellow chrysanthemums that ringed the front of the house and wondered if these were the flowers Lucinda had wanted them to see. Taking in the bowling ball–sized stones that made up the outer walls, Gabriela tried to guess the age of the place. A hundred years? A hundred and fifty?

Behind the house, where the driveway widened into an apron in front of a small barn, Gabriela hit the brakes. Never had she seen anything like it. Multiple gardens stretched in all directions, each crisscrossed with flagstone paths. Some bore the full sun; others sheltered in the shade of four old maple trees. Before Gabriela could shut off the engine and unfasten her seatbelt, Agnese had opened the passenger door and pushed herself to her feet. Gabriela caught up with her at the side of a large vegetable patch.

"*Zucchine, carote, pomodori,*" Agnese exclaimed. "Just like in Italy."

"I take it anyone who cultivates plants like an Italian can't be all bad, eh?" Gabriela gave her mother a wry smile.

"Gardens, they don't lie. To grow good things, you have to be—" Agnese muttered a couple of words in Italian. "Like Mother Nature." Bending slowly, Agnese touched broad dark green leaves growing from a reddish stalk. "This one I know, but not the name."

"Swiss chard," Lucinda said behind them.

"You give me some?" Agnese asked.

"Mama, we're not here to take Lucinda's harvest," Gabriela interjected.

"I have plenty." Lucinda retrieved a pair of gardening shears from a bucket of neatly arranged tools and cut a half dozen stalks. "Cook it tonight if you can, leaves and stalks both."

Gabriela accepted the bouquet of Swiss chard and put it in her car, wondering how it would go with leftover eggplant Parmesan. Returning to the gardens, she followed one of the paths toward an herb patch. She recognized rosemary: spiky like an evergreen, growing in the bright sun and the reflected warmth of a flagstone step.

Lucinda walked up beside her, mumbled something to the rosemary plant, and snipped off a short branch with garden shears. "Good for muscle pains, circulation—and commanding respect. Plus, it's nature's aromatherapy."

Gabriela held the sprig to her nose with one hand and pointed to a bluish-green plant with the other. "Lavender?"

Lucinda nodded, then gestured toward what looked like a miniature conifer. "And that one is juniper. The berries are good for all sorts of things—arthritis, diabetes, stomach issues."

Following Lucinda through the sun-soaked herb garden, Gabriela let the litany of names wash over her: yarrow, meadowsweet, chamomile, coneflower, feverfew, catnip, anise, a bay tree, spearmint, and, on the diagonal far away from its cousin, peppermint. "Can't let those get too close, they'll hybridize," Lucinda explained. "And over there by the driveway is lemon balm—also in the mint family. Loves the sun, hates good soil."

By the small barn converted into a garage, something grew against a high fence—as big as a shrub but with delicate branches and feathery pointed leaves. "*Artemisia vulgaris*," Lucinda announced, "better known as mugwort."

Gabriela shivered a little at the name, though she didn't know why.

"A staple in Chinese and Native American medicines," Lucinda continued. "The Greeks used it. So did Roman soldiers, who lined their sandals with the leaves to keep their feet from getting tired on long marches. Regulates digestion and women's cycles, heals bruising, and promotes lucid dreams."

Gabriela looked around to see where her mother had wandered and found her bending down, fondling a plant's fan-shaped leaves with scalloped edges.

"That's lady's mantel," Lucinda called over to Agnese. "But it doesn't like to be touched. Most plants don't. It bruises them."

"*Scusa*," Agnese said, and Gabriela wondered if her mother apologized to Lucinda or the plant.

As they walked along the serpentine paths, Gabriela became aware of how much time must have passed, far longer than the twenty minutes she'd planned to spend there, but the garden held her captive. Every finely shaped leaf or wide frond, delicate blossom or showy flower begged a second glance, a closer look. Each moment offered another sweet fragrance or heady aroma.

An exotic-looking plant leaned over the sides of a rectangular wood container. *Bamboo?* Gabriela wondered.

"Ginger," Lucinda said. "It grows well enough all summer, but as soon as it starts to get cool, I have to haul it into the greenhouse. Still, it's worth the effort to have my own ginger." Lucinda cocked an eyebrow. "If I don't grow it, it doesn't go in my teas."

Beyond the herb garden, ceramic pots spilled cascades of yellow pansies, red snapdragons, and purple petunias. Insects buzzed everywhere, more than Gabriela had seen in years. "Do you keep bees?" she asked.

"I like to think they keep me," Lucinda replied. "They work in my garden as much as I do."

"And they never sting you, right?" Agnese said, coming up behind them.

"Never," agreed Lucinda.

Gabriela noticed her mother chewing on something and peered closer to see. *Parsley.* She waited for what Lucinda would say, but she didn't seem to react to Agnese grazing through the kitchen herbs, or perhaps that's why they had been planted.

The other half of the backyard was cast in the shade of four old maples that grew in a circle. Below them spread a sea of plants bearing wide leaves with multiple points. "Goldenseal," Lucinda said. "Many medicinal uses, but—" She snapped her head in the other direction, and Gabriela followed her gaze.

Agnese traipsed across the shadowy ground toward a patch of plants on the far side. Lucinda's eyebrows pinched together. "Don't taste anything over there."

Lucinda walked quickly toward Agnese, and Gabriela trailed close behind. A short border fenced a small round garden where three plants grew together. Gabriela waited for the recitation of names, but Lucinda said nothing.

"This one, with the berries," Agnese said, pointing. "I see it before."

"*Atropa belladonna,*" Lucinda replied; "otherwise known as deadly nightshade."

At the name, Gabriela curled her lip reflexively. "What are the other ones?"

Lucinda paused. "Hellebore and monkshood."

The shortened answers contrasted with the long explanations Lucinda had given for all the other herbs and flowers. Here volumes seemed to be left unsaid.

"I take it they're poisonous," Gabriela ventured.

Lucinda hitched up one side of her mouth into a crooked smile. "Almost anything can be toxic in the wrong dose. Let's just say these plants are for a different kind of medicine." She extended her hand toward the house. "Shall we have tea?"

The screen door yawned open on a long spring, then snapped shut behind them. Wooden shelves along one wall of the sunporch held mason jars where plant cuttings dangled long strands of roots into blue-tinted water. In the corner rested a huge orange tabby, his sides rising and falling with his breathing.

"Corky," Lucinda said, and the cat raised his head. "I found him outside one fall day—wet and hungry. I opened the door, and in he walked. That was that."

"Lucky cat," Gabriela said. "And smart."

"You sleep all day? Or you catch mice?" Agnese asked. Corky blinked, then proceeded to give his front paws a tongue bath.

They followed Lucinda into the kitchen where a steady breeze blew through the open window over the sink. The fixtures and counter-top were old but immaculate. Gabriela detected no trace of cooking odors, only the sweet scent of herbs and flowers. Peach-colored paint covered the walls, and brightly printed curtains framed the windows. "What a lovely room," she said.

"It's old, like me. I've been here since I got married—fifty years ago. I'll be seventy-two in December."

The number shocked Gabriela, who would have guessed Lucinda to be closer to sixty.

"My husband died twenty years ago. My daughter, Trudy, lives in Maine."

Agnese made a soft grunt. "Twenty years is a long time. Me, I be seventy-seven in January. But my Vincent, he died only four years ago."

While her mother and Lucinda talked, Gabriela glanced at her phone, which she'd put on silent back at the library in Livery. She scrolled through several text messages: all from the library, and none of them urgent. She'd check the voicemails in a moment.

"All those plants—just for you?" Agnese pointed toward the sun-porch and the gardens beyond.

Lucinda spread her arms wide. "I believe in abundance. When I have extra, I share. But I also receive in return. People bring me a dozen eggs from their backyard chickens or loaves of homemade bread. Pies, preserves, potatoes, apples—occasionally, a nice salmon fillet."

Gabriela groaned with regret. "I'm afraid we've come empty-handed."

Lucinda shook her head. "You put on a program at the library, and I wanted to show my appreciation." She turned on the burner under a teakettle on the stove. "I brewed this while we were out in the garden. It should be just about ready."

"All this time?" Gabriela remarked.

"Good tea can't be rushed," Lucinda replied, getting out a strainer, three mugs, and a honey pot.

"I think that's my problem," Gabriela said. "I don't let my tea steep enough."

Lucinda sat down at the table. "I am hoping you will do something for me. I'd like you to tell me what happened at the chasm."

Agnese swatted Gabriela on the wrist. "*Si!* You never say a word to me."

Gabriela picked up the honey dipper and held it an inch above the pot, watching the amber liquid slide down the grooves of the stick.

"There's not much more to say. Daniel and I were hiking when we came across two people and their canoe. The man was very sick—he was having a seizure. The woman looked like she was dead. She must have been unconscious."

Lucinda poured their tea, drizzled honey into each cup, and slid one toward Gabriela. "Why did you think she was dead?"

"No pulse. Her body was cold."

"Evidence of vomiting?" Lucinda asked.

"Yes, both of them." Gabriela took a sip of the tea, which tasted sweet and not just from the honey. She sniffed the steam and detected anise.

"*Sfortuna!*" Agnese crossed herself. "And you don't tell me."

Gabriela reached around the corner of the table and laid her hand on her mother's arm. "I didn't want you to worry."

"I always worry." Agnese picked up her teacup and sniffed. "It's what mothers do."

"Poisoned—that's my guess," Lucinda replied. "Could be any number of things. Belladonna would do it if they ate enough berries."

"Like in your garden?" Gabriela asked.

"It grows all over the place—a common garden escape."

Gabriela shook her head; she'd never heard the term.

"It goes feral. Creeps out of its confines and spreads. But someone has to plant it first."

Gabriela remembered the tiny garden with the three mysterious plants, sequestered by themselves, and recalled their names again: monkshood, hellebore, and belladonna. She'd google them later. "Well, whatever happened to those people, they got sick but didn't die—fortunately. They left the beach, and they never showed up at any of the hospitals for treatment."

Lucinda placed her palms flat against the table. "There's something funny going on at the chasm. My dear friend Parnella lives out that way. She was coming home late one night—must have been after ten. She saw three black pickup trucks tearing down the road, one after the other."

Pickup trucks roamed every country road, Gabriela thought, and three in a row meant nothing more than people heading to some honky-tonk bar. But the mention of black pickups recalled the trucks she'd seen parked in that godforsaken clear-cut in the woods.

Lucinda pursed her lips. "Parnella says that sometimes at night you can see lights up on the ridge around Still Waters. Not from houses or camps—out in the woods. One time she heard a humming so loud, she thought an earthquake was coming."

"Perhaps it's the state doing some work up there?" Gabriela suggested.

"At night?" Lucinda's forehead furrowed. "You can't find a game warden during the day because of budget cuts. I can't imagine any-body from the state doing something up there at night. Then you come across two dead people who rise up like Lazarus and paddle their canoe away."

No one spoke for nearly a minute. Gabriela's mind raced right back to the scene at Still Waters Lake and her absolute certainty of what she'd witnessed: the woman dead, the man dying. But she had to have been mistaken. Their pulses had slowed, not stopped. They'd been ill, not dead, and somehow recovered. There could be no other explanation, she repeated to herself.

———

As they left the house and walked toward the car, Gabriela sidestepped a tall plant with blue starburst blossoms that bobbed at the edge of the path. As she passed, a half dozen bees took flight and danced a figure eight above her head.

She felt the strength of Lucinda's grip as the older woman pulled her forward. "You're drawn to these flowers. Or rather, they're drawn to you. Close your eyes and quiet your mind."

"I really have to get going," Gabriela said.

Agnese stepped forward and held out her hands. "*Sì*. We do this."

Gabriela set down her purse and a bag of tea Lucinda had given her. Stretching out her fingertips, she felt a tingle—or at least she thought she did. "I'm not very good at this. I can't even do yoga."

"Open your palms toward the flowers. Tell them in your mind that you mean no harm," Lucinda instructed. "Ask if you can approach."

Gabriela felt foolish, talking to flowers, but she overheard her mother making a request in Italian. "*Bei fiori . . .*"

"Now, cup the blossoms the way you would a child's face," Lucinda continued.

The gesture recalled for Gabriela the countless times she had framed Ben's face with her hands and felt the smoothness of his cheeks.

"What do you sense?" Lucinda asked.

Gabriela thought of a dozen things, from needing to get back to Ohnita Harbor to the realization that she hadn't checked the voicemails.

"Not your thoughts—your feelings."

In a fleeting moment of mental quiet, something came to Gabriela, but she dismissed it as nothing more than the power of suggestion. In its wake, she could still name it: resolve, bravery. Before she said those words, her mother spoke aloud, "Courage."

Gabriela gasped. "Yes, I thought the same thing."

Lucinda's face crinkled pleasantly. "As if you were on a mission?"

Gabriela hesitated, not wanting to retrofit whatever she had felt into her mother's word or Lucinda's suggestion. Yet both matched what she had experienced, even if only for a few seconds. "Something like that." She picked up her things from the ground.

"Some people call it starflower, but I prefer its less picturesque name—borage," Lucinda said. "It reminds me of an ancient proverb: 'I, borage, bring always courage.'"

Gabriela scanned the backyard bounty of flowers, vegetables, and herbs. "Your gardens are amazing, but your knowledge is the most impressive of all. Do you consider yourself an herbalist?"

"That's one name for it," Lucinda replied.

A question sent out a tendril from her brain to her tongue, and Gabriela couldn't keep from asking it. "What's the other name?"

Lucinda's dark eyes held hers for a half minute, unblinking. "I'm what they call a green witch, though most people drop the 'green' part."

"Oh—" Gabriela began.

"Like *Bufana*!" Agnese exclaimed. "In Italy, she's a good witch who brings people presents—like you with your tea and vegetables."

Lucinda angled her head to the side. "I just know plants and they know me. I can feel their properties, for healing and for harm." She extended her hand toward a pot of multicolored snapdragons, close but not touching them. "These sweet ladies have a mild energy, but they're good for protection. That's why I plant them here. If someone is coming to my home to fool me, I want to stop that intention in its tracks."

"You think somebody tries to hurt you?" Agnese asked.

"Not directly. But sometimes—" Lucinda shook herself in a little shiver.

Agnese pawed around in her purse and pulled out her rosary. "I give you this. You put this up someplace. Maybe there." She pointed to a crabapple tree between the vegetable patch and the herb garden.

"Mama," Gabriela cautioned, ready to run interference against her mother foisting her beliefs on someone else. But Lucinda accepted the beads with what sounded like genuine gratitude. All three of them walked to the tree, where Lucinda hung the rosary over the fork of two slender branches. The facets of the clear blue beads caught the sun.

Lucinda turned to Agnese. "How long has it been since your chemotherapy?"

The question snapped Gabriela's thinking in a different direction. She hadn't heard her mother mention anything about having cancer or being in recovery. But perhaps she had, or else Lucinda had amazing observational skills.

"Three months. They take the breast too."

"A full mastectomy on the left side," Gabriela explained. "Three years ago, she had a mastectomy of the right breast."

"It makes me tired," Agnese said. "I wish I could be like before."

Lucinda nodded. "I'll give you some dandelion root. Boil it and drink the broth. It's especially good for the liver and will help build your strength."

Not so long ago, strength would have been the last thing anyone would find lacking in her mother, Gabriela thought. Though not quite five feet tall and not much more than a hundred pounds for most of her life, Agnese could command respect and sometimes fear from most people. She remembered her mother arguing so often with the butcher about the accuracy of his scale, the man told her to take her business elsewhere. Her father had needed to smooth things over, promising that in the future Agnese would be on her best behavior, though that hadn't stopped her from giving the butcher a squinting look that broadcast, *I watch your every move.*

Gabriela linked arms with Agnese to keep her mother moving down the path toward the car. As they walked slowly, she heard the rasp between her mother's breaths and felt the bony press of her ribs. This time, Agnese accepted help getting into the passenger seat, a sure sign, Gabriela knew, that the outing had tired her mother.

As they waited for Lucinda to come out of the house with the dandelion root, Gabriela checked her phone, scrolled through the texts again, and listened to the voicemails. The first two came from Daniel, asking and then urging her to call him back. The other two, from a number she didn't recognize, had been left by Trooper Douglas Morrison, who stated that the body of a man had washed up on the opposite side of Still Waters Lake. The corpse matched the description of the man they'd found on the beach.

Sitting in her car behind the steering wheel, Gabriela slowly detached from her surroundings. Her mother's voice echoed at the opposite end of a long tunnel that dimmed her peripheral vision. The buzzing in her ears amplified into a siren shriek, and she slipped into someplace dark and distant.

CHAPTER
FIVE

"Gabriela . . . Gabriela . . ." Someone called her name—the voice soft, yet unfamiliar.

Someone else touched her face. "*Bella,* wake up."

Back into her body and consciousness with a rush, Gabriela tried to focus her eyes. She saw Lucinda, leaning in through the open car door on the driver's side. On the passenger seat sat her mother, who held her hand. Fully aware now, Gabriela pressed her eyes shut against a throbbing headache. Her stomach roiled.

"You fainted," Agnese said.

Lucinda reached inside the car for Gabriela's arm. "I think you should come back inside for a little while."

Gabriela swung her legs out and slowly raised herself to a standing position. "How long was I—?" She hated admitting to losing consciousness.

"Not long," Lucinda replied.

"You see your phone, and you gone," Agnese said. She held up a bottle from her purse. "I put some holy water on you."

"Of course you carry that with you. Doesn't everyone?" Gabriela laughed thinly.

Agnese clucked her tongue. "You look no good."

Lucinda's mouth drew downward into a frown. "So pale."

A sheen of sweat glazed Gabriela's face. "I get triggered sometimes."

Agnese gripped Gabriela's hand tightly as they followed the flagstone path back to Lucinda's house. Corky the cat looked up as they passed through the sunporch and into the kitchen. Settled into a chair, Gabriela accepted a cool, moist cloth from Lucinda and pressed it to her forehead, then the back of her neck. The room spun, and Gabriela shut her eyes as her stomach lurched.

"A bad man—some bigshot in town—he tried to kill Gabriela. Puts a knife here." Agnese pointed to her own neck. "She has a scar there. After that, she's not the same."

"I read about it in the newspaper. Such a horrible thing to happen." Lucinda set a glass of water with mint leaves on the table. "What set it off this time?"

Gabriela opened one eye; the spinning sensation subsided. She picked up the glass and sipped. "A voicemail," she said and related the message about the body found at Still Waters and her needing to identify it.

"No!" Agnese made the sign of the cross twice. "You do enough already."

"I have to, Mama. I'll be okay. Daniel will be with me." Gabriela looked around for her purse, then spied it next to Agnese. "I need to call him."

Daniel answered on the second ring. "Where are you?"

"Up in Livery. Mama and I stopped to have tea with someone." As she spoke on the phone, Gabriela watched Lucinda pull jars from her cupboard. "I got a message from Trooper Morrison. I guess you did, too."

"Yes. I told him I would do whatever they needed," Daniel said. "You don't have to be there."

"I'll go. I have to," Gabriela insisted.

"Do you think that's wise? What if you—you know—have a—"

"Already had it."

"What happened?"

She kicked herself for saying something. It only made Daniel worry, and Gabriela didn't want to be a burden. "I'll be fine. Maybe confronting this will help me get stronger."

In the background, Gabriela heard her mother muttering something in Italian, low and urgent. A complaint or a prayer of thanks, she couldn't tell—and with her mother, they often sounded the same.

Gabriela assured Daniel that she'd be back in Ohnita Harbor in about forty-five minutes and would call as soon as she arrived. Daniel told her he'd contact Trooper Morrison and make the arrangements.

As she ended the conversation, Gabriela rubbed her right thumb over a spot just above her left wrist. The more she scratched, the more it irritated her.

"This will help." Lucinda held up a small cloth sack tied with twine.

Gabriela pressed it to her nose, and the mix of scents made her swoon a little. "What's in here?"

"Mugwort, sage, bay leaves, juniper, rosemary, lavender. And just a bit of wild mistletoe that came down in a storm. I would never cut mistletoe, but if the plant offers a bit of itself, there is no harm in taking it."

Gabriela took a second inhale and her head seemed to clear.

"Just keep it in your pocket. The herbs repel negative energy—what some people call evil."

"*Malocchio*," Agnese muttered.

When Gabriela looked into Lucinda's face, the kindness she read in the woman's expression made her own eyes mist. "Thank you."

Taking a step, Gabriela felt no dizziness and assessed herself safe to drive. "We need to get back."

A knock sounded on the screen door. "Lucinda?" a woman called from outside.

Lucinda flitted toward the door. "That's Wendy—a friend. I'll speak with her on the patio."

Agnese excused herself to use the bathroom, and Gabriela waited for her mother in the kitchen. From the window she watched Lucinda walk through the herb garden with a thin young woman in jeans and a T-shirt, her shoulders rounded, her blonde-brown hair pulled back in a messy ponytail. She carried something in her hand: a long cardboard tube, the kind that might hold a poster. Gabriela turned away to give the two women their privacy.

When Agnese returned to the kitchen, Gabriela ushered her outside. Lucinda beckoned them over to the Adirondack chairs—one bright turquoise, the other deep coral—and a wooden patio table on the other side of the herb garden. As they approached, Gabriela noticed Wendy quickly rolling up a large, yellowed document. Gabriela wished she had gotten a closer look, but now the document was tucked out of sight.

"This is Wendy Haughton. I've known her since she was a little girl," Lucinda said. "I told her how you found an old cross at your library that turned out to be seven hundred years old."

Gabriela recalled Lucinda saying she'd read all about it in the newspaper.

"How did you know how old it was?" Wendy asked.

"My background is in authentication. I used to work at the New York Public Library where I spent many years researching documents."

Wendy sat up straighter. Gabriela noticed the look that passed between the young woman and Lucinda. She had to wonder what that was all about.

"Perhaps Wendy could show you something one day. Something from her family," Lucinda said.

"I'd be happy to look," Gabriela said. "I'm not an appraiser, but I may be able to give you some indication of age or even origin—depending on what it is, of course." She waited for Wendy to elaborate, but nothing more was said.

Wendy twirled the stem of a flower between her fingertips, and Gabriela recognized it as borage. Something in the young woman's manner made Gabriela think she needed courage. She thought of the protection pouch in her purse. "Maybe you should do a program, Lucinda, on the healing property of plants."

Lucinda's grimace took Gabriela by surprise. "Folks around here already know about me and my plants, but not everyone wants to hear about them."

"Really? But so many people seem to love your teas," Gabriela protested.

"And there are others who think I'm a godless heathen."

"Well, I—*uh*." Gabriela wet her lips. "I'll come up with another idea for a program. And when I do, I know I can count on you to tell people about it." She looked over at Wendy, who held the rolled-up paper in her lap. "I hope you'll come too."

When Wendy glanced her way, Gabriela saw dark circles under her eyes and a smudge of yellow with a faint purple streak on her cheek. Gabriela chose her words carefully. "The library has so many useful resources. Not just books to read, but also information on health, safety, and how to find legal advice." Opening her purse, Gabriela took out her business card. "If you ever want me to help you with anything, you can call me."

Wendy dipped her chin as she reached for the card.

Lucinda patted Wendy's hand, then got up to walk Gabriela and Agnese to their car.

"Thank you for everything," Gabriela began before being engulfed in Lucinda's generous hug.

"I'm so glad I met the two of you." Lucinda released Gabriela and embraced Agnese. "No goodbyes. Just see you soon."

Gabriela swung the car around in the yard and drove slowly out of the driveway, fluttering her hand in response to Lucinda's sweeping wave.

As they drove back to Ohnita Harbor, Gabriela tried not to think about going to the county coroner's office to view the body. She'd only seen such things on television and in movies: the sheet peeled back, the head and shoulders uncovered. Bile crawled up the back of her throat, and Gabriela swallowed hard.

"Mama, tell me what you thought of Lucinda." An open-ended question like that, she knew, would launch her mother into a steady stream of conversation.

"She reminds me of someone in Poggibonsi—*Genoveffa*. Big garden like Lucinda."

High praise, Gabriela smiled to herself, for her mother to compare Lucinda to someone she knew back in Italy and, more than that, to someone from her hometown.

"You walk down her street, you smell the basil in the air," Agnese went on, with reminiscences from her native Tuscany—the perfect distractions Gabriela needed for this drive.

———

Forty-five minutes later, they reached Ohnita Harbor. After dropping Agnese at her house, Gabriela headed straight to the library. It was 3:50, almost two hours later than she'd originally planned to return. After entering the building, Gabriela picked up a stack of messages from Delmina and went into her office to call Daniel.

She heard weariness in his voice as he related his latest conversation with Trooper Morrison. They wouldn't have to see the body, only photographs of the face. A coil of tension in Gabriela's chest and gut unwound with that news.

"I told him we'd be there around 4:15. Does that work for you?" Daniel asked.

"That's fine. I'll meet you there."

"No, I—" Daniel paused. "Would you like me to pick you up so we can go together?"

Gabriela thought of the logistics: going to the state police station on the outskirts of town, then coming back to the library for her car so she could finally go home.

"I think we should go there together," he added.

For the first time, Gabriela considered the possibility that Daniel needed her with him. "Okay. I'll be waiting downstairs."

Two flags—the stars and stripes for the nation and the dark blue pennant of New York State—snapped in a steady wind off Lake Ontario. Passing the flagpole planted in the close-cropped lawn of the New York State Police station, Gabriela discerned the two figures on the emblem in the center of the state flag: Liberty on the left, Justice on the right. She started to comment on them to Daniel, but a faraway look in his eyes dissuaded her.

All the way to the front door, Gabriela focused on the seams in the sidewalk, imagining each one as a mile marker that brought her closer to what she had to do, but dreaded doing. As her fingers touched the cold metal of the front door handle, her chest tightened and her pulse beat furiously in her ears. Aware of Daniel's long arm reaching above her head, Gabriela saw the door open a few inches wider, but her body blocked the doorway.

Her constricted throat would not allow the words to pass. Swallowing became impossible. Gulping a breath with her diaphragm, she gasped. "I can't."

"I know, but we have to try," Daniel said, his voice soft but his free hand firmly on her shoulder. "We owe it to the man we tried to save."

Gabriela stepped aside and let Daniel open the door the rest of the way.

A uniformed officer met them at the front desk then disappeared through a door with a frosted pane. A moment later, Trooper Morrison came out and greeted them.

Gabriela braced for the anger she expected to direct toward the state trooper for not believing what they'd witnessed. Instead, she felt only relief at seeing a familiar face. As her body relaxed enough to deepen her shallow breathing, Gabriela discerned another feeling: vindication. She'd been right—they'd been right. It emboldened her to follow Trooper Morrison to an empty desk, its surface unmarred by anything, not even a paper clip. No nameplate, coffee mug, or framed pictures.

"I usually work out of a field office, but the resources are better here," he said. "Probably easier for you folks too."

"Yes, it is. Thank you," Daniel said.

"Where is he?" Gabriela asked. "The body, I mean."

"County medical examiner," Trooper Morrison replied. "They're doing the autopsy now. I have photographs for you to look at." He held up a manila folder.

Daniel sat in one of the two chairs on the opposite side of the desk, and Gabriela slipped in beside him. Resting her hands against her leg, she felt a lump in her pocket: Lucinda's herb pouch. *Mugwort, sage, bay leaves, mistletoe* . . . Silently reciting the contents she could remember, Gabriela felt her body relax and her breathing even out.

The office chair creaked as Trooper Morrison leaned back. "Tell me again, why had you gone to Still Waters that day?"

"For a hike," Daniel replied. "Gabriela had never been there, and it's one of my favorite places."

"You got there at what time?" the officer continued.

"A little after ten," Gabriela said. "I know because I called my mother when we arrived. She was staying at my house with my son. I just wanted to make sure everybody was fine."

"Why wouldn't they be?" Trooper Morrison spoke in a casual tone, but Gabriela knew he expected his question to be answered.

"I'm usually at home with my son on the weekends. He's eleven. But Daniel and I went away for the day."

"How long did it take you to hike to the lake?" the trooper continued.

"We took a detour," Daniel explained. "We found a small path and followed it into the woods. About a mile and a half in, we came across a construction site."

"Total clear-cut," Gabriela added. "Every single tree gone. Someone left a truck with some kind of platform underneath it, and then a bulldozer and more trucks. They put a dirt road in too. We thought maybe the state was doing something up there."

Trooper Morrison shook his head. "Not that I've heard of. Maybe somebody's building a house. About half the land around there is privately owned. The rest belongs to the county and the state. You take any pictures?"

Daniel shook his head. "Never occurred to me. The place was so ugly."

"So, then what?" the state trooper asked.

Daniel recounted everything: seeing the canoe on the beach, finding the man as his body convulsed in a seizure, discovering the woman who seemed to be dead.

Gabriela retrieved the herb pouch from her pocket and clutched it in her hand as she recalled the woman's gray skin, cold to the touch, the wisps of light hair blown across the face, the half-closed eyes.

Trooper Morrison nodded. "What's in the bag?"

Gabriela yanked her mind away from the images. "Herbs. A friend gave them to me. They're calming."

"May I?" He extended his hand, and Gabriela deposited the little sack in his palm. Trooper Morrison held it to his nose then gave it back to her. "Okay, let's take a look at these." He opened the folder. "I have to warn you. These photos are graphic."

Clutching the pouch tightly, Gabriela narrowed her eyes and stole small glances at the first photograph. Purple mottled the swollen face, and the eyelids were opened partway.

"I can't be sure," Daniel said. "I'd guess the guy we saw was thirty-five or so. This person could be any age."

Smelling the lavender and rosemary released by the warmth of her hand, Gabriela recalled the man's red hair, the thin beard, and something else. "He had a mole—here." She pointed high on her right cheekbone.

Trooper Morrison nodded. Shuffling the photos, he brought out one from the opposite side of the face. "This one is pretty gruesome. The lacerations are from the rocks when the body washed up." He laid the photo on the desk.

Daniel turned away. Gabriela glanced down at the mangled mass of flesh and teeth visible through a deep, wide cut across the lower cheek. Her eyes followed Trooper Morrison's finger to the mole visible in the photo. "Yes," she said, then trained her eyes on the yellow walls. A second hand swept slowly around the face of a round clock. No one spoke for half a minute.

Gabriela's brain pounded with questions: When had the man died, what had killed him, had he ever revived at the beach? Suddenly she wanted to know his name more than anything else. She asked Trooper Morrison, but he shook his head. "No wallet, no ID."

But he wasn't a nameless, faceless person. Somewhere this dead man had family and friends, she argued silently. Someone at home waited for him to return—or at least to call. "Are you still looking for the woman?" she asked.

"We haven't stopped looking," the state trooper told her. "From the moment you reported finding those two people, we've been combing the area for them. That's how we found him." He patted the closed folder with the photos inside.

"What about their canoe?" Daniel pulled his phone from his jacket pocket and scrolled through the pictures taken that day. He enlarged the image so that the corner of the upturned canoe became more visible. "It looks new. They make them out of Kevlar these days—a whole lot lighter than fiberglass. That'll wash up someplace."

"Probably," Trooper Morrison agreed.

"If they rented it, someone knows who they are," Daniel added.

"And they didn't paddle that canoe from wherever they came from. They parked a car someplace." The more Gabriela said, the higher her voice rose in pitch.

"We're chasing it all down," Trooper Morrison said. "But what we can't figure out is what happened between when they left the campsite on the west side of Still Waters Lake and the man washed up on the east side."

Gabriela's mouth dropped open, but no sound came out right away. She squeezed the pouch of herbs. "We tried—" Daniel touched her forearm, but she snatched it away from his grip. "We were telling the truth, but you didn't want to go look."

"We did check the shoreline, later that day and the next," the state trooper said evenly. "And we keep searching. But right now, this has got us stumped. The only information we have is what you two told us."

Gabriela mentally pulled away as Trooper Morrison said something about the results of the autopsy being known later that day or the next. She held the cloth bag of herbs against her nose and mouth

53

and imagined herself back in Lucinda's garden, where pansies and snapdragons stood sentry at the end of the walkway and bees flew figure eights over the flowers' bright faces.

CHAPTER
SIX

They rode in silence from the state police station to the library. Out the window of Daniel's SUV, the quiet streets of Ohnita Harbor streamed past: modest houses and a few fancier ones; kids playing on the sidewalks; a teenager riding a bicycle while holding a cell phone. Gabriela watched the quaint hometown panorama, trying to erase the images of a cadaver's face brutalized by rocks and submersion.

"Want me to drive you home? We can come back later and get your car," Daniel offered.

Gabriela cleared her throat. "Thanks, but I want to stop at the grocery store." Hearing these words come out of her mouth, she wondered where this plan had come from.

"You're sure that's not too much?" Daniel slowed to turn into the library parking lot.

"Just have to pick up a few things."

"Okay, I'll try to get to your house by 6:30."

Gabriela's hand gripped the door latch of the SUV. "Sounds good."

Daniel leaned over to give her a quick kiss, and Gabriela offered her cheek. Seeing his eyebrows crimp together, Gabriela scrambled to explain her muddled feelings. "I'm just so—"Her shoulders and upper body angled toward Daniel. Lowering her head, she touched her brow to his upper arm, resting just a moment. "I'm so sorry. About all of it."

"This is not your fault."

"No, but—" She straightened, and her fingers clutched the latch. "I better go. Ben should be home at five."The door swung open. A moment later, she watched him drive out of the library parking lot.

He had worried about her from the very beginning of their relationship, Gabriela knew, recalling Daniel's attentiveness as she recovered from the knife attack. His care had endeared him to her, but now she feared the constant concern would overwhelm him. The first few months of a relationship should be fun and romantic, not constant turmoil. She thought back to Saturday, a perfect outing until that too ended in more trauma, another tragedy. The newness of their relationship made it fragile. Time would strengthen or shatter it.

She had learned that the hard way with her ex-husband, Jim. He had been unable to take the constant money worries of living in New York City and of being working parents juggling babysitters and daycare for Ben, along with the grind of commuting to work in Manhattan each day from their apartment in Brooklyn. He'd escaped their marriage to a much easier life with his girlfriend in California, while she'd come back to Ohnita Harbor, the hometown she'd left at eighteen when she went off to college. Although reconciled to her choice to stay here, with a new role as executive director of the library and a chance to positively impact the community, Gabriela never forgot what had brought her back. "Necessity," she murmured aloud.

Unable to live on her own in New York, she had returned to her hometown because the cost of living was so much less, and her mother needed her. Cheaper, but not easier. Her fingers found the scar on her neck again as she reflected on the last three months: a crescendo of intensity greater than she'd ever known.

She needed to scale it back, Gabriela told herself, not only for Daniel's sake but for her own. She had to be stronger and more resilient, even when she felt like breaking. Instead of giving in to the panic attacks, she would have to ignore them when she could and push through them when she couldn't. Just that thought alone made her feel more in control as she got in her car and turned the key in the ignition.

Stopping at the grocery store would delay her at least fifteen minutes and Ben would probably be home by then, but not going meant she had lied to Daniel, Gabriela reasoned as her car bumped over the pitted grocery store parking lot. She nabbed a prime spot near the entrance when another car backed out. Inside the store, the cart felt like a lumber wagon as she pushed it through the brightly lit aisles where crackling announcements punctuated easy-listening music. She went through produce and picked up the usual items—lettuce, tomatoes, cucumbers, carrots, bananas—then swung by the bakery section for a doughy loaf of Italian bread and the dairy coolers for yogurt and a carton of milk.

She chose the shortest line: one customer at the checkout and one waiting behind. The clerk called for price checks on two items, and Gabriela groaned aloud. Her glance connected with the person directly ahead of her, who only had five things in her cart, Gabriela noticed. She widened her eyes in sympathy for them both.

"What else can they do?" the other customer replied. "They can't guess the prices. Are you in that much of a hurry?"

She should just leave, Gabriela thought—take her purse out of the carrier and leave everything behind. As she contemplated the move, she saw through the wide plate glass windows someone approaching the store: Sharon Davis, who owned A Better Bean, Ohnita Harbor's only coffee roaster. In no mood to be social, Gabriela picked up a copy of *People* magazine from the checkout rack and pretended to study an article about a Hollywood couple she'd never heard of before. A close-up of the couple, their foreheads pressed together, clashed with the lingering mental picture of the drowned man, his face mangled by the rocks. She slammed the magazine shut.

"Gabriela?"

Her smile wide but her jaw tight, Gabriela looked up. "Oh, hi." She stuffed *People* back into the display rack.

"It's good to see you. We miss you at the Bean—it's been a few days."

"Really busy at the library. And I spent most of the day in Livery for an outreach program."

Sharon grimaced. "I can't imagine going all the way out there for anything."

Gabriela took in Sharon's crisp beige slacks that hugged her slim hips and long legs, and the light blue top the same color as her eyes. "Not too bad of a drive," she said. "But it does make for a long day."

"Long nights too, at least from what I hear." Sharon's mouth curled upward. "You're seeing Daniel Red Deer, right?"

Gabriela didn't feel the need to reply; nothing got past anyone in this town, especially not someone like Sharon.

"He's such a good guy," Sharon added.

"Very nice." Gabriela glanced over at the customers ahead of her in line, but still no movement. Looking across the checkout lanes she saw none moved any faster.

Sharon bit her lip—pearly teeth against her bright pink lipstick. "Did he ever mention me to you?"

Gabriela paused. "Who, Daniel? *Um*, no."

"Well, why would he? It was a while ago. We spent some time together. Gary and I were separated at the time. And it was right after Vicki died. Daniel was so lost and lonely."

Her mind reeling, Gabriela couldn't think of how to respond, so she didn't.

"Daniel was doing some work on my house, and sometimes he'd stay for a beer or a glass of wine."

Gabriela willed a neutral expression on her face as her brain hit the accelerator, racing through the undeniable parallels that, like Sharon, she'd hired Daniel to work on her house and ended up dating him.

"Oh, but there's nothing going on between us now." Sharon smiled again. "Gary and I are in a good place. Really good."

Finally, the customer in front left the checkout, and the woman ahead of her rolled forward. Gabriela couldn't wait to start unloading her cart. "I better get moving, you know. Hungry crowd at home."

Sharon pushed her straight blonde hair behind her ears, revealing a pair of tasteful diamond studs. "Tell Daniel I said hi."

"I'll do that." Gabriela directed her reply to the bottom of her shopping cart as the conveyor started to move and the customer ahead of her moved forward. Looking down, she noticed a trail of dark splotches on her skirt—coffee probably, maybe mud. Given where she'd been that day—Livery, Lucinda's backyard, the state police station—it could be anything.

Gabriela saw a flash of pink manicure as Sharon laid a hand on her shoulder. "Are you okay? Let me help you." Sharon reached into the cart and began unloading the contents onto the conveyor.

"Really, I'm fine."

Sharon stepped closer. "After what happened to you, I can't imagine how you're still standing. Everybody in town wonders the same thing."

Everybody in town? Gabriela fingered the scar on her neck, then dropped her hand. "I assure you I'm doing great."

59

The conveyor belt began to move again. Gabriela handed her reusable shopping bag to the clerk. "I've got this, Sharon," she said over her shoulder, then added, "thanks."

Sharon pushed her empty cart in the other direction.

Gabriela paid for her groceries, loaded the bag in the back of her car, and called her house phone, hoping Ben might answer. The line rang and rang, until she heard her own voice on the message loop. As she got in the car, she called her mother, inviting her to dinner. Agnese feigned a lack of appetite, but when Gabriela promised Daniel would be there, her mother changed her mind. As she drove down her block, Gabriela spotted Ben on his bicycle, pedaling fast, a kid trying to beat the clock even though he was still twenty minutes late. She smiled at the normalcy of it.

Standing at her kitchen counter, Gabriela sliced a carrot into rounds. At the thick end, the knife slipped and nicked her finger. "Damn it!" she swore, examining the cut that didn't look long or deep but bled steadily. The sight of the small wound shocked her, and Gabriela's vision wavered slightly. Grabbing a wad of paper towel, she swiped at the counter to erase the red drips then wrapped her finger to staunch the bleeding. With her left hand, she turned on the tap and ran cold water over her finger. A red streak swirled down the drain. Her stomach lurched.

Daniel came in the back door with a small bouquet of pink carnations and feathery greens. "When I stopped to get gas, I saw these—*whoa*, what did you do?" He took her hand and peered at the cut.

"Just a nick with the knife." Gabriela pulled out of his grip. "I was going too fast, as usual, and mistook my own finger for a carrot."

Daniel wrapped a fresh paper towel around the cut. "You have any aloe?"

"I'm not sunburned."

"Nature's antiseptic. It'll take away the sting too."

"And you know this because . . . ?" She thought of Lucinda and her encyclopedic knowledge of plants.

"My grandmother always had aloe in a pot by the back step. Of course that was out west, where it grows like crazy."

Gabriela went into the downstairs bathroom for a Band-Aid. Daniel took it out of the wrapper and bandaged her finger. He kissed the tip. "Good as new."

Stiffening her injured finger, not wanting to reopen the cut, Gabriela reached for one of the tomatoes on the counter. She nearly collided with Daniel. Pushing her heavy dark hair back from her face with the heels of her hands, she gulped a breath. "Need a little space here."

He handed her two tomatoes.

"Just one."

Daniel leaned against the counter where it right-angled from the sink to the stove. "Don't mean to get in your way."

Gabriela sliced the tomato without looking up.

"You feeling okay?"

She wheeled around toward him. "Why is everyone asking me this today? I'm not crying. I'm not catatonic. I'm just trying to get things done."

Daniel stepped away from the counter. "Are you upset that I came over?"

Gabriela planted her left elbow on the counter then leaned over to rest her head in the palm of her hand. "No, I'm glad you're here. It's just—" She raised up, squared her shoulders. "I don't like it when people fuss over me. Today, in the grocery store, Sharon Davis swooped in like she was Mother Teresa because she said I looked tired."

She studied Daniel's face at the mention of Sharon. She saw his lips part as if he were about to say something and wondered just how involved he and Sharon had been and for how long.

"Well, that was nice of her," he said.

"Yeah, but I don't want people acting as if I'm an invalid." Gabriela jammed her fists on her hips. "Sharon actually said that *everybody* in town was worried about me because of what happened. Everybody in Ohnita Harbor—all twelve thousand of them—wringing their hands over me because someone threatened me."

"With a knife that cut you. Someone who gave you the choice of bleeding to death or being pushed off the library tower," Daniel said.

"Yeah, I know. I was there, remember?" Gabriela closed her eyes at the hurt that flashed across his face. "I'm sorry. My sarcasm was uncalled for. And, in case you're wondering, Sharon made a point of telling me how you two used to date, which I didn't know until now. And she says hi."

Daniel wagged his head. "That's a lot."

For her or for him, she wanted to ask, but didn't. She waited for him to offer some explanation or detail, but he just kept looking at her. "*What?*" she asked.

Daniel stretched one arm toward her and kept it there until Gabriela walked slowly into the embrace. She held her body stiffly at first, then relaxed into the hug, pressing her cheek and the palm of her right hand against his chest. Drawing her hand back, she noticed the dark, wet spot on his shirt.

"Oh no." Gabriela stuck her bleeding finger under the faucet again.

Daniel pulled out a chair at the kitchen table, and Gabriela sat down, her hand wrapped in another paper towel. "I'll finish the salad," he said. Rummaging in a basket on the counter, Daniel pulled out a red onion, peeled, and sliced it. "You ever consider that maybe you're afraid to ask for help?"

Gabriela tightened her jaw. "No. I'm just very independent."

The handle smacked against the counter as Daniel plunked the knife down. "Stubborn is a better word for it."

The sound made Gabriela jump, and she saw worry flicker across his face. She closed her eyes and focused on her breathing. "I just want to act normal, be normal, and have everybody see me as normal."

Daniel squatted down beside her chair. Gabriela heard his knee pop and saw him wince for a second. He stayed like that, eye to eye with her, for what seemed like two minutes but probably only spanned fifteen seconds. "We both know that you have some trauma after what happened," he said.

Tears brimmed, and Gabriela rolled her eyes upward to keep them from falling. "I hate getting triggered, feeling out of control."

Daniel leaned forward, resting his forehead against hers. "I get that. But it won't always be this way. Time and safety, right?"

Agnese came into the kitchen, her hair a little mussed from dozing on the sofa. "Why you not wake me? Oh, sorry."

Daniel put a hand on the table to boost himself upright.

Gabriela shifted in her chair. "It's okay, Mama. We were just having a conversation."

"You talk—the two of you. I go back to my own house for dinner."

"We wouldn't hear of it," Daniel said. "I actually helped make the salad."

Agnese peered into the wooden bowl on the counter. "So much onion. The slices are too thick."

"Welcome to my world," Gabriela said, getting up from the table and patting him on the arm as Agnese fished the onion slices out of the salad bowl then chopped them into smaller pieces.

The next day, the *Ohnita Harbor Times-Herald* ran a front-page story about the body found at Still Waters Chasm. Gabriela braced herself as she skimmed the column for her name, hoping the reporter hadn't found it necessary to mention her. But there it was, in the fourth paragraph: "Last Saturday, the state police received a call from two hikers about a man in distress and an unresponsive woman at Still Waters Chasm. Police identified the hikers as local residents Gabriela Domenici and Daniel Red Deer. Domenici is also the executive director of the Ohnita Harbor Public Library."

The reporter had gotten a quote from the coroner, who stated the man had died of poisoning, not drowning. Just as Lucinda had surmised, Gabriela acknowledged. The police believed that he had been severely ill or already dead when his body went into the water. The article never stated the obvious or even hinted at it: How had someone so ill, or even dead from poisoning, gotten back in the canoe then washed up on the other side of the lake? But that wasn't all. Poisoning could be accidental, a case of ingesting the wrong substance, or intentional. Gabriela read the article a second time, but instead of answering questions, it only nagged her with all she did not know.

———

Two days later, Trooper Morrison called Gabriela at the library to say that the woman's body had not been found as yet. However, the toxicology report on the man led the coroner to suspect atropine, probably from a natural source. "I guess there's some plant in the woods with toxic berries."

Gabriela got up from her desk and shut her office door. "Nightshade," she said, recalling what Lucinda had told her.

"You know about this?"

"No, not really. Just something I heard. Working in a library, you pick up a lot of information."

"The coroner wants to rule out ricin, which is far more problematic," the state trooper said.

Gabriela sucked her breath in at the mention of the powerful poison made from castor beans.

"There's something else, unfortunately. If there is ricin in the man's body, you could be at risk since you performed mouth-to-mouth resuscitation. Maybe Daniel too."

"No, only me. He just did chest compressions. I did the rescue breaths."

"Once we have the toxicology reports, you should get tested by a physician—check for organ damage. We'll know more tomorrow," he said. "I just wanted to prepare you."

"Okay," she said softly. "*Wait!* Did you tell Daniel about the ricin?"

"I called you first. He's my next call."

"Don't tell him—please. He's not at risk. Only me. There's no need for him to worry if it turns out to be nothing."

"I get it," Trooper Morrison said. "We'll wait till we hear more."

Gabriela clutched her bag of herbs. Its scent had faded to memory, but she liked holding it. Tears rolled down her face and dripped onto the papers across her desk. It wasn't possible, that having survived a knife attack, she could die because she had tried to help someone. Life could not be that unfair.

A half hour later, Daniel called, just to ask how she was.

"All right—considering the circumstances." Gabriela's mouth dried, and her tongue didn't want to form the words. "I just spoke with Trooper Morrison."

"Oh?" Daniel asked.

"The woman still hasn't been found," Gabriela added quickly.

"Somebody has to have reported them missing."

"You'd think." Gabriela grabbed a pencil on her desk and began doodling jagged lines across the top of a piece of paper. "So how are you doing?"

"I'm okay." Daniel sighed. "And you're alright—that about covers it. I have to work late tonight, so I won't be over. But I'll call you later."

"Okay, bye." Gabriela watched the call disconnect. Relief flooded through her. She couldn't keep up the pretense of everything being fine when she might have been exposed to ricin. She'd read enough on the internet about ricin poisoning to know what her symptoms would be, starting with respiratory problems, but she'd kept herself from reading anything more about it. At the moment, she needed *not* to think about it.

That evening, Gabriela focused solely on Ben, an evening for just the two of them. After showering and putting on their pajamas, they decided to watch *The Mummy Returns*, an old movie and a little scarier than she remembered, but Ben loved it.

They sat on the sofa together, a bowl of popcorn between them until they both had their fill. Gabriela brought the nearly empty bowl back into the kitchen, then snuggled closer to Ben. As the mummies came back to life and waged battles with archaeologists who fought off an ancient curse, she tried to let the Hollywood images of danger and suspense distract her. But she kept returning to the phone call from the state police. Wrapping her arm around him, Gabriela held her son close.

"Are you scared?" Ben asked, swiveling around to look at her.

Gabriela hesitated for a second. "Oh, of the mummies? Yes—yes, they're awful looking." She pretended to shiver a little, while masking the sheer dread she felt inside.

Ben laughed. "It's not real. Just computer stuff."

He settled against her again, and Gabriela closed her eyes and told herself for the hundredth time that everything would be all right. It had to be.

Twenty-two hours later, Trooper Morrison called. Recognizing his number on the caller ID, Gabriela got up from her desk and closed her office door. Sitting down slowly, she braced to hear the worst.

"No ricin was found. You're in the clear."

Gabriela covered her mouth with her hand. "Oh, thank God."

"Maybe I shouldn't have said something yesterday. You worried for nothing. I just wanted to prepare you."

Gabriela tasted bile and swallowed. "It's okay. Everything's fine now."

"We'll keep you informed if we learn anything else."

When she hung up the phone, Gabriela made it as far as the wastebasket before retching until her stomach emptied. Looking up, she saw Delmina peering through the window of her closed office door. Gabriela gave a little wave to let her know she was alright, but Delmina pursed her lips and shook her head slowly.

CHAPTER
SEVEN

The next morning, an unseasonably warm mid-September day, Gabriela drove to work with the windows down. Crossing the bridge over the Ohnita River, she inhaled the fresh air faintly scented with fish and pine. As it flowed to the harbor and poured into Lake Ontario, the river divided the town: the historically working-class east side from the more prosperous west side. Time had evened things economically, but the topography of the two halves of the town remained distinct. The east side had rolling hills, while the west side heaved higher; atop the tallest hill sat the Ohnita Harbor Public Library.

Catching sight of it as the sun hit the facade, Gabriela paused to appreciate not just the architecture but also what this building had stood for over the past 160 years: free and equitable access to learning. Emboldened with a renewed sense of purpose, Gabriela entered the building and headed upstairs to her office, where she began sketching out a series of evening lectures with both historical and holiday themes that could be hosted at the library between mid-November and mid-December. By midmorning, pleased with her initial ideas, she emailed Charmaine Odele, local historian, history professor at the community college, and the library board president. A minute later, Gabriela received an enthusiastic reply that began, "I'm in!"

Descending the stairs with a smile, Gabriela headed toward the circulation desk to offer a half hour of her time in case one of the clerks wanted a break. As she passed patrons browsing shelves and a couple of senior citizens using the computer stations, Gabriela saw heads swiveling toward her, their stares lingering. She tried to dismiss it until she approached the circulation desk, where she saw Pearl Dunham nudge Francine Clarke with her elbow and tell her to shush. "What's going on?" Gabriela asked.

"Nothing." Francine pushed her limp brown hair, threaded with gray, behind both ears then pulled it out and pushed it back again.

Gabriela raised an eyebrow in Pearl's direction. The older woman locked eyes and looked back. "What d'you expect? Of course people are talking about you. You go off on a hike with your boyfriend and you find two dead people. That's not exactly the kinda luck somebody would want to bottle and sell."

Francine made a face. "What Pearl means is that people are concerned. It's an awful strain. You've been in my prayers every day, Gabriela."

A smile split Pearl's face. "Course, if you were in mine, that would really be something."

Pearl leaned over, her face just a few inches away. Gabriela could smell the cigarette smoke on Pearl's breath. "Seriously, you gotta unwind. Take off a day or two. This place hasn't fallen down in 160 years, so you being gone a couple of days won't send it off its foundation."

Gabriela lay the palm of her hand flat against the circulation desk, feeling the nicks and scratches from countless patrons over the years. "I appreciate the thought, but I'm fine—really. If either of you wants a break, let me know, and I can fill in on the desk."

"I just got in," Francine said, "so I'm good."

"We're not busy," Pearl added. "Why don't *you* take the break, Gabriela?"

Without replying, Gabriela turned and walked quickly back to the stairs and up to the second floor. She passed Delmina's desk with only a curt nod to acknowledge the smile aimed at her and shut her office door.

Sitting down at her desk, Gabriela saw Delmina through the window in her door. "Like a fish in a fishbowl," she said aloud, not caring if Delmina heard her.

Swiveling her chair 90 degrees toward the view from the office window, Gabriela stared out over treetops blazing the first of their fall colors against the bright blue of the sky. Everyone meant well, she told herself and recalled how, in the first few weeks after the knife attack, people she encountered had inquired about her health and Friends of the Library members had regularly showed up at her house, bearing everything from cookies to casseroles to scented candles. Now, the same concern had been churned up because of what happened at Still Waters Chasm.

A soft knock turned Gabriela's attention toward the door, and she called for Delmina to come in.

"I figured you didn't want to be disturbed, but you just received two phone calls. One from Trooper Morrison of the state police. He said he tried your cell phone, but it went to voicemail." Gabriela patted her pockets but found her phone in the bottom of her purse, on mute and showing two missed calls and a voicemail. "The other is from Lucinda Nanz of Livery. She left a number but no message."

Gabriela took the pink message slips from Delmina's hand and thanked her. "If you need anything, you just let me know," Delmina said.

"You'll be the first one I ask," Gabriela promised. But all she wanted was peace and quiet and to be left alone.

"Open or closed?" Delmina asked, her hand on the office door.

"Closed." Gabriela glanced up from the phone messages. "Please." She saw Mike Driskie, the library custodian, behind Delmina and waved him in. So much for some privacy to return the calls, she thought, as Mike took a seat opposite her desk.

"Fixed that light by the back door. Wasn't just a burned-out bulb. Whole fixture had to be replaced. Bad wiring," he said.

"Okay, thanks." Gabriela gave him a tight smile.

"That back entrance will be really bright." Mike made his two hands into starbursts.

"That's great, thanks."

"But you shouldn't be coming in here after hours," Mike added.

"I try not to do that."

"I'm just saying. Lights or not, it's not good to be here by yourself."

Delmina reappeared in the doorway. "You do too much, dear. I used to say the same thing to Mary Jo."

Gabriela flashed back to the spring, when Mary Jo had been in this office as the executive director, and she had occupied the office down the hall as circulation director. Thinking of her, Gabriela missed her boss, who was also her best friend and now seemed farther away than the hundred miles to Binghamton. They'd only gotten together once since Mary Jo moved.

"You need to delegate more," Delmina added.

Gabriela pushed her chair away from the desk, but one of the wheels stuck. Getting halfway out of the chair, she managed to inch it back, then stood. She drew in a breath. "We're all doing the best we can, day by day. Thanks for fixing the light, Mike. And thanks, Delmina, for keeping us afloat."

Mike drifted away, but Delmina stayed. "Yes?" Gabriela asked as she sat back down.

"Charmaine also called, just to check in with you." Delmina handed her a third message slip. "She said it was absolutely nothing urgent—her exact words. If you need anything, she wants you to call her immediately."

The mention of the board president's name evoked for Gabriela the vivid image of a lioness: tall and big boned, with a thick mane of white hair that fell in one smooth layer to her jaw. She'd call Charmaine later, Gabriela decided, when things settled down and she would sound less frazzled.

Delmina departed, closing the door behind her. Gabriela dialed the dispatcher at the state police field station, who patched her through to Trooper Morrison. He told Gabriela that one of the pictures Daniel had taken at Still Waters had shown enough of the canoe to trace it to a rental place near Saranac Lake. "We could tell it had a gelcoat finish, and only a half dozen places in the Adirondacks rent canoes like that. The last one we called had an unreturned rental."

Gabriela pictured the canoe: the deep green of the finish that reflected the light. Something about that canoe stuck with her, but for now she had another priority: She wanted to know the names of the dead people they'd found. "Who were they?" she asked.

"Keith Maldon rented the canoe. He was a biologist with the Department of Environmental Conservation."

Gabriela let those details sink in. "And the woman?"

"His girlfriend, Sheena Dowley. She taught geology at a high school in Albany."

Keith and Sheena, biologist and geologist; Still Waters Chasm must have seemed like a paradise at first, Gabriela mused. The lake some six hundred feet deep; the layers of rock that showed the span of eons. Then it had become a dark and deadly place, beauty obliterated by panic and the sensation of choking. She recalled Keith's body convulsing, his lungs unable to draw breath.

"Was it official—the trip, I mean, for the DEC?" Gabriela asked.

"That's not clear," Trooper Morrison replied. "Maldon worked in fisheries, so it's possible he wanted to see Still Waters firsthand. But there were other things going on too, which I can't really discuss at this point."

His reticence annoyed Gabriela. If it weren't for her and Daniel, no one would have known what had happened to Keith and Sheena. "Let me guess. It has something to do with that construction site in the woods. It's not a fire tower, and nobody is building a cabin."

The state trooper said nothing.

"You didn't know about that either until we told you," Gabriela went on.

"It's seismic testing, but you didn't hear it from me."

"What? Somebody's going to drill for oil up there?" That made no sense to her. There had never been much oil and gas drilling in New York State, except for some small activity in the western part of the state.

"I've said all I can—more than I should. Right now, the most important thing is we know who those two people are—or, rather, were. If we can figure out what they were doing up there, we'll get a better indication of whether their deaths were accidental or suspicious."

Gabriela fought against the urge to laugh at the absurdity of it. "Maybe eating poisonous berries could be an accident. But Keith and Sheena did not get into that canoe themselves. They were dead. So, the bigger issue here is how two lifeless bodies got into a canoe and ended up in the lake."

"I know," Trooper Morrison said after a long pause. "And I do believe what you've told me. But other people want to go on the assumption that it was an accidental poisoning. And if you tell anyone I said that, I'll deny it."

Gabriela switched the phone out of her right hand to cool her sweating palm. "So that's why you need to figure out why Keith and Sheena went canoeing that day. Maybe he didn't like what was happening in the chasm and somebody put a stop to him."

"That's your speculation, not mine."

"Sounds like a good theory if you ask me."

Gabriela heard only dead air.

"Have a good afternoon," Trooper Morrison told her. "I thought you'd like to know the names of the two people before the article appears in the newspaper."

Just as she started to disconnect the call, a picture of the canoe flashed in Gabriela's mind. "Wait!" she yelled into the phone. "You there?"

Trooper Morrison's voice returned. "I can't tell you anything more than I already have."

"No, this is about the canoe. I just thought of something." Under her desk, Gabriela wiggled her feet in excitement over the idea. "The canoe was upside down. Before we saw the bodies, I remember noticing how the whole thing, even the hull, was dark green. Overturning a canoe is something you do when you make camp, right?"

"Unless somebody thinks it might rain."

Gabriela focused all her attention on the memory of the overturned canoe next to the tree trunk. "But there wasn't any rain. So, they must have overturned the canoe the night before. If so, where was their tent? Their sleeping bags?"

"Maybe they set up camp away from the water."

"Then where was their stuff? Do you really think these two people—no pulse, no breathing—came to, walked somewhere to take down their tent, packed up all their gear, paddled a canoe, and drowned—all within the time we were gone from the lake?"

Trooper Morrison didn't reply right away.

"Oh, come on!" Gabriela's voice rose the more she spoke. "Those people camped somewhere and came to the beach in the morning. And that's where they died—first Sheena, then Keith. Someone else must have packed up their stuff, wherever it was, and dumped their bodies in the lake. Whoever it was didn't want any trace of them to be found."

"Just be careful," the state trooper said. "There's no reason to think you're in danger, but you never know."

"Unfortunately, I do know." Gabriela's fingers found their way to the scar on her neck. Her excitement cooled to dread as she thought of her new L.L.Bean backpack with the ID tag she'd written out the morning of their hike, and Daniel's dark blue backpack that looked like it had seen a lot of treks. The newspaper article had listed not only her name but also where she worked. If someone wanted to find her, it wouldn't be hard.

When the call ended, Gabriela opened a spreadsheet on her computer screen and worked on her part of a grant proposal from the City of Ohnita Harbor. Last year, the city had been a finalist for an eight-million-dollar state grant, $1.6 million of which would have gone to the library, until the corruption scandal that took down the mayor also meant the city had to withdraw its application. Now the new mayor, Duncan Phillips, insisted they try for a smaller grant: $1.2 million for city beautification, with 10 percent going to the library.

Gabriela stared at the screen, the numbers blurring into rows of dots. Fixing the front steps and replacing the railing could be construed as beautifying the building, especially given its designation on the National Register of Historic Places. She might even be able to hire a part-time assistant to help Mike with the improvements. But the grant allowed no flexibility where the library needed the most help: staffing, including a new director of circulation, her old job.

She rubbed the heels of her hands into her eyes before remembering the makeup she'd applied that morning. Mascara streaked the base of her palms. Grabbing a tissue, Gabriela wet it with her tongue and wiped under her eyes. Just then Delmina walked by and saw her through the window on the door.

"Now she thinks I'm crying," Gabriela murmured. She smiled and waved at Delmina, who returned a look of sympathy.

To avoid any misinterpretation of her mental state getting back to the board, Gabriela called Charmaine. "How are you holding up?" asked the board president.

Gabriela clicked a pen three times before putting it down, knowing Charmaine could probably hear it. "Busy as usual, but no complaints about that."

"You know that I'm referring to the incident at Still Waters," Charmaine replied. "The newspaper article made it sound like quite the grisly scene. I'm sorry you and your friend had to encounter that."

"Yes, that's true." Gabriela searched for a way to pivot the conversation. "Did you hear about our outreach program in Livery? Well attended, especially for the first one. Perhaps you'd like to give a talk sometime on local history. You know everything about this area."

Charmaine made a sound like the idea intrigued her but pointed out that her expertise centered more on the Great Lakes and the Erie Canal. She promised to give it some thought, and Gabriela said she would come back with some suggested dates in the coming months. The phone conversation ended pleasantly, and Gabriela congratulated herself for deflecting unwanted concern.

Another pink message slip sat next to the tissue box. Gabriela punched in the number on her phone. Lucinda greeted her warmly. "Can you come up to see me one day this week—morning, afternoon, evening?"

Gabriela considered her schedule and apologized. "I'll be there in ten days for a children's story hour. Can we see each other then?"

"Oh, we'll have a crowd for that," Lucinda continued. "But this is about Wendy, the woman you met at my house the other day."

The thin woman with the bruises on her face, Gabriela recalled. Perhaps Wendy wanted the number to the county's domestic abuse hotline or information about free legal assistance. "If Wendy needs something right away, I can call her."

"She wants to show you something," Lucinda went on. "Given your expertise, I think you'll find it fascinating."

Gabriela recalled the scroll Wendy had brought to Lucinda's house and how protectively she had held onto it. Clicking on her electronic calendar, Gabriela saw she had a small window on Friday—three days away. She could get to Lucinda's house by 12:45 but would have to be on the road again no later than 2:30 to make a 3:30 meeting at City Hall.

"Splendid," Lucinda said. "Bring Agnese too. It would be nice to see her again."

Friday arrived cool and damp, and a light drizzle changed to a steady rain. Gabriela hugged Lucinda, and Agnese kissed her on both cheeks Italian-style. As they sat down at the table and Lucinda brought over the teapot, Gabriela detected the aroma of ginger and something else—a mix of wood and mint.

"Catnip. It's good for calming anxiety," Lucinda said as she poured three cups. "But not enough to put you to sleep."

"Won't Corky be jealous?" Gabriela joked, then took a sip.

"Oh, he gets plenty—right out of the garden."

Agnese opened a plastic container of almond cookies she'd baked that morning. "You try. They good for you too."

Lucinda's smile reached all the way to her eyes. "Baked with love, so I know they are."

Gabriela thought she heard something in the driveway and turned expectantly, hoping Wendy had arrived.

"She'll be here," Lucinda promised. "It's hard for her to get away sometimes, but she told me this morning she'd leave as soon as she made J.J. his lunch."

Given the bruise she'd seen on Wendy's face, J.J. should be served a restraining order and divorce papers, Gabriela opined silently, but kept her thoughts to herself.

"J.J. is working these days, so Wendy doesn't want to upset him," Lucinda added.

"What does he do that's so important?" Gabriela's lip curled with every word.

"He restores campers. People come from as far away as Lake Placid or even Syracuse to bring him a camper to work on. He gets a crew together and they tear everything out and refurbish them." Lucinda took a bite of an almond cookie and a sip of tea. "Do you remember Jake from your program on fishing? That's his father—Jake Haughton. So he's Jake Junior, but everybody calls him J.J."

Gabriela scowled. "Jake Senior didn't seem to be the friendliest person, but I gather this J.J. is worse than his father."

Lucinda nodded. "Jake is ornery, but J.J. is just plain mean."

"I noticed the bruise." Gabriela raised her teacup to take another sip.

"He's threatened to kill her a couple of times, but Wendy says it's only when he's been really drunk."

Gabriela put her cup down on the saucer with the force of her outrage, and tea sloshed over the rim. "When a woman is murdered, more than half the time a spouse or a partner killed her—current or former. We have to help her."

"That's why I asked you here," Lucinda said.

"There's a women's shelter in Ohnita Harbor. I can take her there today. We'll see about getting her legal protection."

79

Lucinda poured from the teapot to top off everyone's cup. "Wendy needs money so she can get away from J.J. and go a lot farther away than Ohnita Harbor."

Through the window, Gabriela saw a small blue car pull in the yard. "I don't have that kind of resource." She watched the driver's side door swing open and Wendy step out. The young woman reached back inside the car and drew out something wrapped in a black garbage bag.

Lucinda scurried to the door. "No one is asking for money. We need different help. You'll see."

The change from "Wendy needs help" to "we need help" didn't escape Gabriela's notice. Lucinda clearly played a part in whatever involved Wendy.

Hair dripping, her jeans and shirt soaked, Wendy stepped into the kitchen, clutching a garbage bag wrapped around something. She appeared even younger than the other day, and Gabriela adjusted her assessment to about twenty-five.

"J.J. fell asleep after lunch, so I just got in the car and left. I didn't dare open the closet and get my slicker 'cause the door squeaks, and I didn't want to wake him."

Lucinda wrapped a cardigan sweater around Wendy's thin shoulders then poured her a cup of tea. "You remember Gabriela and her mother, Agnese, from the other day?"

Wendy bobbed her head in the affirmative, but she didn't make eye contact.

"I'm glad to see you again," Gabriela began.

"What you bring with you?" Agnese asked.

Gabriela nudged her foot against her mother's shoe under the table.

"It stay dry?" Agnese continued.

Gabriela tapped her mother harder this time. Agnese's shoe scraped against the floor as she slid it back.

"I'll show you." Wendy opened the top of the black garbage bag. "It's really old."

"Oh, like me!" Agnese said.

"Older than that." Wendy pulled out a cardboard tube and unsealed one end. Sticking her fingers inside, she extracted a large, rolled sheet of paper so yellowed, it appeared brown in some places.

Seeing the coloration, Gabriela stifled a groan at the lack of protection for what appeared to be an antique.

"Let's roll it out flat," Lucinda said, beckoning them all to follow her into the next room, where a long dining room table stood on six carved legs. Lucinda removed a vase of fresh flowers from the center and flicked a few petals from the tablecloth.

As Wendy smoothed out the document, Gabriela visually measured the dimensions: about three feet wide and two feet high. Noticing the vertical lines imprinted on the paper, Gabriela gasped. Such markings indicated what was known as laid paper made from cotton rags shredded into a pulp and spread on a wire-mesh screen to dry. She knew that antique maps and other documents dating before 1800 often used laid paper. After that date, smoother, more uniform woven paper became increasingly common.

Her eyes shifted to the drawing: an intricate pen-and-ink rendering of a tall center post and two angled supports at the bottom, around which billowed an oval shape. "Gerald Shumler, 1808" had been written with great flourish in the bottom right-hand corner.

"He was my great-great-great-great-great-grandfather." Wendy ticked off five greats on her fingers. "It's really old, so I guess that means it's valuable—right?"

So that's the plan, Gabriela thought. Wendy wanted to sell an old document and get away from her husband. "Hard to say what it could be worth." Gabriela fingered the paper and the familiar feel of old documents returned to her. "But I can tell you this should lie flat, ideally in a climate-controlled space. Rolling it up will ruin it."

Wendy's forehead wrinkled. "I was given it this way."

Gabriela pressed her lips together, then curled her mouth upward. "From now on, let's keep it flat. Do you know what it's a drawing of?"

"Gerald was a sailmaker—that's what my dad told me. So I guess this is some kind of sail design?" Wendy's voice rose at the end, turning a statement into a question.

As Gabriela pored over the drawing, she noticed the thickness of the lines at one end where a pen nib deposited maximum ink into the paper, then thinning at the other end. One corner was creased, but she resisted the urge to unfold it, for fear of further damaging the document. What little she knew about sailing, from an exhibition she'd helped arrange at the New York Public Library, ships in the 1800s had three masts and square sails like giant bedsheets, as well as triangular ones that helped catch the wind—jibs, she recalled.

This sail resembled nothing she'd ever seen before. Its irregular shape lacked symmetry: two long sides and four short ones. Lines like spiderwebs indicated ropes that tethered and moved the sail. Maybe it depicted an early parachute or a hang glider prototype, Gabriela guessed. "Does your dad know any more about it?"

Wendy shook her head. "He died about a year ago. When he got sick, he gave this to me. He said it's been in my family for more than two hundred years."

"Did your family live around here?" Gabriela asked, hoping the location might give some clue about this strange drawing.

Wendy nodded. "I grew up in Natural Bridge."

"Is that a town?"

"Yeah, really small. It's on the way to the Adirondacks. Not many people stop there, though."

"Oh, but some interesting people did," Lucinda chimed in. "No less than Napoleon's brother."

Gabriela blinked twice. "Napoleon—as in Bonaparte?"

"The one and only." Lucinda squared her shoulders and tucked her hand against her stomach in a quick imitation of Napoleon's famous pose. She explained that his brother Joseph Bonaparte had been king of Naples and then king of Spain. But after being deposed, he came to the New World, bought land in the Adirondacks, and settled in Natural Bridge. "They named the lake up there after him."

"Napoleon—he was Italian!" Agnese blurted out. "From Corsica."

Unable to resist following this tangent, Gabriela did a quick Google search on her phone and read aloud a short description of Lake Bonaparte and its history: "*Having bought more than 25,000 acres in the Adirondacks, Joseph Bonaparte established a camp for himself, with plans that his brother, Napoleon, would join him there in security and seclusion. Although the Adirondack dwelling was built as a hunting camp, it contained fine art and tapestries—and some say meals were eaten off plates of solid gold. For pleasure, Joseph and his guests rode in a six-oared gondola on what they called Lake Diana in honor of the Roman Goddess, which later became known as Lake Bonaparte.*"

Gabriela stopped reading, her eyes wide and eyebrows raised.

Lucinda chuckled. "The North Country is full of interesting characters."

"We used to fish there—on Lake Bonaparte, I mean," Wendy said.

Gabriela tapped a finger against her pursed lips. "Your ancestor—Gerald Shumler. He lived in Natural Bridge too?"

"I guess so—for a while. He's buried there. All I know is, my dad told me this paper was really old and really important. He called it our family treasure."

Gabriela wondered what a sailmaker would be doing in a land-locked area on the edge of the Adirondacks, but maybe he made sails for smaller crafts that plied inland lakes. Her curiosity piqued, she weighed the possibility that Gerald Shumler and Joseph Bonaparte might have known each other. Another Google search put a date of 1818 on Joseph Bonaparte's land purchase in the Adirondacks.

As she quickly scrolled, a name and a date jumped out at her: Count Le Ray de Chaumont, described as "an old friend of Joseph Bonaparte," came to the Americas in the late 1790s and became a permanent resident of the area near Natural Bridge starting in 1808—the same date as the Shumler drawing. A coincidence, yes, but also an apparent intersection between a sailmaker who lived in Natural Bridge and a French exile and a close associate of the Bonaparte family who lived in the area at the same time. But she knew it would take more than paths crossing in time and place to establish any connection between Shumler, the drawing, and the Bonaparte brothers.

Agnese placed her hand on Wendy's arm. "You'll see. Gabriela, she find out for you. Then you'll know everything."

Gabriela cast a quick glance at her mother, annoyed at such a sweeping promise. She thought for a moment. Old nautical drawings, sea charts, and navigation maps could be valuable, but Gabriela wasn't sure about a schematic for some kind of sail. The key would be finding out more about Gerald Shumler. "I used to know someone at the Mystic Seaport Museum in Connecticut. I don't know if they're still there, but I'll make some inquiries."

"What I tell you! She knows somebody. And that somebody gonna know somebody else," Agnese said. "That's how it works."

Gabriela took several photos of the drawing with her phone, including two close-ups of the name and date. "From now on, this drawing has to be stored flat—no exceptions."

"I don't have a place for it," Wendy said. "J.J. doesn't—"

Like it? Know about it? Gabriela finished the sentence in her head when Wendy didn't.

"You can store it right here." Lucinda opened the top drawer of a large sideboard in the dining room and removed two long, folded tablecloths. The drawing fitted snugly inside.

Wendy's eyes stayed on the drawer. "Who are you going to tell about it?"

"Researchers—people who have expertise in these kinds of things." Gabriela opened the drawer to take one more photo.

"I've been hiding this at my mother's. But I told her I have to sell it." Wendy traced her finger around a swirl of woodgrain on the sideboard.

Gabriela wanted to tell Wendy about more help than just an appraisal of an old drawing. She could go somewhere safe, talk to legal experts who could keep J.J. away for her. "You don't have to live like this," she began.

Wendy jolted. "Like what?"

Gabriela knew from articles she'd read that many women who suffered abuse often denied it out of shame or fear of incrimination, and abusers sometimes convinced women that they were to blame. She mulled the best response. "You seem a little afraid."

Agnese put her arm around Wendy's waist. "You gonna be okay! You need anything, you tell us, okay? You call Lucinda—" She pronounced it *Lu-chin-da*. "And she tell us."

Wendy swiped at her cheeks, and Agnese embraced her.

"For sure, we'll help any way we can," Gabriela agreed. As she watched Agnese with Wendy, she tried to remember the last time her mother had hugged her like that.

CHAPTER
EIGHT

On Saturday night, Gabriela bustled around the house in her bathrobe, alternating between stirring butter and milk into macaroni
and cheese for Ben's dinner and testing the iron as it heated up. She
had changed her clothes twice already, discarding a sage green dress
with muted yellow flowers that turned her complexion sallow, as
well as a skirt that cinched her waist uncomfortably. Now a pair of
navy slacks stretched across the ironing board and a white blouse
needed pressing. Before smoothing the wrinkles out of her clothes,
she spooned a lumpy orange mound on a plate and called for Ben.

Gabriela dressed in the downstairs bathroom. When she came
out, she saw the blandness of her outfit and nearly dove back into her
closet for something else to wear but didn't have time. This would
have to do. While Ben ate, Gabriela drove to her mother's house
to pick her up. On the five-minute return trip, neither woman said
much. Then, as she pulled into her own driveway, Gabriela heard her
mother's deep sigh, which ended in a few muttered words of Italian.
"What time you coming home?"

"I told you, Mama. I'll be home in the morning."

"And what you gonna tell your son? That you sleep with Daniel?"

Gabriela stared out the side window of the car, fighting the bitterness that soured her thoughts. "If Ben asks, I will tell him that I'm staying at Daniel's house. He doesn't need to know more than that."

"You think you so smart, but you act like a *puttana* and then he won't marry you."

Gabriela slammed the car into park and shut off the engine. "Don't you dare use that word with me." She started to count to ten in her head but stopped at three. "Jim moved out and started living with someone while we were still married. But what did I do? I moved back here to take care of my son—and you. I've done everything for everyone else. Now I am enjoying my life and a relationship with Daniel for however long it lasts."

"And what then?" Agnese spat out. "You say, 'Okay. Too bad,' and you find somebody else?"

Gabriela felt the strangle of the seatbelt as she spun around in her seat. "I don't know what's going to happen, Mama. But I've been alone and lonely for so long."

Agnese curled one side of her lip. "You take me home. You don't have a babysitter, then you don't go off and do this."

Gabriela started the engine. "Fine. I'll call someone else."

Agnese slapped the dashboard with her hand. "You would have a stranger stay with Ben so you can be with this man? Okay, I stay—but for Ben, not for what you're doing."

Gabriela's scalp prickled as if with a sudden rash of heat and her hand went to her throat, fingering the scar. "If we go inside, you're not going to say another word about this—and never in front of Ben."

Agnese opened the door and got out. Gabriela gave her mother a head start toward the house, needing every bit of increased distance between them. Once her mother climbed half the steps to the small deck behind the house, Gabriela put herself in motion.

———

Daniel arrived a half hour later in jeans and an open-neck white shirt, the long sleeves folded back neatly to expose his tanned forearms. Gabriela tried to hurry them both out of the house, but Daniel lingered to talk with Agnese. Gabriela braced for what her mother might say.

"So where you going tonight?" Agnese asked him.

"A little place not far from here—great fish and right on the water," Daniel replied.

"Fine, I come too. Like when you go out walking with a boy and the old mamas follow you."

"You'll chaperone?" Gabriela offered.

"*Si.* That's what I do. *Shop-a-rone.*" Agnese laughed, but Gabriela caught the glint in her mother's coal-dark eyes and felt the point of the dagger in that joke.

Leaving the two of them in the living room, Gabriela went upstairs one more time to Ben's room, finding him flopped across the floor, surrounded by Legos, which he hadn't touched in the past several months. "Where you guys going?" the boy asked.

"To dinner and then we're going to watch a movie at Daniel's house." She squatted down and stroked her son's hair.

"You could watch it here."

Gabriela paused as if considering the suggestion. "We could, but I haven't been to Daniel's house to watch a movie."

Ben snapped and unsnapped two Lego pieces with a series of sharp clicks. "If you guys get married, where are you going to live?"

Gabriela slipped out of her crouching position and sat on the floor. "Nobody is talking about moving anywhere."

"Dad moved to California with Shelley. Are you going to move in with Daniel?"

Gabriela recalled the advice of the counselor she had seen back in Brooklyn after Jim left: Answer the question that's being asked—no more, no less. "I have no plans to move anywhere. You and I are going to live here for a long time."

She waited while Ben snapped the Lego pieces together and pulled them apart three more times. "Can we go fishing again? You and me and Daniel?"

Gabriela wrapped her arms around him, not caring if her slacks and shirt got wrinkled. "Yeah, we can go—lots and lots."

<hr />

They headed north along twisting and hilly roads and arrived forty minutes later at The Lakeside, aptly named for its location overlooking a remote stretch of Lake Ontario's rocky shoreline. A blonde woman with an ample figure showing a lot of sunburned cleavage greeted Daniel by name and led them to their table along the window. The hostess set both menus down on Daniel's side of the table. He handed one to Gabriela.

"Guess you're a regular," she said.

"Off and on. The fried perch dinner here is the best." He snapped the menu shut.

Gabriela read the ingredients of the Cobb salad but figured the turkey and ham would probably be deli meat and opted for the fish sandwich with coleslaw instead of fries.

The sun had already set, but a pink glow lingered outside the plate glass window. Gabriela watched it fade and wondered who Daniel had taken here before. Vicki, for sure. Maybe Sharon Davis. Reining in her thoughts, Gabriela scolded herself for being ridiculous. But something in the hostess's familiarity made her wonder if Daniel had a reputation for bringing different women to this place. Or maybe he ate alone at that bar, as several men were doing right now, and flirted with the female staff.

As if on cue, the hostess returned to their table. "You getting the perch? Fresh caught today." She smiled at Daniel.

"Am I that predictable?" he laughed.

"What kind of fish is in the sandwich?" Gabriela asked.

The hostess glanced over at her. "Cod. Comes frozen."

Gabriela waited to hear more of an explanation, but the hostess merely looked at her. "All righty then," Gabriela muttered as the hostess left their table to greet a couple entering the restaurant.

"Dotty is harmless." Daniel fidgeted with his fork. "She's just—"

"Rude to other women?"

Seeing the pinch of Daniel's eyebrows, Gabriela focused her attention on the menu. "I'm going to have the fish sandwich, so we don't order the same thing."

"You're missing out," Daniel said. "Ordering two perch dinners wouldn't make Dotty think any less of us."

"Oh, she already thinks highly of you, and I doubt she's ever going to change her opinion of me." Gabriela set the menu down and rested her elbows on the table. Daniel said nothing.

After their food arrived, Gabriela looked at the mound of narrow perch filets that filled a small platter in front of Daniel. "The chef must love you too."

He cut off a small piece of fried perch and held his fork out to her. She leaned forward for the bite. The tang of the tartar sauce, the crunch of the batter, and the sweetness of the fish mixed in her mouth. "For the record, that's ten times better than my fish sandwich."

"Next time, we'll trade," Daniel said.

Gabriela wiped tartar sauce from her fingers and wondered how she could eat this sandwich without wearing it. "Next time we'll both get the perch."

As they made small talk, Gabriela noticed a man sitting at the bar glancing their way numerous times. He could be looking out the window behind them, she considered, although the sky had darkened and the lights along the pier outside glowed with more utility than attractiveness. She leaned forward to speak in a low voice to Daniel. "That guy keeps staring over here."

"Maybe he's just admiring the lovely woman I'm having dinner with."

Gabriela cast a quick look at the man. "He's creeping me out."

Daniel reached for her hand and brushed his thumb across the back of it. "Just ignore him."

The waitress asked if they wanted dessert, and they declined. As they waited for the check, the man got off his barstool and approached their table. Gabriela stiffened her spine and sat up straight. Instinctively, she observed everything about him: about five-foot-ten, his hair shorn military short. He wore jeans—like nearly everyone else in this place, but with a hoodie with an insignia splashed across the front that she couldn't read.

Daniel turned in his chair. The man stopped a few feet from their table. "You're Red Deer. I've seen you here before, and I remember your name."

"Not many Red Deers around here. Think I'm the only one." Daniel folded his hands on the table.

"I read in the paper about two people who found those bodies at Still Waters. One was Red Deer, and I figured that had to be you. The other was a woman."

"That would be me, Gabriela Domenici." She considered extending her hand but decided against it. "And who are you?"

He eyed her, and Gabriela fought the urge to look away. "Colby."

At closer range now, she studied the logo on his sweatshirt: a large leafless tree, spreading an empty crown, and a stump with an axe protruding from it. A woodcutter, she guessed.

"So, what happened out there? At Still Waters," Colby asked.

Daniel tugged on the collar of his shirt, adjusting it. "Some kind of accident, I guess."

"We don't know more than what's been in the newspaper," Gabriela added. "I think the police suspect poisoning—berries or something they ate."

Colby took a half step closer. "I don't believe that." He shook his head and frowned. "Something in that lake. Never eat the fish outta there. Too much mercury."

"Huh?" Gabriela cast a glance at Daniel, widening her eyes slightly. She suspected Colby had been overserved at the bar.

"Maybe you're right. But the perch here tonight was good," Daniel said. He looked around for the waitress and signaled again for the bill.

Colby leaned down, and Gabriela could smell the beer on his breath. She angled her head backward. "I'm telling you—it's the water. I thought you people could sense that stuff."

"You people?" Daniel asked.

"Indians. You know—"

"*Mmmm.* I must have been absent from Indian camp that week."

Gabriela noticed the tightening of Daniel's jaw and felt a stab in her chest. She had no idea what to say.

The waitress set a small plastic tray bearing the bill on the table. Daniel pulled out his wallet. "Thanks for stopping to say hello, Colby," Daniel said. "You have a good evening."

Colby took a step backward, still looking at them, then turned and walked back to the bar. As Daniel counted out twenties to cover the bill and a generous tip, Gabriela kept her eye on Colby. She saw him drain his drink and head for the door.

Gabriela used the restroom, and Daniel waited for her nearby. When they left the restaurant, their feet crunched on the gravel parking lot. The noise seemed overly loud to Gabriela, announcing their every step. Daniel opened the passenger side door and, after she got in, Gabriela watched him check in all directions as he walked to the driver's side door. The locks clicked before Daniel started the engine.

"That's the only problem with this place on a Saturday night. It can get a rougher crowd. That guy never would have said anything to me if my name were Smith or Jones."

Gabriela touched his arm. "Does that happen often?"

"Often enough to piss me off. There's a lot of prejudice out there."

Growing up, Gabriela had borne jabs at her name. She remembered crying over a kid in fifth grade who'd chanted "Greasy Domenici" every time she passed him in the hallway. When the girls in seventh-grade gym class called her "Gaby Gorilla" because of the dark hair on her unshaven legs, she had begged her mother for a razor, then had taken her father's without permission to do the job. For her, such comments had stopped when she became an adult, but Daniel still faced prejudice because of his ethnicity. "I'm sorry that happened. But this evening is for us, and I'm not going to let anything change that," she said softly.

Daniel rested his hand on her knee. "I'm glad to hear that. I feel the same way."

They drove for about a half hour before Daniel made a right turn that Gabriela recognized as the road leading to his house. A short while later, they pulled into a long driveway, triggering the motion sensor on the side of the house. Gabriela caught a glimpse of something small scurrying out of the flood of light, a raccoon, maybe, or an opossum.

Standing in the backyard, Gabriela listened to the wind fanning the branches of the tall evergreen trees with a sound like waves against a beach. Daniel took her hand and led her through the back door and into the kitchen with its tall cabinets, many with panes of glass in their doors to reveal the neatly arranged dishes inside. Daniel opened one cupboard, took out two wineglasses. "I got the red you like." He reached for an unopened bottle on the counter.

Gabriela drifted from the kitchen into the open space of the main floor, where all but one weight-bearing wall had been taken down. In the area nearest the kitchen stood a table with six chairs; in the opposite corner clustered a sofa and two comfortable chairs, facing a wall-mounted television. Daniel's framed artwork took up the rest of the space: oil paintings, watercolors, and charcoal sketches.

Accepting a glass of wine from Daniel, Gabriela took it to the sofa. He clicked a remote and the sound system engaged, filling the room with the sound of a saxophone and an upbeat jazz tune that Gabriela recognized but couldn't name. Daniel sat beside her, his long legs stretched out, feet on the coffee table. A bachelor's habit, Gabriela thought, and imagined Vicki scolding him for it. The scene, all too vivid, brought with it an unwelcome reality. She and Daniel had made love at his house before, but she'd never spent the night. Tonight, she would sleep in the bed he had shared with Vicki, maybe even on the same mattress and pillows. The intimacy of it—not just the two of them, but the memory of Vicki as well—gave her second thoughts about staying. If she said she had to get home to Ben, Daniel would understand, Gabriela told herself. But she wanted to spend the night with him; she just needed to stop thinking about Vicki and the bed.

Take it slow, Gabriela told herself as she shifted her posture, crossing one leg over the other, and leaned forward. "Someone showed me something interesting the other day."

"Oh?" Daniel set his wine down and turned toward her.

Giggling at the unintended innuendo, Gabriela rushed to explain. "Something historic. The person asked me to keep it confidential. I promised to only share the image with experts and researchers."

"Do I qualify?" Daniel winked at her.

"As an artist, perhaps. But seriously, please keep this between us." Gabriela scrolled through her phone to the photos of the schematic drawing.

Daniel took her phone and enlarged the image, then swiped to the next one. "1808—that's impressive. You think it's original?"

"Yeah, I do. The paper has the right feel and markings. And real ink—not just a copy. We know Gerald Shumler was a sailmaker, but what is this a drawing of? To me, it looks like some kind of parachute prototype."

Daniel studied the image. "You see how the mast looks like it bends here, right above where the two supports angle in? I think is a foldable sail. When the ropes loosened, I bet this thing folded up like a tent."

"A foldable sail. So this was small, like an umbrella?"

"Not necessarily. I've seen large ones."

"Really? Where? Any idea how big this one could have been?"

Daniel put up his hands as if to slow the stream of questions. "The only foldable sail I saw was not antique. It was a polyester and fiberglass combination for a canoe."

Gabriela cocked an eyebrow. "A sail for a canoe?"

"I'm serious. If the wind is right, a canoe can really fly across the water."

When Daniel finished examining the images, Gabriela took back the phone and studied the drawings. "At least I will have something more specific to ask the museum at Mystic when I call. I can tell them I think it's an antique drawing of a foldable sail."

Daniel reached over and touched her hair, winding a curl gently around his index finger. "Why are you doing this, with everything else you have to do?"

Gabriela clicked off the photos and set her phone aside. "The person who asked me is in trouble. She really needs help."

"Help with an antique drawing?"

"Bigger than that. But the part I can help with is getting some idea of what this is and what it might be worth."

"I take it this person you are helping needs money." Daniel took Gabriela's wineglass out of her grasp and reached for her hand.

"She needs to escape."

"You're such a good person. You never think of yourself."

Gabriela slid over and relaxed against Daniel's chest. "Sometimes I do." She raised her face to kiss him, at first light and gentle, then stronger and more urgent. "I'm thinking about what I want to do right now."

Daniel fumbled with the buttons on her blouse, and Gabriela undid them, then stood to take off her slacks. With every touch and sensation, her longing intensified with an almost painful urgency. They made love on the sofa, with the lights on and the music playing, and afterward they lay together, bodies entwined. Gabriela's eyelids drooped as Daniel traced slow circles on her shoulder with his fingertips. She dozed off, then roused when she felt a tug on her hand. Daniel led her up narrow stairs to the sleeping loft overlooking the main room. A king-size bed took up most of the space, flanked by two dressers: one a dark wood chest of drawers she assumed was Daniel's; the other, shorter and wider with a honey-colored finish.

"You want some water?" Daniel headed back toward the stairs.

"Yes, please," Gabriela replied. She watched as Daniel descended the stairs, but instead of going into the kitchen, he headed to the bathroom. Hearing the door close, she swept her eyes around the loft, fixating on the lighter-colored dresser. Slowly, she opened the drawers, feeling the drag of wood on wood. The first two were empty, and the third jammed at an angle. Gabriela couldn't pull it out or push it in, and now she heard Daniel in the kitchen: opening a cupboard, taking out glasses, running water in the sink.

Bracing herself, Gabriela pushed with both hands. The wood squeaked—loud enough for Daniel to hear, she assumed—and the drawer inched back in place. Peering over the loft railing, she watched Daniel walking naked through the house, taking their wineglasses to the kitchen, then turning off lights. She looked back at the dresser and opened the last drawer. Inside was a lilac-colored sweater and a photograph of Daniel and Vicki sitting together in an Adirondack chair, her long legs over his, both of them laughing and Vicki wearing the lilac sweater. Hearing Daniel's first step on the stairs, she slipped the photograph back inside the drawer and pushed it shut. When his head and shoulders appeared above the top landing, Gabriela sat down on the side of the bed nearest the dresser.

Smiling, Daniel handed a glass of water to her, and Gabriela drank. Watching Daniel settle in—punching the pillow into shape and patting the other side of the mattress for her—she assumed he was in his familiar space. That meant she occupied what had been Vicki's side of the bed.

After a kiss, he reached for a switch on the wall, and the room darkened. Gabriela sat up, fingering the edge of the sheet. She looked over but couldn't make out Daniel's face. "Are you glad I stayed?" she asked, her voice barely above a whisper.

"Of course," Daniel replied. "Why wouldn't I be?"

Gabriela waited to hear more, but he said nothing. She felt his hand under the sheets, seeking her out. Lying down, she curled into his body, his arm around her waist. She heard Daniel's breathing deepen, but Gabriela stayed awake. She stared into the dark room until her eyes felt dry and gritty and she had to close them. Eventually, she slept.

CHAPTER

NINE

Story hour at the Livery library a few days later brought a full house. Gabriela counted eleven young children, eight mothers, and some older women who might have been grandmothers or perhaps senior citizens looking for something to do. Todd Watson, county supervisor for Livery, had unlocked the building, helped Gabriela set up, then stayed for the program. At a table at the side of the room, Agnese handed out juice pouches and homemade oatmeal raisin cookies. An unopened tin behind the refreshment table contained a batch of Agnese's almond cookies—a gift for Lucinda, who also attended.

As Gabriela finished reading the first story, she noticed a woman walk into the library and stand toward the back. Tall and athletic looking, with short graying hair, she wore jeans and a beige T-shirt with a picture of the Earth and the slogan *Love Your Mother*. Lucinda and the woman exchanged a brief hug. Gabriela started reading the second story, turning the pages around for the kids to look at the illustrations. Each time she raised her eyes, she observed Lucinda and the woman standing close to each other. Once, she thought she saw their fingers intertwine.

When the story concluded, Gabriela distributed paper and crayons. Kids sat on the floor and started to draw or scribble. A few of the children fidgeted and tried to run around, but their mothers corralled them and refocused their attention. As Gabriela made her way toward the back of the room, one little boy held up a smiling stick figure. "That's you!" he cried.

Seeing the scrawled dark cloud around the lollipop head, Gabriela had to admit the boy captured both her out-of-control hair and the dizzying swirl of her thoughts. When Lucinda beckoned her over, Gabriela tried to gather her hair with both hands and press it against her scalp, but the curls sprang out again.

"I'd like you to meet Parnella Richards. She's back with us after almost two years."

Parnella extended her hand to Gabriela in a firm shake. "Got a farm out this way. Bought it after I retired. Rented it out for the past couple of years while I did some traveling. But it was time for me to come back." She looked at Lucinda and smiled.

"Parnella used to teach botany," Lucinda said. "You can imagine the discussions we've had about plants."

"You taught at the community college?" Gabriela asked. "That's quite a commute."

Parnella shook her head. "Syracuse University. Almost two hours each way." She grinned, flashing white teeth against a suntanned face. "Slept in my office plenty of nights during the winters."

"What brings you back?" Gabriela asked.

Parnella exchanged a look with Lucinda, then replied in a muffled voice. "Lucinda and I always stayed in touch. And I don't like much of what I'm hearing around here."

"The trucks," Lucinda added. "Like the ones you saw at Still Waters Chasm."

Gabriela remembered what Trooper Morrison had said about seismic testing and kept her word to say nothing about that, but she saw no harm in describing what she'd found there. "The entire site has been clear-cut, and there's a road through the woods."

"And parked in the middle are heavy-duty trucks with compressors on the back," Parnella said.

"Oh," Gabriela replied. "You saw the truck?"

"*Trucks.* Two of them now," Parnella corrected. "Thumper trucks. They shoot shockwaves into the ground to map the rock below the surface. Somebody's got the idea there's natural gas up there."

Gabriela's eyes widened. "They're going to drill?"

"Uh-uh." Parnella stepped closer to Gabriela. "Fracking."

Gabriela had read enough about fracking over the years that the thought of it in a place as pristine as Still Waters Chasm knotted her stomach. "Isn't fracking illegal in New York State now?"

"High-volume hydraulic fracturing is banned, but gelled propane fracking isn't completely illegal yet. It seems they're betting on sky-high energy prices to bring back fracking," Parnella said. "That and a political change in the governor's office."

"Gabriela!" She heard Todd Watson's voice and waved to acknowledge him. He rubbed his eyes with his thumb and forefinger then pointed toward the center of the room where children chased one another around a circle of bored-looking parents.

"I better get back to story hour," Gabriela said.

"Come back to Lucinda's, if you can." Parnella said.

"Can't today. I have to be in Ohnita Harbor this afternoon. Another time, for sure."

As Gabriela rushed past Todd, he grabbed her arm. "You can't keep order if you're gossiping in the corner."

Gabriela straightened her spine and drew back an inch. "The program is over. The children will be leaving momentarily."

Todd squinted at her and rubbed his eyes again. When he took his hands away, the whites of his eyes had reddened. Allergies, Gabriela guessed, but said nothing more as she continued to the front of the room and instructed the children to line up with their pictures. After a round of applause, she thanked everyone for coming and told them she'd be back next month.

"And don't forget we have another program for the adults in two weeks on local history," Gabriela called out over the noise of the chairs scraping across the floor. "It should be very interesting."

Gabriela began taking up the chairs and stacking them against the far wall. Todd carried a chair under each arm toward her. "Nice program for the children," he said.

"Good turnout. It just takes a little time and organization, but no budget to speak of."

"This should just be for children," he continued.

"And their parents or grandparents. It's good to see a mix of the generations. We need more of that in our communities."

Todd set a chair down with a thud. "Parnella Richards has no children or grandchildren. She's just here because there's a crowd, and she loves an audience."

Gabriela cast a glance over to Lucinda and Parnella, who looked back at her. "I think people are just curious. I'm never going to turn away anyone from the community who is respectful and poses no threat or harm to the children."

"Then the county needs to rethink this program," he shot back.

"The county?" Gabriela slammed a folded chair against the stack. "This program is sponsored by the Ohnita Harbor Public Library. It has nothing to do with the board of supervisors."

Todd picked up another chair and set it down against the wall. His slow deliberate movements made Gabriela think of a chess player. "Except we own the building."

As she sat in her office the next morning, Gabriela couldn't keep her attention on the library budget, programming, or the dozen other things that vied for her attention. Instead, she tried to think of an offensive strike to ensure that the county board of supervisors would continue allowing programs at the Livery library. She began drafting an email, citing attendance for the first program on fishing and the popularity of story hour as examples of community engagement and emphasized that it cost the county taxpayers nothing. It wasn't just the town of Livery; in time, other community libraries around the county would benefit from programs she could establish with a network of volunteers.

She smiled as she wrote, feeling good about the soundness of her logic. As she reread the email, Delmina tapped on her door and informed her of a call on hold from Todd Watson.

Gabriela took a few seconds to compose herself and answered the call with as much friendliness and enthusiasm as she could muster. "I was just writing to you," she said, before even saying hello.

Todd replied with a palpable chilliness. From the echo of his voice on the line, Gabriela knew she was on speaker.

"I'm calling to inform you that the county board of supervisors is discontinuing our support for the outreach program in Livery," Todd told her.

Gabriela held the phone receiver in a shaking hand. "Why? It costs nothing, and it brings joy and enrichment to the community."

"We appreciate what you're doing for Livery," he continued. "I know you come all the way out there on your own dime, without any reimbursement from the county. And the two programs you organized were well attended."

With an opening like that, Gabriela knew the next word was going to be *but*.

"But there are concerns," Todd went on. "The Livery library building is old and in need of repair. You saw what happened yesterday—the children running all over the place. It's not a gymnasium."

"They just got a little restless at the end. We'll—I'll—take care of that next time." Gabriela picked a pen up from her desk and clicked the point up and down repeatedly.

"There won't be a next time. We can't take the chance of the children getting hurt and the county being liable. Besides, the children in this county get plenty of reading in school."

Gabriela dropped the pen with a clatter on her desk. "Not the preschoolers! County statistics show that most children under the age of five are at home with a parent or an adult babysitter. These children need exposure to reading at an early age."

A woman's voice sounded on the phone. "Ms. Dominic?"

"Domenici," Gabriela corrected, wondering who else was on the line with Todd.

"This is Betty Graudler."

Gabriela recognized the name: the supervisor from Newlan, another township in the county.

"Your passion and enthusiasm are to be commended," Betty continued, "but we cannot allow the program to continue. We're sorry. The Livery library is being permanently shut down."

"Who else is on the line?" Gabriela demanded.

Neither Todd nor Betty spoke.

"Who else? If this is an official call, I deserve to know to whom I'm talking."

"Bruce Woltzer—Mandeville."

Livery, Newlan, and Mandeville—the three townships surrounding Still Waters Chasm, Gabriela realized. "This is because of Parnella Richards, isn't it? For whatever reason, you didn't like it that she showed up, and now you're shutting down an outreach program for the community."

"I'm afraid I don't know who that is," Betty Graudler said.

"I doubt that, but I know Todd knows her."

Gabriela heard a low murmur on the other end of the line and surmised they were sitting together.

"I told you how I felt after the story hour," Todd said. "Parnella had no business crashing the event."

"Crashing? Like a party?" Gabriela stifled a laugh. "Listen, I'm not going to discontinue this program no matter what the three of you say. I'm contacting the full board of supervisors, and I'll be at the next meeting to overrule this ridiculous—" She didn't want to give it the permanence of calling it a decision. "Opinion."

"Maybe you better take care of your business at home," Bruce interjected. "Your own library will be falling down while you gallivant around the county."

Gabriela clicked off the cordless receiver then threw it against the opposite wall, cracking the black plastic and spilling the double-A batteries in the handset across the floor. Storming out of her office, ignoring Delmina's inquiries about what was wrong, she stomped down the stairs and out the library's front door.

For the first several blocks, Gabriela's heels pounded the sidewalk, marking time with the pulse of her angry thoughts about the arbitrariness of the decision to pull support for the library outreach. She would take the matter up with the county attorney if she had to. The attendance numbers spoke to the need in the community.

But did they really? Gabriela asked herself. How many of the attendees for the fishing lecture had come because they'd heard she had found two bodies at Still Waters Chasm? Story hour, while lively, had attracted just eleven children.

Anger gave way to the emotion lurking underneath, and Gabriela allowed the tears to well in her eyes. She'd always been on the side of the underdog. The outreach program had given her a mission and a deeper sense of purpose than merely trying to manage a budget deficit at her own library. Pushing deeper into her motives, Gabriela had to admit another truth, one she didn't like about herself. Her need to rescue could be ego-driven at times, a desire for recognition and acknowledgment. In personal relationships, including the early years of her marriage to Jim, she had often confused being needed and being loved.

After Gabriela reached the park along the Ohnita River, she sat on a bench, watching as the current slowed, as if surrendering to the fate of being swallowed by Lake Ontario. Her shallow, angry breaths deepened to inner calmness. No one in Livery had asked for the programs; she'd come up with the idea on her own. Going forward, she needed to get the community's input about what they wanted.

Before returning to the library, Gabriela decided to call Lucinda. She owed her an explanation that all library outreach had been canceled because of safety issues over the building.

"What a crock!" Lucinda retorted when Gabriela told her about the call with the county supervisors. "We'll find another place."

Gabriela interrupted. "Let's see what happens. If the community really wants these programs, a door will open."

Lucinda sputtered a little, then agreed. "Still galls me, though. Say, any luck on Wendy's project? She asked me yesterday if you had heard anything."

"A little." Gabriela told Lucinda about the theory that the sketch might depict a foldable sail, feeling a pinch of guilt that she had inflated her conversation with Daniel to research.

"Well, that sounds very interesting," Lucinda said.

Gabriela promised to return with more details soon, then ended the call. Back at the library, she searched online for the Mystic Seaport Museum in Connecticut but could not find the person she had known there years ago. After wandering around the site for far longer than she'd intended, Gabriela clicked on a generic email for the collections department and wrote a succinct inquiry about speaking to someone at the museum regarding an antique schematic believed to be for a folding sail. She'd look for other places to contact later.

That evening, while folding laundry in the living room, Gabriela turned on the local news out of Syracuse to listen to the weather report. She reached for Ben's favorite T-shirt—blue, with a white stencil of a curling wave and *Santa Monica* across the chest, a souvenir from his trip to visit Jim and Shelley early in the summer. She folded the sleeves inward and tucked in the bottom. For weeks afterward, Ben had talked about California, and now his father wanted him to return over Christmas break. Of course he should go, but the mere thought of it triggered an anticipatory ache of missing her son.

An image flashed on the TV screen—a smiling gray-haired man with glasses. Then Gabriela read the name. "Oh, my God!" she shouted, and the folded T-shirt fell in a heap on the living room floor.

The newscaster announced in a somber tone that the body of Ohnita County Supervisor Todd Watson had been discovered along a road about a mile from his home in Livery. "Watson's wife told police that he had gone for a walk. When he didn't return after an hour and a half, she went out looking for him and found his body on the side of the road," said the man on TV. "The apparent cause of Watson's death is a heart attack."

Gabriela replayed her shouting match with Todd, then imagined him storming out of his house to take a walk, just as she had done. But the walk that had calmed her down hadn't done anything for Todd. Their argument must have killed him. *It was her fault.* The crush of responsibility hit Gabriela like a body blow, sending her back onto the sofa, crumpling the freshly folded laundry.

CHAPTER

TEN

Every space in the funeral home parking lot held a vehicle, and cars lined both sides of the pavement. Gabriela cruised down the street, hoping someone would pull away from the curb. It was 7:15, and evening calling hours for Todd Watson's wake had just started. With this many people there already, no one would miss her if she skipped it, Gabriela told herself; besides, she might not be welcome. Even so, she reminded herself, her role in the North Country Library Association and interactions with the Ohnita County Board of Supervisors obligated her to attend. When a car pulled away, opening a space, Gabriela quickly parallel parked.

Inside the funeral home, Gabriela joined the end of a long line that stretched to the front door. Seeing the *Kindly silence your phones* sign, she checked hers for messages and texts, then shut it off to save the battery, which showed only 20 percent power. The people ahead of her inched forward, and Gabriela advanced two steps. After an hour, she stood third in line to give her condolences to a gray-haired Mrs. Watson in a black dress. Four years ago, she remembered, her own mother had stood the same way beside her father's casket. All afternoon and evening, Agnese had refused to sit down, and her feet had swelled so badly she could barely get her shoes on for the funeral the next day. The memory lodged like a millstone on her chest, and Gabriela struggled to take a deep breath.

The line moved again, and the couple in front of her stepped up to speak to Mrs. Watson for a few minutes then moved on. Now it was Gabriela's turn. She took in a breath and introduced herself, explaining how she knew Todd from the library association.

"Oh, yes, Gabriela," Mrs. Watson replied.

Gabriela swallowed and clenched her hands.

"Todd told me all about your program—the one on fishing," Mrs. Watson continued. "He said it was very well attended—and you did it out of the goodness of your heart."

"That's kind of you to say." She paused, waiting for any indication that Mrs. Watson knew about her argument with Todd, ready to apologize and explain.

"Thank you for coming," the widow said. "It's very good of you."

Stepping away, Gabriela paused at the open casket, where a faded color wedding picture was propped against the satin lining, along with smaller snapshots of two adult children and four grandchildren. She'd seen the daughter earlier, carrying a toddler toward the restroom. Gabriela thought of Ben, only seven at the time of her father's death— sad and bored and confused during the services. Bowing her head, as if in prayer, she whispered, "I'm sorry, Todd."

A man about thirty, in gray pants and a navy blazer with an open-neck shirt, stepped up beside her. He introduced himself as Brady Watson. "Dad talked about you."

I'm sure he did, Gabriela groaned silently.

"When you had story hour, Dad wanted to take Jason, but he'd had a little cold. We should have let him go. Now he'll never go with his grandpa."

And no one else will get to go to the program either. Gabriela pushed away the uncharitable thought. "I'm glad I got to know your dad. You have every reason to be proud of him. He cared very deeply for the town."

Brady nodded and swiped at his tears with his hand. "Thanks."

Gabriela made her way toward the back of the room, threading through clots of people she didn't recognize. The back of her neck dampened and her mouth dried. The smell of the floral arrangements—the heady lilies, the sweet roses—in the hot room gave her a headache.

"Shall we?" An arm linked through hers, steering Gabriela toward the door.

Turning to acknowledge Lucinda, Gabriela said she had to get some fresh air. When Lucinda headed toward the parking lot, Gabriela pointed in the opposite direction. "My car is down the street."

"Meet me at the house," Lucinda said.

"I can't. It's late, and I've got a long drive home." Gabriela fished her car keys out of her purse.

"Please. It won't take long."

"It's—" Gabriela shut her eyes for ten seconds and calmed herself. The loss of a contemporary could be hard on people, she told herself. Lucinda probably did not want to walk into her house alone. "A very fast visit." It was already 8:35.

As she drove toward Lucinda's house, Gabriela caught up with a car headed in the same direction. Surmising it was Lucinda's but unable to tell in the dark, Gabriela followed the vehicle all the way to the familiar stone cottage set back from the road. The car in front slowed down almost to a complete stop, as if ready to pull in the yard. Then the driver hit the accelerator and shot past the house. The taillights narrowed to two red dots and disappeared over the crest of the next hill.

Slowly, Gabriela made her way down the gravel drive to the back where illuminated kitchen windows showed two people sitting at the table—one of them Lucinda and the other Parnella Richards. So much for her theory on Lucinda not wanting to enter her house alone, Gabriela thought as she got out of the car. She knocked, then let herself into the sunporch.

"We're in the kitchen," Lucinda called out.

"The strangest thing just happened," Gabriela began, and told them about the car she'd followed.

"Nothing would surprise me at this point." Lucinda got up from the table, turned on a stove burner, and set a teakettle on it.

Gabriela remained standing but put her purse down on a chair against the wall. "I don't get it. I thought everybody knows you and where you live."

"But they don't know where *I* am," Parnella interjected. "I decided not to stay at my farm for a while. Too much going on for Lucinda to be alone right now."

That didn't make sense to Gabriela, but she figured it might be something personal between the two women. Picking up one of the articles covering the kitchen table, she read how the South Dakota state government had backed down from enforcing stricter anti-protest laws, a victory for people campaigning against a fracking project in that state. She selected another article that described the growth of hydraulic fracking over the past decade to become the dominant technique for natural gas production in the United States. Gabriela sifted through protest flyers, pamphlets, and a map of Ohnita County, with a circle drawn in red marker around Still Waters Chasm.

"I'm sure you've guessed already. We're trying to stop the seismic testing," Parnella said. She held up one article after another about places ruined by fracking—towns in north Texas, Oklahoma, Pennsylvania, Ohio. Water, soil, and even food supplies affected. Cancer rates skyrocketing among adults and children.

Gabriela stepped closer to scan the headlines. "Someone put in a road through the woods and clear-cut the testing site. Who has that kind of money?"

"Investors," Parnella said. "Something called Still Waters Resources has been buying up land around the chasm. They started two years ago—ten acres here, twenty acres there. Word was, someone planned to build cottages, maybe a wilderness resort. There was even talk of another fishery. People cashed in by selling their land, then waited for all the new tourism money to come pouring in."

"And it hasn't happened." Gabriela sighed.

"It never will. Still Waters Resources owns nearly a hundred acres of land. That's where they're doing the seismic testing."

"But a hundred acres? Is that enough?" Gabriela had imagined they would need to own the entire chasm.

"You can thank technology for that. You can sit on a parcel of land and conduct a seismic survey of all the adjacent property. You don't even have to get permission from the other landowners to do it," Parnella explained.

"But they can't just start fracking without permits or a license or something. Besides, it's illegal in the state," Gabriela said.

The teakettle rattled on the stove, and Gabriela flinched at the noise. Glancing at the kitchen clock, she saw that it was almost nine. If she left right now, she wouldn't get home until quarter to ten.

Lucinda brought the kettle and two mugs to the table. "Don't worry, it's herbal," she said to Gabriela. "Made it this evening and just reheated it."

"I'm good with this." Parnella raised a cordial glass by its narrow stem. "J.J. may be a son of a bitch, but he makes a helluva nice elderberry wine."

"Wendy brought us a bottle yesterday," Lucinda added. "Said he wouldn't miss one."

"J.J.?" Gabriela asked. "He doesn't exactly seem like the craft wine type."

"Folks around here brew all kinds of things. Back during Prohibition, J.J.'s family, the Haughtons, were moonshiners," Lucinda went on. "And elderberry wine has been a home remedy back to the earliest settlers." She enumerated all its health benefits, from better immunity to a stronger heart.

"Too bad it doesn't improve J.J.'s disposition," Gabriela remarked, and Parnella laughed.

"Maybe we need to give him a little belladonna," Parnella added.

"Isn't that poisonous?"

"Just a pinch." Parnella held her thumb and index finger close together. "Mellow him out a little."

Lucinda poured the tea, and Gabriela added a little honey. At her first sip, she tasted chamomile and lavender.

Parnella got up from the table to refill her glass of elderberry wine. "I forgot to ask: How was the wake? The Watsons run you out of there?"

Gabriela opened her mouth, ready with a retort, then looked away. "Actually, everyone was very nice. It surprised me. Mrs. Watson and her son both told me how much Todd liked the library programs."

Parnella's laugh rang out sharp and loud. "Of course, he did—until I showed up."

Gabriela wouldn't argue with that. "Why did you come to story hour?"

Parnella smirked. "Lucinda invited me. I'd heard great things about you—how you were one of the few people from outside this community who actually gave a damn about Livery. I hope that's still the case."

Gabriela's jaw tightened. "I do care—and I have no agenda other than bringing programs to a community that lost its library. Right now, I'm on hiatus."

"Who's to stop you?" Parnella raised both hands in the air. "Todd's dead. Somebody in town has to have a key to that old library."

Gabriela took one more sip from her mug of tea. "It's late, and I've got to get home."

"I'll walk you out," Lucinda said. "I want to cut some herbs for you and your mother." Lucinda slipped on a sweater and retrieved a pair of kitchen shears from the drawer.

Gabriela found the switch for the floodlight in the backyard, and something scampered toward the woods. She recalled how the same thing had happened at Daniel's place on Saturday evening and wished she had called him before coming over to Lucinda's, just to hear his voice. It was too late now.

"Probably a deer," Lucinda said, coming up behind her. She led the way into the garden, where she snipped sprigs of rosemary, thyme, and lavender and broad basil leaves. "Don't let Parnella scare you off. She can be abrasive, but she has a heart of gold. I'd trust her with my life."

The softness of Lucinda's tone spoke of the deep bond between the women, far more than friendship, Gabriela suspected. "It's obvious Parnella is passionate about protecting Still Waters."

Lucinda whirled around. Enough diffused light caught her face to illuminate her angry expression. "Do you know what happened here in the '70s? Someone set up an incinerator to burn chemical waste. It violated every possible state and federal standard, but it took seven years to shut it down."

Lucinda recited the details of the DEC's discovery at the site: more than ten thousand drums of toxic waste, many of them leaking PCB, oil, and who-knows-what-else into the groundwater. Within a year, the cancer rate in that part of the county had doubled. "And how did that happen? Because people assumed at first that the incinerator had to be okay, because there must be permits and approvals. So nobody stopped it. Well, we're not going to let that happen again."

Lucinda bent down and snipped two more sprigs of lavender. Gabriela accepted the bouquet of herbs and lowered her face to inhale the scent. Maybe Keith Maldon, the DEC biologist, and his girlfriend, Sheena Dowley, had come to Still Waters to investigate, she thought. Perhaps they'd heard about the seismic testing and wanted to see the extent of the operation. They could have easily canoed to Still Waters Chasm then hiked up the trail from the lake. Maybe the boot prints she and Daniel had followed to the thumper truck had been theirs.

Gabriela fingered one spiky leaf of the rosemary, crushing it between her fingers, releasing its pungent scent. Had someone seen Keith and Sheena up there? And then what—poisoned them? It did not make sense.

Her brain fogged from fatigue. "Take care, Lucinda."

"That sounds like a pretty final goodbye." Lucinda reached over to embrace her. "You've got ties here now, Gabriela. Please don't break them."

"I won't," Gabriela assured her and got into her car.

All the way home, Gabriela drove with the radio on and the window down to stay alert. Her shoulders tensed and her neck ached until she crossed the Ohnita Harbor city limits. Then relief set off a chain reaction of yawns that made her eyes water.

Daniel's truck was at the curb in front of her house. Seeing it, Gabriela's heart raced with worry that something had happened to her mother or Ben. She pulled in the driveway but left her car outside. As she ran toward her back door, it opened, and there stood Daniel. "What's wrong?" she blurted out.

Daniel stepped back and ushered her in with a sweeping gesture. "You tell us. Agnese and I have been sitting here for the better part of an hour. When I couldn't reach you on your phone—"

"Shit! I turned it off at the wake." Gabriela pulled the lifeless device from her purse and held up the blank screen.

"—I came over to see if you were here. I found Agnese pacing the floor and Ben on the sofa, refusing to go to sleep."

"But you knew I went to Todd Watson's wake." Gabriela looked from her mother's sullen face to Daniel's frowning expression. "I ran into Lucinda Nanz. She asked me to stop by, and I did but only for a little while. She gave me some herbs for you."

"You're spending an awful lot of time up there," Daniel said. "First, the library programs, and then a wake for someone you didn't know that well and just had an argument with. And this Lucinda person is constantly inviting you to visit her."

"What's wrong with that?" Gabriela asked.

Daniel ran his toe over the nap of the carpet. "You're never home."

Gabriela's mouth dropped open. "I'm *always* home. I never go anywhere except for my job or to go somewhere with you."

"You know what I mean," Daniel said.

Gabriela raised her voice to talk over him. "Otherwise, I'm here. And *nobody*—" she narrowed her eyes at him and her mother "—has any right to criticize me where Ben is concerned."

Daniel blew out his cheeks. "I never said anything about Ben. You're a terrific mother."

"Yeah? Then what is this about?"

Agnese coughed and reached for a glass of water on the end table beside the sofa. Gabriela handed it to her. "*Grazie.*" Agnese took a sip. "You go too far, and you out too late. You need to rest. He's worried. I'm worried."

"About what?" Gabriela raised her eyes toward the staircase, listening for Ben who surely wouldn't sleep through this arguing.

Daniel reached for her hand, but she snatched it away. "It's only been a few months since the attack," he said. "You're jumpy and irritable. Anybody can see you're getting triggered."

"Well, pardon me for not being Miss Congeniality. Have you forgotten what the past couple of weeks have been like?" Gabriela pressed her fingertips against her eyelids, which felt hot. "Look, I'm exhausted. I'm really sorry my phone was off and that you worried. But I'm going to bed."

Daniel stroked her shoulder, and Gabriela let him. "We—I just want you to take care of yourself."

Gabriela twitched the corner of her mouth into a half smile. *Take care of yourself.* That was exactly what Jim had said to her when he left for California. *Take care of yourself* meant one thing: *I won't be around to do it.* "You want me to drive you home?" she asked her mother.

"I'll do it," Daniel offered. "Unless you want to stay here, Agnese."

Rising to her feet, Agnese accepted Daniel's offer for a ride. She took Gabriela by the elbow. "Come to the kitchen with me."

"No, Mama. It's so late."

"*Si.* Now." Agnese headed toward the kitchen.

Gabriela pulled a chair out at the kitchen table and sat down. "Two minutes, Mama."

"I take one." Agnese lowered herself into a chair and leaned forward. "Daniel, he sit with me for one hour, waiting for you. Why he do that?"

"He's a nice person," Gabriela replied. "I'm glad he was with you."

Agnese slapped the table. "He loves you."

Gabriela toyed with the fringed edge of a placemat. She had no doubt Daniel cared for her, as she did for him. But when it came to love, she felt equally sure that his deepest attachment still belonged to the woman in the photograph she'd found—the two of them in the Adirondack chair, long legs entwined, laughing into the camera. Daniel loved Vicki—always had, always would. Her death had not changed that.

"I'm sorry I made you worry, Mama," Gabriela said. "I promise. I'll be home more often."

CHAPTER
ELEVEN

After a fitful sleep, Gabriela awakened with a headache and scrambled to get herself and Ben ready for work and school. The boy flopped on the sofa, complaining that his stomach hurt, but Gabriela didn't fall for it. "You'll feel better once you get some fresh air. It's too late to take your bike. Do you want to ride the bus, or should I drive you?"

Ben's shrug sent his shoulders up to his ears and back.

"Fine. I'll drive you. We're leaving in ten minutes."

"Why were you yelling last night?" he asked. "I heard you."

Gabriela shook her head. "We were just talking. Maybe our voices got too loud."

Ben jutted out his lower lip. "Daniel said something, and then you yelled that you don't go anywhere but work."

"Oh, we were just talking about how late I came home last night. The place I went to was so crowded. A ton of people. It took me forever just to get in the door and out again." Gabriela rolled her eyes. "Today I'm going to work and then come right home."

She waited for another question, but Ben seemed to accept what she'd said. "So, speaking of home," she added, "do you want me to pick you up at the park after school?"

"Yeah, okay." Ben grabbed his backpack and the lunch she'd made for him and headed out the back door.

When Gabriela arrived at the library, she called Daniel but only reached his voicemail. She composed a text that read "Good morning," added a smiling sun emoji, then deleted it. Three other messages also fell to the backspace arrow. Gabriela decided to wait until she heard from him.

After checking in with the staff and ensuring that the library was running smoothly, Gabriela called the Mystic Seaport Museum in Connecticut, spoke with a friendly person in the curation department, and left her contact information. But when Gabriela had to repeat "Ohnita Harbor" twice and explain its geographic location, she knew the phone message would have a far lower priority than during her days at Archives and Documents at the New York Public Library. Back then, people took her calls immediately.

Opening the photos on her phone, Gabriela scrolled to the shots of Gerald Shumler's schematic. She traced the lines of the fan-shaped sail with her finger, the folding masts, the hinged supports. Her attention turned repeatedly to the only solid information on the drawing: Shumler's name and the date, 1808. She toyed with the idea of contacting Charmaine Odele because of her knowledge of nineteenth-century Great Lakes shipping. But as library board president, Charmaine was also her boss, and Gabriela didn't want to cross the lines between her professional responsibilities and a personal project.

As she considered other options, Gabriela realized that instead of trying to track down the sail design, she needed to find out more about Shumler, the designer. His connection with the hamlet of Natural Bridge, on the western edge of Adirondack Park, gave Gabriela another idea. She looked up the number for the Adirondack Museum, which she had visited as a child on a rare road trip with her parents to the Adirondack Mountains. Only vague memories remained, the most vivid being a huge taxidermy bear, standing menacingly on its hindlegs and brandishing a forepaw and a huge grandfather clock that boomed the hours in a tone so deep and ominous, it had scared her even more than the bear.

A Google search revealed the museum name had changed to the Adirondack Experience, the Museum on Blue Mountain Lake. Two phone transfers later, she reached Dr. Cynthia Rahlberg, the director, who also headed Documents and Archives. Gabriela explained both her current role as executive director of the Ohnita Harbor Public Library and her former role at the New York Public Library.

Without disclosing Wendy's identity, Gabriela explained to Dr. Rahlberg the schematic, her belief that the type of paper used was consistent with a document dated 1808, and the possibility of it being a design for a foldable sail. Gabriela squeezed the pen in her hand as she spoke. "The person who owns the drawing is highly motivated to learn more about it. Any help you can provide would be most appreciated."

"I'd like to check one thing," Dr. Rahlberg replied.

As Gabriela heard typing in the background, she closed her eyes and hoped for good news.

"I thought the name sounded familiar," the museum director responded. "I just checked our digital directory, and we have two Shumler drawings in our collection. I don't know much about him."

"Can we see the drawings? Are they online?" Gabriela asked.

"Ohnita Harbor isn't that far away. Any chance you could come to the museum and see them in person? I'd love to look at your drawing, and we can make some comparisons."

Gabriela considered the time commitment and the planning, knowing it would take a full day, and a long one at that. Another day away from the library, another day away from her family—unless. "Could we come on a Saturday?"

When Dr. Rahlberg agreed, they set a date for a week from the coming Saturday. Gabriela's hands shook with excitement when she punched in the next phone number. Her knee bounced up and down under her desk through three long rings.

As soon as the call was answered, Gabriela blurted out the news. "Gerald Shumler was definitely a sailmaker. There are drawings of his at Adirondack Experience. I spoke with the museum director. I'm going to see them."

"I'm sorry, who's calling?" the woman queried.

"Gabriela." She looked at the number she'd dialed—off by one digit.

"Oh, are you the lady from the library?" the woman asked.

"I misdialed. I'm so sorry to have troubled you." Gabriela disconnected quickly.

Tipping her head toward the ceiling, she sat with her eyes closed, trying to control her racing heart. She was overreacting, Gabriela told herself. The woman she reached accidentally wouldn't remember anything other than her name. No way would she remember or repeat anything else.

Pressing each number deliberately, Gabriela placed the next call. Even when she heard the familiar voice, she double checked. "Is this Lucinda?"

"Who else would I be?" Lucinda laughed. "I was just thinking of you."

Gabriela repeated the conversation with the museum director and the arrangement she'd made to visit at the end of the following week. "Can you ask Wendy if I can pick up the drawing from you and bring it to the museum?"

"I'm sure it's no problem. Just swing by the house on your way to Blue Mountain Lake," Lucinda said. "I'll have it all ready for you."

Gabriela sent off an email to Dr. Rahlberg, confirming their upcoming visit, and received a friendly reply that began, "Call me Cynthia—and I can't wait to meet you." She then explained how she'd looked up Gabriela online and found an article she'd written years ago for *Modern Conservator* on using invitations and other social memorabilia as primary material.

Reading the email, Gabriela felt the pinch of just how long ago she had written that scholarly article. That one, she recalled, had been requested by the magazine editors after she had authenticated several documents as having belonged to the daughters of Cornelius Vanderbilt, the nineteenth-century shipping and railroad magnate, based on handwriting comparisons with RSVP and thank-you cards in the New York Public Library's collection. A duller ache set in with the knowledge that those days had passed, that her current position lacked the cachet to capture an editor's attention. At least she had the opportunity to authenticate something, Gabriela consoled herself. Gerald Shumler's drawing might not belong to the Vanderbilts, but it was historic and had to be locally significant.

With so much accomplished for Wendy, Gabriela dove into her library to-do list with vigor, determined to make a sizable dent in it. After an hour at her desk, she made another round of the departments, stopping in the Children's Room to speak with the new program director, in the position less than a month after someone else had walked off the job in protest over her book budget being cut. Gabriela then moved on to Circulation.

"Is it really you? Or am I dreaming?" Pearl Dunham clutched her chest for effect and laughed at her own antics.

Francine Clarke pressed her lips together and dropped her gaze, but not before Gabriela heard her snicker.

"I'm a figment of your imagination, come to haunt you." Gabriela calculated that it had been at least three days since she'd spent any time on the circulation desk.

"Just giving you a hard time." Pearl scanned a book to check it, and the machine beeped. "Every time I didn't see you, I kept hoping you were taking a day off. But no, Delmina always said you were up in Livery. Those people are gonna put up a statue of you or make you queen or something."

"Hardly." Gabriela assessed the fullness of the book return bin, pleased by so many materials in circulation. "But my outreach is on hold for a while, so I'll be underfoot."

Mike rounded the corner of the reference stacks, hands shoved in his pockets. Gabriela sent a smile in his direction, but his expression remained pinched. "You got a minute?" he asked.

"That usually means something is broken." Gabriela's groan ended with a short laugh.

"That's why the gods gave us duct tape." Pearl clasped her hands together and rolled her eyes skyward.

Gabriela met Mike where he stood, between a set of reference encyclopedias and four oversized volumes of literary criticism. "What's up?"

"Come down to my office." Mike walked away before she had time to reply.

Gabriela followed him across the main floor and down the stairs in the rear to the lower level, nicknamed "the dungeon." As they descended, Nathaniel the cat bounded upward with something in his mouth. Gabriela shuddered to think it might be a mouse. If so, then having Nathaniel around was definitely a benefit in an old building.

At the lower level, Gabriela passed a large workroom and continued down a dimly lit hallway toward the boiler room and a small windowless space that Mike called his office.

"I didn't want anybody else to see this, not until you did," he told her.

Gabriela crossed her arms in front of her body and rubbed her upper arms. "What is it?"

Mike pushed the door open, and at first Gabriela didn't see anything out of the ordinary in the room with its cement-block walls painted bright yellow. Then she saw them. Leaning up against the side of the old wooden desk cast off from some city department stood her backpack and Daniel's. "Oh my God." She rushed over and grasped hers by the loop at the top. "Where did you get them?"

"I found them about a half hour ago right by the back door. These are the ones you lost at Still Waters, right?"

Gabriela nodded as she grasped the large zipper and opened it, not heeding the inner voice that cautioned against touching anything. Opening the backpack wider, she noted the contents: extra socks, another sweatshirt, a flattened granola bar—just as she had packed them more than two weeks ago. Then she saw something out of place. Someone had taken her half-full water bottle out of the side pocket and put it inside. That stopped her from touching or moving anything else.

Using Mike's desk phone, because cell reception was sketchy in the basement, Gabriela called the state police and left a message with the dispatcher for Trooper Douglas Morrison. When she related the details, the dispatcher promised to contact him as soon as possible.

As she headed back upstairs, Gabriela phoned Daniel on her cell. He picked up immediately but sounded a bit cool.

"You'll never guess what Mike Driskie found outside the back door of the library," she began.

"I don't know, Gabriela. Just tell me."

Hearing his exasperation, Gabriela stopped, then cleared her throat softly. "Our backpacks. Someone brought them here. I just opened mine. Everything's in here."

"Don't touch anything. Call the state police." Daniel's voice rose in pitch and volume.

"I already did." Gabriela heard a beep, indicating an incoming call. "This is him now. Can you get over here?"

Daniel promised to be there in fifteen minutes.

When Trooper Morrison came in the front door of the library, Pearl and Francine crowded together at the circulation desk, and even Delmina made a rare appearance on the main floor. The buzz among the patrons became audible, and Gabriela overheard one person ask another if the library had been robbed. Gabriela shook the state trooper's hand and ushered him toward the stairs to the lower level, explaining that Daniel should arrive any minute.

"I'm here," Daniel called from behind them.

Turning toward him, Gabriela saw the crease between his eyebrows deepen. She stopped, her arms hanging limply at her side. "I'm glad you got here so fast."

"Wasn't far away," Daniel added.

As their footsteps thudded against the stair treads, Gabriela told them she had already opened her backpack but hadn't touched anything. "I just wanted to see if my stuff was there. I noticed that someone had taken my water bottle out of the side pocket and put it inside the pack. I thought perhaps there were fingerprints, and didn't want to mess them up."

"Your prints are already on the bottle," Trooper Morrison said.

"Well, I didn't need to add any more of them."

Mike got up from the chair at his desk and nodded to both men and Gabriela. Trooper Morrison grabbed a dowel from a worktable and threaded it through the handle on top of Daniel's backpack to pick it up and set it down on Mike's desk. "You okay with me opening this?" he asked Daniel, who nodded.

Trooper Morrison put on vinyl gloves and tugged on the main zipper of Daniel's backpack, sliding it open carefully. He peered inside, using the dowel to move the contents aside. "Sweatshirt, socks, first-aid kit, an apple that's seen better days." He extracted the bruised and battered fruit. "Anything missing?"

Daniel shook his head. "Wait. My water bottle—it was in the side pocket."

The state policeman opened the other pockets, one containing tissues, the others nothing. Then he picked up Gabriela's backpack and opened it.

Watching him search inside, Gabriela noticed the dirt on the side of the backpack, making it look worn. "It's new. I just ordered it." She pointed to a small tear, like a puncture, in the front.

"Yeah, somebody roughed this up. I'll ask the lab to see what they can lift from it. Maybe prints, maybe fibers or hair. The fact that it's new helps." Trooper Morrison opened the last pocket in the front, the flap falling all the way open. Inside was a smaller pocket, just big enough for keys or an emergency stash of money. Something yellow protruded.

Trooper Morrison pulled out a piece of paper. As he unfolded it, Gabriela could see thin blue lines striped one side of it, and the bottom right corner bore the words "Amount Due."

"That's not mine." Gabriela recognized the paper as some kind of invoice or at least part of one. "I didn't buy anything the morning we went hiking. I packed a few things at home, but that's it."

Daniel rested his hand against her back, touching her for the first time since he'd arrived. "I know," he said softly.

"Obviously, it's not yours." Trooper Morrison turned the paper around.

Gabriela sucked her breath in and leaned against Daniel. The words on the paper, written in block letters, read: "Be careful."

CHAPTER

TWELVE

The small interior room in the basement suddenly seemed airless, and Gabriela struggled to take a deep breath. She tried stepping backward toward the door, but Daniel stood behind her. His arm moved from her waist to her shoulders, gathering her closer to him. He meant to comfort her, she knew, but it felt like restraint. Sweat beaded her upper lip and ran down the back of her neck.

Across the scratched and pitted wooden desk, Mike Driskie slid the chair toward her. "You wanna sit down?"

Gabriela feigned a smile and shook her head. "I'm okay."

Daniel loosened his arm from her shoulders and stepped closer to the state trooper, who was still studying the half sheet of a blank invoice and the message written on the back. "What is it, a warning or a threat?" he asked.

"You could read it both ways." Trooper Morrison set the paper down. "Since someone took the trouble of coming all this way, returning the backpacks with a note inside, I'm inclined to think it's a warning."

129

"About what?" Gabriela asked. "All we've done since the incident is answer your questions and go about our business."

Daniel's hand rested on her shoulder again. "Not exactly. You've been going to Livery quite often. Maybe you need to keep your distance."

Gabriela wheeled around quickly, breaking his grasp. "For library programs. Children's story hour. How threatening is that?"

She saw the muscle twitch in Daniel's jaw. "You told me yourself you had a shouting match with Todd Watson not long before he died."

"Wait—when was this?" Trooper Morrison asked.

Gabriela shook her head. "It's nothing. We had a heated discussion over the phone."

"Heated? You told me he yelled at you, and you practically screamed at him," Daniel shot back.

She glared at him, unfiltered. "We were having a disagreement over the library outreach—that's all."

Trooper Morrison cocked his head in Gabriela's direction. "Back up and tell me about that conversation."

She swallowed, then related the call from Todd and the supervisors from the other townships who informed her that she could no longer use the Livery library building. "Someone Todd didn't like showed up at story hour—Parnella Richards." Gabriela paused to see if the name registered, but Trooper Morrison's expression didn't change. "She's an environmental activist."

"What the hell does that have to do with story hour?" the state trooper asked.

Gabriela suppressed a sigh. "Parnella wanted to introduce herself to me, and Todd got mad that she was there. Next thing I know, the county banned me from using the library building."

"Then Todd goes out for a walk and has a heart attack." Trooper Morrison picked up the piece of paper and folded it carefully along its creases. "This Parnella, does she know anything about what's going on up on the ridge at Still Waters?"

130

Gabriela repeated what Parnella had told her about Still Waters Resources buying up land and conducting seismic testing, all with the expectation of a change in Albany that would reinstate natural gas fracking in the state.

Daniel threw his hands up in the air. "Why can't you just stay out of this? It's not enough that we go on a hike and find two dead bodies. You keep going up to Livery, meeting with these people who are mixed up in this."

Gabriela traced an arc with the toe of her shoe. "The outreach programs were planned long before we went to Still Waters. I made a promise to that community, and I'm not going to break it."

"What about your promise to your son, to your mother—to take care of yourself?" As he spoke, Gabriela heard the catch in Daniel's voice. "Three months ago, someone attacked you right here, in this building. The doctors told you needed to rest, but you never took off any time. Now this. It's taking a toll on you, but you can't see it."

Gabriela took a step in closer. "Doctors?" She emphasized the plural. "I went to the emergency room for stitches and then saw a therapist a few times. So when you say 'doctors,' are you talking about me or someone else?"

Daniel spun around and made a move toward the door. "I've got crews working on two houses, and I need to get back." He turned to Trooper Morrison. "You need anything from me, you know where I am."

Gabriela turned away from the door but heard every step Daniel took up the stairs. She made eye contact with Mike, who seemed embarrassed, and then Trooper Morrison, who was in the process of putting the backpacks into plastic bags.

"I'll see you out," she told the state trooper. "I have a couple of questions for you."

As she left the room, Gabriela stopped and turned back to Mike. "Thanks for everything. I'd appreciate your discretion on this."

"Don't worry about it," Mike said. "But what do I tell Pearl and Francine? You know they're going to pester me the minute I go upstairs."

Trooper Morrison spoke up. "Tell them I came in to speak to Gabriela. Any more than that, nobody needs to know."

"Got it," Mike said.

———

Patrons swiveled their heads for a better look as Gabriela escorted the state trooper out of the library. Francine jumped up from her chair behind the circulation desk, and Pearl stepped around to the front, as if she meant to stop them on their way out the door. When Trooper Morrison tipped his hat in their direction, Gabriela overheard Pearl say, "Somethin' about a man in uniform."

"Pearl is a bit of a character," Gabriela began, then dropped it. She walked in silence the rest of the way to the state trooper's vehicle in a no parking zone in front of the library. "I know this is sensitive, but—" She looked back toward the library and then down at the pavement. "Was an autopsy performed on Todd Watson?"

Trooper Morrison seemed to study her. "Why do you ask?"

"Someone from the DEC is poisoned and presumably his girlfriend, as well. Two weeks later, Todd Watson drops dead. All of them have ties to Still Waters."

"The fact that Todd lived in Livery is only a coincidence, unless you know of some other tie," the state trooper replied.

"Todd Watson was one of three county supervisors whose jurisdiction borders the chasm. I never talked to Todd about the seismic testing, but I do know that he became apoplectic when Parnella showed up for a library program at Livery."

Trooper Morrison took a step forward. "So you think Parnella could have harmed Todd?"

"I didn't say that," Gabriela replied quickly. "I'm just suggesting that these deaths could have some connection. How, I don't know. But if a toxicology analysis was performed on Todd's body, you might find out something."

Trooper Morrison opened the back of the squad car and put the plastic bags containing the backpacks inside. "So now it's my turn to ask for some discretion. Do I have your word?"

Gabriela nodded, but the state trooper kept looking at her, expectantly. "Yes, my word," she said.

"A clinical autopsy was performed on Todd's body. The coroner confirmed damage to his heart, which indicated that he'd died of a heart attack. The toxicology report indicated he had a high concentration of digoxin in his bloodstream. Digoxin is a form of digitalis."

"The heart medicine," Gabriela acknowledged and imagined the scenario: Todd feeling stressed after their argument, maybe experiencing chest pains, then taking an extra pill in hopes of warding off a heart attack.

"Here's the thing, Todd had never been prescribed digitalis."

Gabriela's eyes widened. She'd read about people taking pain medications and even antidepressants that weren't prescribed for them. But heart medication?

"It's possible he got hold of somebody's prescription, maybe took it by mistake. But there's another possibility: that it came from a natural substance."

"Natural as in—?" Gabriela prompted.

"A flower called foxgloves."

Gabriela blinked rapidly. "Really? My mother grows that in her garden. Very pretty—all these little bell-shaped flowers."

"Tell her to be careful; the plant's toxic. Somebody chews the leaves, flowers, stems, or seeds, and they can end up with convulsions and heart arrythmia. Enough of it can be fatal."

"So Todd was poisoned by ingesting a plant?" Gabriela asked.

"You tell me," Trooper Morrison said. "If you think of anything, I'm sure you'll call."

Gabriela stepped onto the sidewalk. "Of course. Thanks for coming today. Let me know if anything turns up with the backpacks."

"You bet." The state trooper opened the driver's side door, looked back at her, then got in.

Biting down on her lip, Gabriela remained on the sidewalk long after the squad car had pulled away, her mind reeling with one thought: What had Lucinda put in Todd's tea?

———

Ignoring Delmina's inquiring gaze, Gabriela headed straight to her office and closed the door. She plunged into the staffing schedule for the next two months, figuring out how to run the facility with a skeleton crew. The only solution was for her to fill in wherever needed, on the circulation desk and in the Children's Room. Friends of the Library volunteers could be counted on to pick up the slack—repairing damaged books, sorting returns to be shelved, reading at story hour. Maybe Delmina could help with circulation if they got into a bind.

Her fingers hovered above the computer keyboard.

The note had been inside her backpack. Not Daniel's—hers. Whether threat or warning, it had been meant for her. Gabriela rolled her chair a few inches from her desk and rested her back against the thin padding. And no matter what the message meant, she realized, the messenger had also shown just how easy it was to reach her—undetected. Built on the highest hill in town, the library resembled a fortress, but one with an open door that welcomed everyone, she thought. Here, in a small town where it seemed that everyone knew everyone else, exposure could not be avoided. Anyone could get to her.

A tap sounded on her door. Through the glass Gabriela glimpsed a man, his body angled away from her as if speaking to Delmina. For a split second she imagined it might be Daniel. Then he turned and she saw Mike Driskie. She waved him in.

"What's up?" She gathered the papers scattered across her desk in a loose pile.

"Wanted to see if you were okay." Mike slipped into a chair across from her desk.

Gabriela gave him a wry smile. "Maybe I'd be better if I didn't keep looking for trouble."

Mike made a face. "What? You didn't mean to find those bodies that day. You just crossed paths with something bad."

"Maybe I attract it, like a lightning rod." She attempted a laugh.

Mike clasped his hands on the edge of her desk, and Gabriela saw the ridges of old scars around his right forefinger and thumb, running up to his wrist, where he'd been burned badly as a child. She knew that Mike believed his scars had diminished and that more feeling had returned to his hand after they had found the medieval cross, the one the library board president had tried to steal, not caring if he had to kill her to get it. Her fingers fluttered up to her neck and her own scar.

"I don't think that at all," Mike replied. "You stand up for what's right. And sometimes that puts you in the middle of things."

Gabriela considered his words as she thought of how enmeshed she'd become in Still Waters Chasm. She hadn't gone looking for that trouble; it had found her. The next time it made a pass at her, she'd be prepared.

Mike stepped back toward the door. "You should know that a lot of people care about you. Starting with everybody here. We'd do anything for you."

Tears bit at the corner of her eyes. "Thanks, Mike. I guess I know that, but it's good to hear."

Mike rested his hand on the doorknob. "You think we could get some funds for a security system? Maybe with that grant?"

Gabriela shook her head. "I'd like that too. But I think we'd be hard-pressed to call security cameras beautification. It seems we can make it pretty around here, just not any safer."

Mike shook his head. "That's bureaucracy for you."

By the end of the workday, Gabriela had tackled the most urgent of her workload, returned the most important calls, and prepared materials for next month's quarterly board meeting. When Ben showed up at 4:45, she gathered her things and took the grant proposal folder home with her to work on in the evening. She said good night to Delmina and descended the stairs. Pearl had gone home already, but Francine worked the circulation desk until five o'clock, according to the schedule. Two patrons stood in line to check out books before closing.

Mike met Gabriela on her way out the back door to the parking lot. "I'm gonna do the lockup with Francine. I'll make sure Delmina's out of here by then too."

She smiled at him. "Thanks, Mike."

"You make sure your mom doesn't work too hard tonight," Mike told Ben.

The boy shrugged. "She's always working."

"Well, not tonight." Gabriela hoisted her tote bag on her shoulder. To keep that promise, she'd have to work on the grant proposal after Ben went to bed.

Sitting on her back deck that evening, Gabriela nursed a cup of coffee to keep herself awake. As the autumnal equinox approached, the days evened out with sunrise and sunset right around seven o'clock. Now it was almost eight o'clock, and the sky had darkened enough to allow the brightest stars to appear through the haze of city lights and a wisp of clouds. She wished she could sit here all night.

An engine sounded in her driveway. Gabriela got up quickly and descended the steps of the deck. The headlights extinguished, and Gabriela could see the blue pickup Daniel used for work. A wave of relief flooded her eyes with tears. She quickly brushed them away.

"Hey," he said, closing the truck door and moving slowly toward her.

"Hey, yourself." She fought the urge to run down the driveway and into his arms.

"Came by to see how you are." As Daniel approached, Gabriela took several steps forward to meet him halfway.

She would have embraced him, but Daniel stuffed his hands in his back pockets, angling his elbows out at a sharp angle. Her arms hung at her sides. "I'm okay. You hungry? You want something?"

Daniel shook his head. "I, uh, grabbed something before I came over."

His words stung, since he almost never turned down dinner, even leftovers, when he came by after work. Gabriela folded her arms against her chest. "Coffee?"

"Sure."

With Daniel trailing behind her, Gabriela went into the kitchen where Ben sat at the table, dawdling over his homework. One look from her and he got down to business. Daniel greeted the boy, who smiled up at him with a look that pinched Gabriela's heart. She never should have let her son get close to Daniel this soon. But even before they started dating, she and Daniel had become friends, and that friendship had included Ben.

Gabriela busied herself with the coffeemaker, brewing one cup for Daniel. Handing him the mug, she suggested they sit outside. On her way to the deck, she told Ben to go upstairs to take his shower when he finished his homework. She'd check it over later.

Daniel slid the two chairs on the deck next to each other. Gabriela sat down at the edge of hers, her spine straight, feet flat on the wooden planks.

"I didn't like the way I left today," Daniel said.

Gabriela nodded. "I didn't like it either—what I said, I mean."

"It's getting to me." Daniel recited the litany of everything that had happened on their hike and afterward. "Now somebody makes a point to come to the library with our backpacks. I feel like we're being cornered. Every day, I'm looking over my shoulder. I'm suspicious of everybody. At the gas station yesterday, some guy started walking up to me. I had my phone out to call 9-1-1, and all he wanted was directions. I hate living like this."

Gabriela stared out just beyond the pool of light from the house, to where her backyard transitioned to darkness. "And you blame me."

"No, of course not." He reached out, touched her arm gently. "It's not your fault. But I do feel that you're not taking care of yourself. We both know you still get triggered. And yet you keep going up to Livery and spending time so close to where something weird is going on."

Gabriela sat back in her chair. "I'm so tired of being scared. That day in the library, I really thought Don Andreesen was going to kill me. I had two choices of how he was going to do it. All I could think of was Ben; how if I jumped, he would grow up wondering why I had killed myself. I chose the knife, for him—so he would know I didn't want to die and leave him."

Hot tears rolled faster and faster down her face. "When I fought Don off, I felt such relief, but the fear never went away. But I can't—I won't—let it defeat me. Because then Don will win. I'll still be alive, but I'll have lost my life just the same. Can you understand that?"

Daniel nodded. "Yeah, I can. When Vicki got her diagnosis, we knew there wasn't much hope. The cancer had already spread to her liver and pancreas. But she refused to give up one day of living. She insisted we take one more trip together, even though she was exhausted and so sick. We drove to Montreal." His voice trailed off. "I get it. The people who are the most alive aren't afraid to die."

"Oh, I'm afraid all right," Gabriela corrected. "I just push through it. And I'm not going to stop."

Daniel reached over and took her hand. "But you do have to be careful. You're not invincible. And I don't want anything to happen to you. You mean a lot to me."

Gabriela laid her other hand over both of theirs. "I don't want anything to happen to me either. Or to you. We're both in this, you know."

Daniel shook his head. "You're in the public more than I am, and I can't keep you safe."

She reached for him first, feeling his arms wrap slowly around her. She felt the embrace tighten, almost to the point of being uncomfortable, and intuited his fear of losing someone else close to him.

CHAPTER

THIRTEEN

Over the next week, peaceful efficiency enveloped the library and its tiny staff. Everyone worked everywhere: Pearl and Francine helped out in the Children's Room, Delmina assisted with shelving returned books, and Mike kept the place spotless and even worked the circulation desk for the last hour of the day. Now, a few weeks into the school year, eighth graders looked for book titles put on reserve by their teachers, and tenth graders wandered the stacks with faces bewildered by the prospect of researching and writing their first term papers. Eleventh graders waded through the American classics: Herman Melville, James Fenimore Cooper, Emily Dickinson, and Nathaniel Hawthorne, whose portrait adorned the wall behind the reading nook on the main floor of the library, where the stray cat named for him loved to nap. And every day after school, Gabriela stood in for the reference librarian, who had retired a few years ago and had never been replaced, answering questions and helping young scholars with their projects. No matter how much other work she had to do, Gabriela loved introducing students to research, not online but with books.

When yet another teenager said she wanted to write about Emily Dickinson, Gabriela mentioned that several students had already chosen the Belle of Amherst as their topic. "But I want to compare her with Amanda Gorman," the student said. "Both women and both reached a worldwide audience."

Excitement broadened Gabriela's smile. "Yes, and both did so very differently—Emily as a recluse and Amanda as a voice for our times." Together they dove into the poetry section for both poets' works, scanned Biography for books on Dickinson, and went to Periodicals for a recent profile of Gorman.

By the time the inquisitive student left, Gabriela had come up with an "Ask the Librarian" poster for the lobby, informing students that if they had research questions, there were people who could help. By people, Gabriela admitted, she meant herself.

On Wednesday she called Trooper Morrison about the forensic tests on their backpacks. When he had nothing to report, she pressed him further. "So will you return my backpack, or are you running more tests?"

"Do you really want it back? It's been in a canoe with two dead or dying people and in the possession of a probable murderer."

Gabriela seized on the last word. "So, the state police are finally calling this a double murder, not just suspicious deaths? What about Todd Watson?"

Trooper Morrison's sigh blasted through the phone. "You are way too involved in this investigation."

"Are you forgetting that *we* found those campers? And those backpacks showed up here, where I work?"

"Trust me, those facts are never far from my mind. But I suggest that you distance yourself from all this, for the sake of the investigation and your own protection."

Gabriela grabbed a strand of her hair and curled it around her finger. "Look, I'm not trying to interfere, but I learned a long time ago that information is the best protection."

Trooper Morrison paused so long that Gabriela thought the call might have disconnected. Just as she was about to say something else, he spoke up: "There's just a lot more going on here than meets the eye. So lay low, go about your business, and don't go poking into anything that doesn't involve you. Please."

The plea she heard in his comment stopped her questioning but amped up her worries about Still Waters. Her mind whirled, connecting the seismic testing and the dead campers. But where did Todd fit in? His anger at seeing Parnella indicated that he probably had been pro-fracking. That, presumably, would have put him in opposition to the campers. Unless—could Keith and Sheena have been working for Still Waters Resources, maybe on the side?

"I have no intention of going back up to Still Waters Chasm," Gabriela said quickly. But that didn't mean she wouldn't keep a watchful eye on everyone around her. She had overlooked Don Andreesen's threat, even though he had come to the library nearly every day before attacking her. She would not be caught off guard again.

That evening, when her mother came over for dinner, Gabriela presented her plan to visit the Adirondack Experience. Prepared for any possible complaints from Ben, Gabriela recited the exhibits and activities, including an archery program on Saturday morning. Afterward, she promised, they could try zip-lining.

"You'll come too, Mama," Gabriela announced. "It will be a nice ride."

Agnese pushed a piece of wilted spinach across her plate. "We'll see."

Gabriela wrinkled her nose. "You're waiting for a better offer?"

Agnese put her fork down. "I thought maybe Daniel go with you."

"Nope, just us. While you two have all the fun, I have to meet with the museum director."

Agnese narrowed her eyes. "What you up to?"

"The curator wants to see Wendy's drawing. We're bringing it with us."

"*Sfortuna*," Agnese muttered. "Okay, I go. Somebody has to protect you."

On Friday night, Agnese promised to make homemade pizza. Daniel called twice from his last job, pleading with Agnese not to roll out and toss the dough until he got there. He burst in the door in a cloud of sweat, dust, and roof tar from repairs on an old house.

"*Whew*, no offense, but you stink," Gabriela said after accepting a light kiss.

Daniel scrubbed up in the bathroom, while Gabriela searched through her workout clothes for an oversized T-shirt. She found an old one that had belonged to Jim and handed it to Daniel without explaining its origins.

Examining a mound of rising dough, Agnese proclaimed it ready. She sprinkled white and wheat flour across the counter and wielded a rolling pin with deft strokes. "You try." She handed it to Daniel and coached him in how to smooth the dough in all directions.

"Now you take like this." She peeled the dough from the floured surface and held it across her two hands, stretching it with her fingertips.

Gabriela stood in the doorway to the kitchen, watching her mother just as she used to do as a child. In her mind, she saw her mother, dark haired and trim figured, standing next to her father, who always tried to get his hands on the pizza dough. Her mother would acquiesce only after scolding him not to ruin it or get the floor dirty. Her father would toss the circle of dough high in the air, catch it on his fingertips, and put it back on the counter. Only once did Gabriela remember the dough tearing.

When she looked back to the counter, her mother stood beside Daniel. "Now, we toss." Her mother flipped the dough into the air with a slight spin, and centrifugal force and the weight of the dough enlarged the circle. Gabriela held her breath for a second until her mother caught it.

Daniel cheered and put his arm around Agnese's shoulders. "That was amazing."

Stepping closer to them, Gabriela spied her mother's smile and knew the enormity of joy behind that expression. Agnese spread the dough in the pizza pan, while Gabriela readied the toppings: sauce, cheese, oregano, thinly sliced pepperoni, and crumbles of cooked Italian sausage. They slid it into a hot oven and set the timer.

Ben dragged his feet into the kitchen, complaining that he was about to die of hunger. Gabriela held out a slice of leftover pepperoni to her son. He gobbled it eagerly.

"I'm going zip-lining," Ben said, his mouth full.

"Manners," Gabriela interrupted.

Daniel walked his fingers across the counter and snagged a piece of pepperoni. "Really? Where?"

Ben shrugged. "Mom's taking me."

"We're going up to Blue Mountain Lake tomorrow. Day trip." Gabriela reached for a bottle of red wine to uncork.

Daniel chewed and swallowed. "That's a long way."

"Three hours each way," Gabriela said with a shrug. "We'll leave around 7:30."

"That's too early," Ben complained.

Gabriela pressed her forehead to his before he ducked away. "Yes, 7:30. We'll stay until 3:30 or 4:00, then come back. If we have a late lunch, we can drive straight through."

Behind her, Agnese hummed a tuneless song.

"Mama is coming with us," Gabriela added. "It will be a nice day."

"I've got a bunch of jobs going on or else I'd go with you," Daniel told her. "Text me when you get there, okay?"

"I promise." Gabriela opened the oven door a crack and a waft of pizza aroma escaped.

"Is it done?" Ben asked.

"Five more minutes," Gabriela told him.

"Three—maybe four," Agnese corrected.

Gabriela rolled her eyes but smiled. When it came to pizza, Mama was always right.

They ate every slice, right down to the last piece of crust. Gabriela shooed her mother into the living room, where Ben flopped down on the sofa to watch television. When she returned to the kitchen, Daniel had begun washing the dishes; she dried and put them away.

"So why Blue Mountain Lake?" he asked.

"There's a museum there, full of Adirondack history. And I found a place where Ben could zip-line." Gabriela took the pizza pan out of the drainer and began wiping.

"Went to an art show there once, but that was years ago." Daniel rinsed a froth of soap suds from a plate.

Gabriela knew she had an opening to talk about meeting with the museum director to discuss the Shumler drawing of the foldable sail, but that could turn the discussion into why she kept helping people in Livery. *I'm only helping Wendy*, she wanted to tell him. If Daniel could see how frightened this young woman was, he'd understand that she couldn't turn her back on Wendy.

"Wish I could see Ben zip-line," Daniel said, as he scrubbed the inside of the large mixing bowl Agnese had used to make the pizza dough.

146

"You ever try?" Gabriela asked.

"Once, a few years ago." Daniel shook his head. "I crawl on roofs and spend half my life on ladders. But the first time I dangled over a chasm from a wire, I thought I'd die."

Gabriela laughed at the image.

"Vicki was a natural, completely fearless. She'd stand on the other side, cheering me on."

Gabriela turned her attention back to the sink, her throat tightening. Even zip-lining had a Vicki memory wrapped around it.

———

The next morning, Gabriela only needed to call for Ben once. He appeared five minutes later, dressed and ready to go. She gave him a bowl of cereal and finished a second cup of coffee while packing a lunch for the two of them and Agnese: sandwiches, fruit, packages of crackers and cheese, and bottles of water. She checked the stove, even though she hadn't used it that morning, tested the front and back doors, backed the car out of the garage, and assured herself with a glance at the fuel gauge that she had plenty of gas to get there.

Agnese stood on her front step, wearing dark slacks and a white blouse, a sweater draped over her shoulders. Seeing the basket at Agnese's feet, Gabriela asked Ben to help her.

The boy sprang into action, reaching his grandmother in a few strides. When Agnese yielded it to him, Ben had to carry the basket with two hands. "Nonna's got rocks in here," he complained.

Standing at the trunk of her car, Gabriela took the basket from her son, surprised at the heft of it. Raising the dish towel that covered the top, she spied several rectangles wrapped in aluminum foil and caught a whiff of what smelled like Parmesan, and something in glass. "Did you bring a quart of pickles? Wait—is that giardiniera?"

"It's good with sandwiches." Agnese opened the front passenger door. "*Avanti*. We go far today."

Ben chattered the first half hour, talking nonstop about zip-lining—how high, how fast, how far—then looked out the window. Agnese sat with her hands folded, her rosary in her lap. This one, Gabriela noticed, had tiny pink stones, replacing the blue one she'd left in Lucinda's tree.

"You drive, I pray. We get there fast and safe," Agnese said.

"I think it's one or the other." Gabriela shot her mother a smile. "Today I'll go for safe."

Agnese gave her beads a shake. "You need to say two of these. You don't tell Daniel where we go, what we do. He thinks this is just for Ben."

"This is for Ben. He's so excited about zip-lining."

"But you don't tell the whole truth. You bring this drawing to the museum. Why can't he know? If you tell lies in something small, you will do it in something big."

"I didn't lie," Gabriela said, annoyed that her mother would mention this in front of Ben, but she couldn't deny that she hadn't told the entire truth.

———

The road to Lucinda's house had become so familiar, Gabriela drove automatically, without reading the tiny signs at the edges of intersections or searching for landmarks along unmarked roads. They arrived at precisely 8:15, exactly the time she'd promised. Lucinda opened the front door and waved, then disappeared back inside.

Five minutes later, Lucinda came down the driveway with a basket over one arm and the drawing draped in plastic in the other.

"Oh shit," Gabriela said. The plan had been to pick up the drawing and go.

"I heard that, Mom," Ben called out.

"I didn't realize you were coming with us," Gabriela said as she exited the driver's side door.

"Two set of ears are better than one for listening to details. Oh, hello, Agnese! Didn't see you there." Lucinda waited by the trunk of the car with her basket.

"What you bring?" Agnese asked, getting out of the car.

"Some sandwiches, a thermos of soup, and cake—lemon with lavender seeds."

Ben stuck his face out of the window. "Lavender seeds?"

"*Shush*. I bring cookies for you," Agnese told him.

Gabriela put Lucinda's basket in the trunk next to her mother's, along with the bag of sandwiches and snacks she'd made that morning. They had enough food for four days.

Agnese offered to sit in the back with Ben, and Lucinda got in the front passenger seat. She balanced the Shumler drawing atop her lap. When Gabriela started the engine and put the car in drive, Lucinda reached over and touched her forearm. "We have one more stop to make. Wendy's coming with us."

Lucinda called out directions, a complicated series of left and right turns that seemed to take them farther off course. As Gabriela slowed to make a turn by an old cemetery, an elaborate black iron fence caught her eye. An oval sign had been welded into the metal curlicue design over a tall gate. Gabriela read it—"Town of Livery Cemetery"—and considered for a moment how interesting it would be to wander among the old headstones and get a sense of who settled this area and when.

"See that barn up ahead and the house set back?" Lucinda told her. "There's a driveway between them."

Gabriela pulled in just far enough to get the car off the road. From where they waited, she could see the barn had once been painted red but now showed large gray patches. The small white house with no shutters had a sagging porch. Grass grew tall in the front yard.

The door opened and Wendy stepped out. She looked in both directions then headed to the car, wearing jeans and a plain blue sweatshirt, her hair pulled into a ponytail.

"She goes absolutely nowhere and really wanted to come," Lucinda explained. "And if this drawing is worth something, Wendy ought to hear it firsthand."

In the rearview mirror, Gabriela watched Wendy slump in the seat, as if making herself invisible. Each time a car came up behind them, Wendy slid even lower.

"Where's J.J.?" Gabriela asked.

Wendy's gaze snapped forward to meet hers in the rearview mirror. "He'll be gone all day. He told me to stay home, but I want to come with you."

"Where'd he go?" Ben piped up.

"J.J.? He went to pick up a camper on the other side of Syracuse," Wendy replied.

"He's going camping?" the boy asked.

"Not exactly," Wendy said. "He restores old campers, the kind that people pull behind a car or a truck. Sometimes he works on RVs, but not usually. People hire him mostly. But he actually bought this one. He's gonna restore and sell it."

"Cool," Ben said.

"You like camping?" Wendy asked.

"Never went," Ben shrugged. "My dad said he'd take me sometime. He lives in California."

Gabriela adjusted her hands on the steering wheel. A West Coast camping trip? That was news to her. "Maybe you and I could go in the Adirondacks, Ben."

"You'd be afraid. Probably want your hair dryer or something."

"*Whoa*, don't make assumptions like that," Gabriela said. "My dad used to take me fishing." Once—maybe twice, she added mentally.

"I think your mom could do anything she set her mind to," Lucinda interjected. "And your grandmother too."

Gabriela glanced over at Lucinda. "He's eleven, so moms are no longer cool."

Lucinda nodded. "My daughter, Trudy, wishes I was a little less cool. I'm too out there for her sensibilities. She lives in Maine and doesn't see me very much."

Gabriela wondered if herbalism put Lucinda on the fringe in her daughter's mind or if there was something else.

"Camping is so fun," Wendy told Ben and launched into a description of some of her favorite destinations across New York State, Vermont, New Hampshire, Maine, and, on one trip, Nova Scotia. "That's way up in Canada, on the Atlantic Ocean. I went there with my parents. My dad always wanted to go to the Grand Canyon, but he never did."

"Why not?" Ben asked.

"Well, it's far, and it costs a lot to go there. Then he got sick and passed away."

"Oh," Ben said, and the sound of that one word sent a pang through Gabriela's chest. She wondered if he worried about something happening to her or to his father.

"My dad went lots of other places," Wendy continued. "But that trip to Nova Scotia was the best."

While Wendy continued her travelogue from long-ago trips with her parents, Gabriela concentrated on the road. They were making good time. This outing, she decided, would be good for everyone.

CHAPTER

FOURTEEN

The road twisted—winding up a mountain, slaloming down the other side, then rising again. The farther they drove, the taller the mountains became. Gabriela's ears popped a few times, and she had to give the car more gas to keep up the momentum of every climb. Ben spotted the first tourism sign for the Adirondack Experience, shouting out from the back seat.

"Where's the zip-lining?" he asked.

"Not far," Gabriela replied, looking at him in the rearview mirror. Her focus back on the road, she dropped her voice and told Lucinda that zip-lining had been her ploy to get Ben to agree to the outing.

"Sounds like fun," Lucinda said, then closed her eyes. "I didn't sleep much last night; Parnella and I were up late. If I can nap even for ten minutes, I'll be refreshed."

Gabriela recalled Lucinda's table, littered with news clippings and scientific articles on fracking, and wondered if the two women had been hatching an activist plot. Glancing over, she saw Lucinda's head loll to the side, apparently asleep already. Like this, in her slacks

153

and sensible shoes, Lucinda looked like somebody's grandmother. But outward appearances, Gabriela knew, rarely told the whole story.

The visitor center at the museum resembled a huge mountain lodge with a gabled entrance and a shingled roof. Dr. Cynthia Rahlberg, a smiling woman with chin-length auburn hair, met them at the front door. After exchanging introductions and pleasantries, Cynthia led them into the center, past displays of Adirondack history. "If you'll wait here, I'll put your Shumler drawing in the administration offices. Do you want to come with me, Wendy?" Cynthia asked.

Wendy nodded and followed Cynthia out of the center, carrying the drawing.

Gabriela stopped in front of a panorama of the tallest peaks and took out her cell phone. She thumbed a text to Daniel, letting him know they had arrived, and hit Send. Nothing happened. She tried two more times. Her phone wavered between one bar and no cell service.

"You try mine. It's old, so maybe it works better." Agnese held up the old flip phone that she rarely used and staunchly refused to upgrade.

"Mama, if mine won't get a signal, yours certainly can't. And yours isn't for texting."

"Try." Agnese pushed the phone into her hands.

Gabriela studied the screen; there were two bars. She punched in Daniel's number, but it went to voicemail. She left a cheery message, laughing about old technology winning out, and assured him they were having a wonderful day.

At the end of the call, Agnese smiled smugly and put her phone back into her purse.

Trailing the others, Gabriela scanned the displays, her eyes gobbling up facts and images. A strip of ancient beadwork recalled the Iroquois peoples, who had arrived as early as four thousand years ago. The Mohawk tribe gave the place its name, derived from *adiro-daks* or "tree-eaters," as they had derisively called the nearby Algonquin tribe. On the next display, Gabriela found a portrait of a man in profile, and read about Samuel de Champlain, the first European to enter the Adirondacks in 1609. Gabriela skimmed maps, drawings, and captions, until her gaze landed on a painting of a slim man in a dark jacket trimmed with gold brocade and knee-length breeches worn with white stockings, a ruffle of lace at his throat. The sword at his hip and sash across his chest confirmed what she had suspected: This was Joseph Bonaparte, Napoleon's brother, former king of Naples and Spain, and one of the most famous of the Adirondacks' early European residents. Recalling the discussion a few weeks ago at Lucinda's house, Gabriela read about the man born Guiseppe Buonaparte in 1768 in Corsica, registering that her mother had been right about the Bonaparte brothers being Italian:

Napoleon's defeat at Waterloo in 1815 spelled the end for the French leader. He and his brother, Joseph, met secretly with a French American businessman named James Le Ray de Chaumont, who in the late 1700s had purchased vast tracts of land in the Adirondacks in a speculation scheme. The Bonaparte brothers saw this land as a way for Napoleon to escape capture by the British. After purchasing 26,000 acres—supposedly with the proceeds of a few crown jewels and the last of the Spanish treasury—Joseph went on ahead to establish a luxurious camp in the wilderness. Napoleon never arrived. The British captured Napoleon and banished him to St. Helena, where he lived the rest of his days.

The 1808 date on Gerald Shumler's schematic reignited her imagination—the sailmaker might have been acquainted with Le Ray de Chaumont and, a few years later, Joseph Bonaparte. Her logical researcher's mind quelled the speculation as nothing beyond coincidence. But surely there couldn't have been that many people living in this region at the time, she argued with herself, making the chances of them meeting each other all but assured.

Pulling herself away from the exhibit, Gabriela looked around for the others but didn't see them. She pivoted in a tight circle, but displays cut the space into small compartments meant to create full immersion without distraction. Then, through the glass panes of a door that led outside, she caught a glimpse of Lucinda and went outside to join the others.

The museum's large deck overlooked Blue Mountain Lake and the surrounding lush pines and thick woods where maples, oaks, and beeches showed ample streaks of their fall colors. A continuous planter lining the deck railing bloomed with red, white, and purple-blue petunias, burnt orange and yellow zinnias, and coleus with green and red variegated leaves. A dappled sky of clouds and sun played with the surface of the lake, turning from gray to the blue of its name.

After a few minutes of taking photos with their phones, the group followed Cynthia inside. A young man with an ID around his neck introduced himself as Josh and explained his role as program coordinator. "I basically get to play all day," he said, smiling at Ben. "Today, I'm thinking archery could be fun. You want to join me?"

Ben rocked up on his toes. "I'm going."

"And when we're through with that, there's a short nature trail we can walk, in case your mom gets really tied up in meetings."

"He may never come home," Gabriela laughed and watched her son take off with Josh.

Cynthia led them out of the visitor center to the main building of the museum campus. A large room held a topographical map of the Adirondacks the size of a conference table. "I remember this when I was a kid!" Gabriela squealed and ran her finger down an interactive panel that lit up towns, rivers, mountains, and lakes on the map. She pushed the button for Whiteface Mountain, a well-known ski area in the state, and a light illuminated not far from Lake Placid.

"Nobody outgrows that map, including the staff," Cynthia said with a smile.

A stone fireplace dominated the end of the room and, above it, a moose head with a rack of broad antlers that Gabriela estimated to be seven feet across.

"They terrify me," Wendy said with a grimace. "One charged J.J. He just made it to his truck."

Lucinda bent her head toward Gabriela. "Smart moose. Wish it had nailed J.J."

Cynthia gave the moose head an affectionate pat on the nose. "He's our doorman for the reading room." She stepped around a display panel dedicated to early European settlers, and the others followed.

At first, Gabriela saw only rough-hewn paneling and the stones of the massive fireplace. Then Cynthia pressed a dull metal plate on the wall, and a section of the paneling opened inward.

The doorway led to a small space with floor-to-ceiling bookshelves. Gabriela scanned the titles visible on the spines, most of them local and regional histories. A red volume with gold lettering bore the name *The Voyages of Samuel de Champlain*. Along the side wall stood a card catalog with dozens of tiny drawers. Gabriela looped her finger through a brass pull and slid a drawer open, revealing a long file of cards, one for each book in the collection.

"We still use it," Cynthia said. "This isn't a public library, so it's sufficient for our purposes; and given the historic nature of our collection, I think it's fitting."

Gabriela tore her attention away from the old card catalog and focused on the oval table that filled nearly all the floor space in the room. Intricate carvings of oak leaves and acorns, pinecones, and sprigs of pine covered the legs and ringed the sides of the massive table.

"A donation from one of the old Adirondack estates," Cynthia explained. "Every time we have a meeting here, I always think we should be serving Thanksgiving dinner instead." She reached for a large folio on the desk in the corner and brought it to the table. After distributing white cotton gloves to each of them, Cynthia opened the cover and took out three drawings. Gabriela searched for the grid markings of laid paper. Two of the drawings had that design; the third had a watermark more common with paper made from fibers woven together.

"We don't know a lot about Gerald Shumler, except he came to the Adirondacks from southern Lake Champlain," Cynthia said. "We don't know why, exactly, but these drawings indicate he was here between 1806 and 1810. We don't know what happened to him after that."

Wendy ran a gloved finger along the name at the corner of her schematic. "He's buried in Natural Bridge. My family is from there."

"Really? You've seen Shumler's grave?" Cynthia asked.

Wendy glanced at Gabriela, as if asking permission to speak. Gabriela nodded reflexively, then regretted reinforcing Wendy's need to get approval to assert herself.

"There's an old cemetery at the Methodist church. He's in the back," Wendy explained. "His inscription is sort of strange: 'God made a wind to pass over the earth.' It's from Genesis."

"Seems like we should be asking you questions. You know far more about Gerald Shumler than the rest of us," Cynthia said.

"I don't think so. A lot of nonsense rolling around up there." She tapped her temple with her finger. "That's what J.J. tells me. He's my husband."

"You know a lot," Cynthia said. "I'm glad you came today so we can learn from you."

Wendy's faced reddened, but Gabriela discerned from the smile and blush that Cynthia's comment had pleased the young woman.

They studied the museum's drawings of traditional sail designs that differed starkly from Wendy's schematic. Cynthia pointed to a drawing of square-shaped sails and explained it had been made for the *Echelon*, a schooner on Lake Champlain. The other depicted a triangular sail for a sailboat. "I'm no maritime expert, but your drawing, Wendy, looks like nothing I've ever seen. It seems so experimental. I can see where it looks like it folds here—and the double rigging."

"Perhaps it's significant because of that?" Gabriela suggested.

Wendy clasped and unclasped her hands. "It has to be worth something—to someone."

Cynthia held up a finger. "I have an idea." Getting up from the reading room table, she went to the desk in the corner. "He called yesterday, so I don't know why I didn't think of him earlier." Cynthia punched several buttons on a landline phone. "Earl Buntley has donated so much in our navigation exhibit." Her explanation ended, and Cynthia engaged in a conversation with someone on the phone. When the call ended and Cynthia rejoined the others, she explained that Earl could meet them at the museum warehouse around two that afternoon. "In the meantime, shall we have lunch and continue our conversation? The café here has some nice selections."

Agnese spoke up. "We treat you. We brought a feast."

Gabriela offered to help Cynthia set up some tables in the staff room. She gave her car keys to Lucinda so that she and Wendy could bring in the picnic baskets. "Call Daniel," Agnese said, pointing to the office phone, before she left with the others.

"As soon as I collect Ben," Gabriela agreed.

"Now," Agnese insisted. "You promised him."

"Do you mind?" Gabriela asked Cynthia, who gestured toward her desk in response. She called Daniel's cell again, but it went straight to voicemail. She left a message, promising to call again later.

Ben rushed in the front door of the building, with Josh behind him. The boy's face flushed as he talked about an "almost" bull's-eye in archery, the deer they'd seen on the trail, and a place where they could canoe. Gabriela listened as Josh steered her and Ben toward the staff room where Lucinda, Wendy, and Agnese had spread out the lunch. Seeing how much food they had, Cynthia invited a few more staff members to join them.

Agnese rapped her knuckles lightly against Gabriela's wrist. "You see? If I didn't bring so much, we would run out."

Gabriela wanted to explain that they had to feed a lot of people because of the amount of food Agnese and Lucinda had brought. But seeing her mother's smile as people loaded their plates, Gabriela agreed that it was a very good thing. As everyone ate, Gabriela excused herself to use the office phone a second time to call Daniel, but again only reached his voicemail. Without a cellular connection, sending a text was futile, but she tried anyway, and wasn't surprised when the screen read "undelivered."

As soon as she came back, Ben started pestering her about zip-lining. Agnese already looked tired, Gabriela noticed, and Wendy seemed anxious about being away from home for so long. "When, Mom?" Ben repeated.

Gabriela turned to Josh. "How far is the zip-lining place? Any chance I could get Ben there before going to the warehouse?"

Josh set down his sandwich and wiped his mouth with a paper napkin. "There's a place outside Lake Placid, but it's almost an hour away."

Gabriela groaned. It was nearly one o'clock. "I didn't know it was so far." The disappointment on Ben's face tore at her heart.

Lucinda came up behind her and set her hand on her shoulder. "Move your meeting with Earl Buntley to four o'clock. He's going to be at the warehouse anyway. We'll go now. Ben can take a few runs, and we'll be back here by four."

Noticing that Wendy and her mother had already started clearing the lunch spread and seemed ready to go, Gabriela called Wendy aside. "If we take Ben zip-lining, we won't get home until 8:30. What about J.J.?"

Wendy shrugged. "When he's out on the road, he may not even come home. It'll be okay."

Gabriela tried to make eye contact as Wendy averted her gaze. "You need to tell me the truth. I can always bring Ben back here another day."

"It's good. And if J.J. gets home before I do, I'll say I went over to see a friend."

"Okay, if you're sure. We need to get this group on the road."

Josh stood back until they finished talking. When Gabriela turned toward him, he smiled broadly at her. "I just spoke to Cynthia. She'll confirm everything with Earl." He jangled car keys. "And she's letting me go with you." He called to Ben. "Buddy, you want to ride with me?"

———

They made it to Zip Adirondack in fifty-three minutes, thanks to light traffic and a shortcut Josh knew about. Ben sprang out of Josh's car as soon as the brake lights illuminated. Gabriela pulled into the next space and shut off the engine. "Wait up, Ben!" she called as she got out of her car.

"You go on ahead," Lucinda told her. "We'll catch up."

Gabriela reached back in the car for her purse. "Looks like there are some tables up ahead. Maybe you could sit there while Ben goes on the zip line."

"What?" Lucinda lowered her chin and smiled. "We're going, too."

Gabriela shook her head. "I'm not sure I'm up for this."

Lucinda hooked her arm through Wendy's. "Well, then you can sit and wave at us. But we're going."

Agnese tipped her head up toward the low mountain. "Maybe I go too."

Gabriela put up both hands, palms out. "Mama, zip-lining isn't like riding in some gondola. It's wearing this little harness that slides really fast along a wire suspended up in the air."

"*Si,* I know this. I see on television. They say it's very safe."

Lucinda started to chuckle, and Gabriela heard Wendy's soft laugh as well. "Mama, you can't be serious. Dr. Granger would have a fit."

Agnese turned to the left and right, her arms outstretched. "Where is he? I don't see him. So, I'm going."

Gabriela decided to ignore her mother's bravado and caught up to Josh and Ben, who were talking to a young man in a Zip Adirondacks T-shirt. He introduced himself as Tim and told her that Dr. Rahlberg had already called and informed them of a party coming from the museum. "So we have what—three people? Four?"

"I thought this would only be Josh and Ben, but Lucinda and Wendy say they want to go."

"That's cool," Tim said. "This course is really good for beginners."

Gabriela looked up the mountain, where a row of ski lift chairs began moving up the cable. Just then she saw someone zip along horizontally from the ski lift platform toward the trees on the other side. "I guess I'll go too. But my mother—"

"I tell her it's safe," Agnese interjected. "I'm seventy-six, but very healthy."

"Mom, you had cancer surgery a few months ago."

162

Tim raised his eyebrows. "So, maybe this isn't a good idea."

Agnese waved her hands as if to shush Gabriela. "My heart is good. My lungs are good. And I'm not afraid."

Gabriela planted her hands on her mother's shoulders, feeling the delicate bones. "I'm sure it's safe, Mama. But it's strenuous. What if you got hurt? Even a hard landing could break your hip."

Agnese put her hands atop Gabriela's. "I have cancer twice. Both times I think, maybe I die. But I don't. I'm here—and I want to live." Lifting one hand, she pointed toward Ben. "Then my grandson will know his Nonna is brave."

Gabriela shook her head. "She wants to go," she told the Zip Adirondack staff.

"The only restrictions we have are height, weight, pregnancy, and people with bad backs." Tim ticked them off on his fingers. "I also heard you guys are really tight on time, so we should go."

Gabriela insisted on buying everyone's ticket and gave her credit card to Tim, who returned with six harnesses and a colleague, Melissa, who led them to two Jeeps to take them up a service road to the platform, instead of waiting for the ski lift.

As they bounced up the rutted track, Gabriela also noticed that they seemed to be cutting in line ahead of two other parties. When she asked Tim, he told her not to worry. "Everybody knows we got a VIP group from the museum."

"Hardly," Gabriela replied. Another zip-liner streaked across the sky, and she tensed.

When they reached the base of the landing platform, they had to climb three long flights of wooden stairs. Gabriela heard her mother's wheezing breath and asked her again to reconsider. Agnese said nothing until they reached the top of the platform. "I say I go, so I go."

"Mama, this is not safe for you," Gabriela insisted.

"But it's safe for Ben?" her mother shot back. "If he can go, I can go. I am an old woman. I've never done anything like this before—like flying."

Gabriela took her mother's arm. "Then I will be with you. Ahead of you or behind you, whichever you wish."

After a round of safety instructions, tips for steering, and what to do if they got stuck in the middle, a prospect Gabriela preferred not to imagine, they began putting on their harnesses. Josh jumped first, flinging himself off the platform with enough velocity to take him across the first expanse. Ben followed, getting a helpful shove from Tim to start off with enough speed to carry him the entire way. Gabriela gulped a breath and held it as Ben sailed along. Two Zip Adirondack staff caught him on the other side.

Lucinda went next, whooping the entire way. Wendy's hands shook so much, she couldn't tighten the chinstrap on her helmet, and Melissa had to do it for her. Then the young woman flung herself off like she had done this a dozen times before.

Gabriela led Agnese up to the platform. "My mother weighs about a hundred pounds," she said to Tim. "She's going to need help."

Tim leaned down, hands on his thighs, until he reached Agnese's eye level. "Do you mind if I throw you off?"

"*Si,* you do this." Agnese tightened her helmet.

Gabriela's eyes blurred as Tim picked her mother up in his arms and tossed her over the side. "Go, Mama!" she yelled, clapping and nearly sobbing as the Zip Adirondacks staff caught her and set her down.

Gabriela's heart hammered and her pulse thrummed in her ears. She glanced across the thirty-yard gap where Ben jumped up and down on the landing platform behind the Zip Adirondack crew. "Come on, Mom!" he yelled, and his voice echoed a little.

Below, the tops of slender trees waved in the wind, and the rocky domes of boulders broke through the grass below. *If I fall, I will die.* The thought pierced her, nailing her consciousness in that deadly moment at the library tower when she had faced an impossible choice. Not live or die, but how to die—jumping from the library tower or getting her throat slit.

Green swam into browns as her eyes flooded. She jerked her head away as Melissa of Zip Adirondack clipped her to the line.

"Hey, if you don't want to do this," Melissa said.

Gabriela's eyes snapped open. That day at the library tower, dying had not been her only option; she had fought back and lived. "I want to do this. I *need* to do this for a lot of reasons, starting with that boy over there." She waved to Ben.

"Know what to do?" Melissa ran through the instructions quickly. Gabriela nodded. "On the count of three—one, two—JUMP!"

Gabriela soared through the air, wind tearing at her hair. She landed, shaky with adrenaline. "I did it!" she crowed, knowing she had crossed far more than thirty yards. She had found a bridge out of the trauma that had dogged her for months. She would not let it paralyze her life.

Grabbing her phone, she composed a text to Daniel. *Took Ben zip-lining and I JUMPED. Felt like I flew*—she inserted a bird emoji—*right out of all the bad stuff. Never again! I'm over it!!*

As she waited for Daniel's reply, Gabriela watched the screen. It came back: "Not delivered." The mountains blocked the cell signal.

Her spirits deflated, she waited at the back of the group on the platform. Tim pointed to a suspension bridge. "That's where we're going, and the jump on the other side is twice as long."

All six of them made the next jump, but on the final run, Melissa suggested that Agnese might not want to attempt it. "If you don't have enough velocity, you could get stuck. We'd come get you, but it's a little nerve-wracking."

"You're right—I do enough. You go." Agnese curled her arm around Ben's shoulders. "But now we know what it's like to have wings."

One after the other, they took off, with Ben getting tossed off the platform so he could clear the distance. At her turn, Gabriela looked at the expanse before her.

"Don't steer," Melissa said. "When you do that, it causes friction—like a brake. You need to let go. You'll be safe."

Gabriela ran three steps and flung herself off. The wind caught her, turning her to the left and right. She gripped the straps and fought the urge to steer. In those few seconds, she felt fear and freedom. Slowing down as she got to the landing platform, she reached out with her toes toward the extended hands of the Zip Adirondack team, then put her feet down on the wooden boards.

As a team member helped her unlock the harness, Gabriela savored the obvious meaning of what had just happened: By letting go of all control, she'd gone the distance and safely reached the other side.

CHAPTER

FIFTEEN

At five minutes to four, Earl Buntley met them at the museum warehouse, set back in the woods that looked like a cross between a barn and boat storage. A rotund man with thick white hair that stood up straight from his scalp, he wore a beige short-sleeved cotton shirt that strained at the buttons and jeans held up by suspenders. After shaking Earl's hand and introducing herself, Gabriela glanced around at the canoes, horse-drawn carriages, and a few vintage automobiles stored inside the cavernous building. Deep metal shelving covered one wall, lined with cartons and crates. Stepping closer, Gabriela read a few labels: "Saranac Lake, schoolhouse—1903"; "Lake Placid, antique skates, c. 1895."

Cynthia Rahlberg came around the corner carrying a small box, which she set down on a wooden table. "Oh, you're here—right on time. How was zip-lining?"

"Awesome!" Ben interjected. "Nonna went too."

Cynthia's eyes widened. "Really? Agnese, I'm impressed."

As Gabriela turned to smile at her mother, she saw the weariness in Agnese's eyes, and worry began edging out the liberation she had claimed for herself on the last zip-line run. "Any chance of getting some coffee?"

"I'm way ahead of you," Cynthia replied. "A couple of our staff members volunteered to stop by with refreshments on their way home. They'll be here by 4:30."

Cynthia guided them toward a corner of the room where Wendy's drawing covered the center of a table. Lucinda took Agnese's arm and walked her slowly toward the table. Josh came up beside Gabriela and explained that he'd like to show Ben some stuff that would be more interesting for an eleven-year-old than an old drawing.

Gabriela thanked him and watched as Ben went off with Josh toward the rear of the warehouse. She stole a glance at her phone; 4:20 already. They needed to be on the road by five o'clock, no matter what. As she put the phone back in her purse, she saw again "no service" in the upper left-hand corner of the screen.

Earl disappeared into the larger items on display and brought out a velvet Queen Anne chair with arms and legs carved in a delicate curlicue design. He set it down near Agnese and brushed his hand along the seat, as if clearing dust. "Fit for a queen."

"*Grazie mille.*" Agnese lowered herself into the chair.

Gabriela invited Earl to tell them about his interest in maritime history, hoping this would help break the ice with Wendy, who appeared nervous in front of him. He obliged by starting with his personal story; he had been born in Buffalo, graduated from Colgate University, and spent a long advertising career in New York City. In the 1980s he bought a cottage near Blue Mountain Lake and had remodeled it three times since then. "If it were up to me, I'd live here full-time, but my wife likes spending the winter in the city," he said. "We come back every spring, as soon as the snow starts melting. The museum is my second home."

Earl launched into a story about buying a painting depicting a battle on the Great Lakes during the War of 1812. "Did some research on the artist and discovered that he had been in that battle. I was hooked. My collection is mostly 1800s, though I do have a few Revolutionary War–era pieces. And I own a couple of Shumler drawings."

Wendy clasped her hands together. "Really? Like mine?"

"My drawings are sail designs for a sloop that sailed on Lake George. I've never seen anything like yours," Earl replied.

When Earl asked how she came to be in possession of her Shumler drawing, Wendy explained the family connection. Gabriela half-listened, her attention more on her mother, who seemed paler, the furrows between her eyebrows deeper. Agnese caught her eye and frowned, and Gabriela knew what that meant: *Don't make a fuss.*

Joining the conversation, Gabriela asked about the unusual design: the hinged mast, the supports that fanned out from the bottom, the double rigging. "A foldable sail?" she asked.

Earl's grin grew into a wide smile. "I thought that too. Foldable sails were not particularly common in the nineteenth century, at least not on traditional vessels. And considering the date on the drawing, I can't help but make a connection in my mind—Robert Fulton."

Just then the staff arrived with refreshments: a large coffee decanter, cream and sugar, and a tray of cookies. Gabriela poured a cup of black coffee for her mother and gave her a chocolate chip cookie on a paper napkin. After a few sips, Agnese seemed to revive.

Earl pulled over a metal stool and perched on the edge of it. Between bites of a cookie and sips of coffee, he began telling them about Robert Fulton: the American inventor who had failed as a painter before turning his attention toward engineering and navigation. He designed all sorts of things—aqueducts, canals, bridges, and boats—all of them with unique, even fanciful concepts. His most ingenious plan was the *Nautilus*, a submarine.

"One of the distinguishing characteristics of Fulton's submarine design was a collapsible sail and mast," Earl said. He explained that the sail propelled the submarine toward its destination. Once there, the sail could be folded up, and the submarine submerged to just below the water's surface. A two-man crew turned a screwlike turbine to bring the submarine the rest of the way to its target.

"Fulton traveled to Paris in 1797 in hopes of meeting with Napoleon to present his idea of the French using his submarine to defeat the British," Earl continued.

"Wait—you know about Napoleon's brother, right?" Lucinda interrupted. "He lived in Natural Bridge, where Shumler is buried."

Earl's mouth twitched. "Well, then, it's probably a good guess that Shumler knew Joseph Bonaparte and his entourage. Although—" his grin disappeared "—the French were never really sold on Fulton's idea."

He explained that Fulton had proposed the *Nautilus* to the French as a secret weapon, capable of creeping unseen, right up to British warships, and leaving bombs filled with gunpowder near their hulls. The bombs would explode once the submarine reached a safe distance away. After multiple experiments and demonstrations, design modifications, and rounds of negotiation, Fulton failed to convince the French of the need for a submarine fleet to defeat the British. "His idea was ahead of its time, to say the least."

The French government's rejection didn't stop Fulton, though, Earl went on. Fulton proposed his submarine design to the British government. But then Lord Nelson defeated the French in the naval battle at Trafalgar, and Britain claimed undisputed control of the seas for the next hundred years. "After that victory, the British didn't need Fulton's experimental submarine," Earl added.

"So where is the *Nautilus*?" Wendy asked.

"Fulton scrapped it. But his drawings for it are in the British Museum."

"Did Shumler do those drawings?" Lucinda asked.

Earl shook his head. "No, they are Fulton's own designs." He continued the story, explaining that after the British rejected the submarine, Fulton returned to the States and engaged in various experiments with submersibles, but soon put all his energy into the steamboats that brought him enormous success. In 1807 his steamboat prototype made it from New York to Albany far faster than the sailing sloops used on that route.

"If—and it's a big if—this foldable sail was designed by Shumler for Fulton, it would suggest that he didn't give up on submarines," Earl went on. "Perhaps he kept working on them in secret."

"So, how do we find out?" Wendy asked.

"We dig around, see if we can find a connection between Shumler and Fulton," Earl said. "Right now, we have a theory, but it's an intriguing one."

"I used to be the assistant director of Archives and Documents at the New York Public Library," Gabriela interjected. "I can contact my former colleagues there and see if there are any Shumler documents—letters, perhaps."

Earl nodded. "I'll ask around too. Maritime collectors are a tight-knit community. They'll love this theory."

"Wait!" Wendy called out. "I don't want a lot of people knowing about this. Can't we just look around ourselves?"

Earl looked from Cynthia to Gabriela and then back to Wendy. "I thought you wanted to authenticate this."

"I don't want my husband to find out about it," Wendy said. "He'll pawn it or try to sell it. He might even get mad at me and burn it. We have to keep it away from J.J."

Earl nodded. "Why don't we keep it here at the Adirondack Experience, just for now? Cynthia can safeguard it, and if we need to send photos of it to dealers or researchers, we won't mention your name. Does that work for you?"

Gabriela caught the plea in Wendy's eyes as the young woman looked at her. "I think that's a great idea," she said. "J.J. will never hear about it, and it will be better preserved here."

"We can have you sign a release form, giving the museum authorization to store it for you," Cynthia added.

Gabriela looked at the time again: 5:15. Her mother, she noticed, rested her head against the back of the chair. "Can you send the documents later by email?"

"No," Wendy said. "J.J. reads all my emails. I trust you. If you need to reach me, leave a message with Gabriela or Lucinda."

"Wendy, if you need any other assistance, it's available to you," Cynthia began.

"I know—Gabriela told me. But I'm not ready. I need money. Once I have that, I can leave him."

Cynthia's arms opened and, to Gabriela's surprise, Wendy stepped into the hug. "You've got a lot of people who want to help you. Not just your friends, but Earl and me, as well. We're here for you, Wendy. And if you're in real danger, you have to tell us."

Wendy wiped her eyes. "I'm okay. Really."

The tug-of-war tightened around Gabriela—on one side, wanting to give Wendy the positive reinforcement of these kind people; on the other, knowing she needed to get her mother home as soon as possible. Hearing Wendy promise to call Cynthia in a few days, Gabriela spoke up. "We really have to go. Mama is exhausted, we all are. And it's a long—"

The lights flickered and went out. The warehouse plunged into darkness. Wendy screamed, and Gabriela shot her hands out toward her mother, gripping Agnese's thin shoulders.

"Don't worry," Cynthia said. "We lose power all the time. Just takes a good gust of wind."

Gabriela heard Ben calling for her and answered him with a light tone. "It's okay, honey. Just stay where you are."

Her phone didn't have a signal, but the screen illuminated, and the flashlight app turned the warehouse into a maze of objects half hidden in darkness. Gabriela kept up a stream of questions for Ben— What had he seen? What was the coolest thing in the warehouse?—as she headed toward the glow of Josh, waving his cell phone in the air.

Holding her son tightly, Gabriela swooned with relief, recognizing in her overreaction all the signs of emotional and physical fatigue. A minute later, the lights came back on. Cynthia ushered them out of the warehouse, and Earl offered his arm to Agnese as they walked toward the parking lot. In the fading sunlight, Gabriela felt the urgency to depart, but didn't want to rush their goodbyes. "I can't thank you enough," she said, hugging Cynthia.

"This is our pleasure—believe me," Cynthia replied. "We'll keep you apprised of what we learn, and I know you'll do the same."

Josh and Ben slapped high fives. "Come back and we'll do more fun stuff," Josh said.

"Can we?" Ben asked Gabriela.

"Absolutely," she promised.

They loaded into the car: Gabriela and Lucinda in the front; Agnese and Wendy in the back, with Ben between them. Lucinda let out a whoop. "Robert Fulton—can you imagine? If that's who commissioned your drawing, Wendy, you're probably sitting on a million dollars. Right, Gabriela?"

Gabriela squinted against the glare of the sun lowering in the sky. "I couldn't venture a guess, but the Robert Fulton theory is an interesting one. Earl seemed to think so."

Lucinda kept spinning the tale, imagining how Shumler, Fulton, and Joseph Bonaparte could be connected. "Maybe the submarine was for him, something to sail around his lake, along with his six-oared gondolas."

Gabriela felt a hand on the back of her seat. She glanced in the rearview mirror and saw Ben leaning forward. "Mom, can we go zip-lining again? Maybe Josh can go with us?"

"We'll look for some other zip-lining places; maybe there are some closer to home," she said. "We'll see Josh when we come back to the museum."

Ben chattered on about zip-lining, overtaking the conversation, but no one seemed to mind. "You were the best," Lucinda said, swiveling in the front seat to address him. "Completely fearless."

Gabriela focused on the winding road through the Adirondacks, trying to drive at the speed limit, but every time she crested a rise the sun blasted into her eyes and she had to slow down. Her phone rang twice, but when she answered using the car's Bluetooth connection, the calls dropped. The third time, she let the call go to voicemail.

As she drove on, Gabriela thought of how she would tell Daniel the story of everything that had happened: learning more about Gerald Shumler, the possible Robert Fulton connection, and the zip-lining adventure. After hearing how well it all went, Daniel couldn't possibly be angry at her for not mentioning her meeting at the museum.

The car quieted, conversation separated by longer pauses.

"Ben sleeps," Agnese said, her voice low. "His head in my lap."

A sweet pang hit Gabriela in the solar plexus. Her eleven-year-old son would never allow himself to do such a thing other than here, in the cocoon of a car.

As she neared Livery, Gabriela spied the bright lights of a service station and minimart and pulled in. She'd filled up after zip-lining, and now the tank was down to half. Getting out of the car at the gasoline pump, she felt the stiffness in her back and the cramp in her neck from hunching over the steering wheel. Raising her shoulders to her ears and dropping them again, she felt a pleasant crack and sighed—almost home. After the pump clicked off, she went inside to use the restroom. Lucinda and Agnese came in as Gabriela headed out, still drying her hands on a brown paper towel.

A pickup truck with oversized wheels rolled into the parking lot, pulling a trailer. As it maneuvered under the awning, stopping in front of a diesel pump, Gabriela saw the pitted siding on the trailer and the rust marks where the metal trim gapped. The front passenger door swung open, and a man in a dark hoodie jumped out.

The back door of her car opened, and Gabriela turned her attention to Wendy, who pointed to the convenience store and explained that she wanted to get a bottle of water. After grabbing the squeegee to clean her windshield, Gabriela rounded the front of her car. A shadow fell across her feet, amorphous at first, then sharpening into the shape of a man. Gabriela wheeled around, taking in the man's face, semi-cloaked by the hood of the sweatshirt pulled past his ears, then the design across the chest: the bare tree, the stump with the axe. She searched the man's face, recognizing him as the one who had approached their table the night she and Daniel had gone to The Lakeside. "Colby," she said aloud before being sure she should.

His lips parted as if he had something to say, then hardened into a firm line when another man got out of the driver's side of the truck. "What the hell are you doing?" the man bellowed.

"Lady asked me directions," Colby replied.

Gabriela put the squeegee back in a bucket by the gas pumps.

"I gotta piss," the man said.

"Who wants snacks?" Wendy called out from the door of the service station.

Gabriela turned just as the paper bag Wendy carried hit the pavement. A water bottle rolled away from her.

"J.J.," Wendy said.

Gabriela snapped her attention to him, committing every detail to memory. Six feet, jet-black hair, and stubble on his cheeks. Heavy eyebrows and a scowling expression hid his eyes.

J.J. crossed his arms across his stocky body. "Where d'you go all day?"

Wendy bent over, picking up the water bottle, a Diet Coke, and a bag of chips she'd dropped. "We went to a museum. Gabriela took us."

"Museum? Since when d'you ever go to a place like that?" J.J.'s sneer landed on Gabriela.

"I'm the executive director of the Ohnita Harbor Public Library," Gabriela began.

"And what's that got to do with me?" J.J. retorted.

Gabriela fisted her hands, her short nails digging into her palms. "I took my son and my mother to the museum today and invited Wendy to join us."

"Yeah? Who else is in that car?" When he leaned toward the window, Gabriela rushed to block him, not wanting him to see Ben.

"Is there some guy in there?" J.J. shouted.

"My son. He's eleven." Gabriela's voice trembled with more anger than fear.

A car door swung open. "She's with me, J.J. Leave her alone." Lucinda stood up slowly, hanging onto the doorframe.

J.J. straightened and squared his shoulders. "This is between my wife and me."

Stay in the car, stay in the car, Gabriela telegraphed to her mother and Ben.

"So, this is the trailer?" Wendy approached him slowly.

"No, it's a pony cart. What the hell you think?" J.J. grabbed Wendy by the arm.

An image crystallized in Gabriela's mind of the first time she saw Wendy: slumped in one of the Adirondack chairs at Lucinda's, keeping

176

her head turned to hide a yellowed bruise on her cheek. "You don't have to go with him. You can come with us," Gabriela called out to her.

"With you? You one of them too?" J.J. shoved Wendy toward the truck.

Wendy opened the truck cab and got in. As the cab door swung shut, Wendy's wide eyes caught Gabriela's. "Call me," Gabriela mouthed, but couldn't be sure Wendy had seen it.

J.J. came toward Lucinda, stabbing the air with his finger. "You stay away from her. She don't need your kinda thoughts."

Lucinda tossed her head. "I'm not afraid of you. And if you hurt her again, I'll make sure you suffer."

Gabriela sucked in her breath at Lucinda's threat, feeling the almost-violent intensity of her words.

"You just try, old lady," J.J. said.

Colby appeared then, walking so close to Gabriela that she side-stepped to avoid him. "You want me to ride in the back?" he said to J.J., pointing toward the truck bed.

"There's room up front. Wendy can fit in the middle."

When J.J. rounded the front of the truck, Colby wheeled and faced Gabriela. Seeing the flash of a knife blade, she gulped for air, straining like a fish out of water.

Colby walked toward the truck cab, hands in his pockets. The knife had only been imaginary, Gabriela realized, a figment from past trauma she hadn't escaped, no matter how much she wanted to be free of it.

The pickup's engine roared to life and the rig pulled out, the camper swaying on its hitch as the truck bumped through potholes.

Gabriela covered her face with her hands. "What's going to happen to her? Can't we do something?"

"He knows we're watching him, watching her. He'll mind his step. Better yet, I'll call his father. Jake will keep J.J. in line. And if he doesn't, I will." Lucinda drew her phone out of her purse. "That's why I haven't heard from Parnella." She shook her head. "Turned the doggone thing off at the museum and forgot to turn it back on."

Gabriela stuck her head in the car to see Ben cowering next to Agnese. "Who's that guy?" he asked. "Why did Wendy go with him?"

"He's her husband," Gabriela said. "He's just a lot of noise. You two okay? We're going home right now."

"*Va bene*," Agnese replied. "Time to sleep soon."

"Oh, my God!" Lucinda shouted. Startled, Gabriela straightened so quickly she clipped her shoulder on the roof of the car. Lucinda stared at her phone, which played back a voicemail. "The sheriff's department—they came to my house."

Coldness creeped up Gabriela's back, prickling her scalp. She clamped her hands on the back of her own neck. "Why?"

Lucinda's mouth went slack. "Parnella said they had a warrant. They took everything—my teas, my herbs. They trampled my garden."

"Why?" Gabriela repeated, dreading the answer.

"They think I poisoned Todd Watson."

———

Gabriela sat alone on her back deck that night, staring into a night sky that threatened rain by morning. Not a single star penetrated the clouds. No light streamed from the house or the outside fixtures. Gabriela wanted darkness, surrounded only by vague forms where her backyard gardens and shrubs should be. Dampness chilled her, and a shiver shook her shoulders. The numbness in her hands and at the tip of her nose matched what she felt inside her mind—too tired, too overwhelmed to think or feel.

In her mind she replayed her phone conversation with Daniel from just an hour ago: the happier details of the day's events completely overshadowed by what had happened in the last half hour of their trip. Describing it to Daniel, she had pictured Wendy's frightened face as J.J. forced her into the truck, and Lucinda collapsing into sobs when Parnella met them at the service station to bring her to the sheriff's department.

Looking back, she would have preferred endless silence to the words that Daniel finally spoke: "You don't trust me."

The echo of Daniel's comment brought tears to eyes that burned with fatigue. Cold penetrated deeper into her body. Gabriela got up to go inside, but stopped when headlights shone down the driveaway then extinguished. She knew who had arrived, and as much as she wanted to see Daniel, she also feared what he would have to say. When she heard the truck door open, she leaned over the deck and called down the driveway. "I'm out here."

"Okay," Daniel replied.

In the quiet, she heard the thick soles of his work boots thud against the driveway. When he climbed the steps to the deck, Gabriela rose to greet him, hoping for a hug. His arms stayed at his sides, and she sank back in her chair. Daniel pulled another chair over a few inches and sat down, clasped hands dangling between his knees.

Gabriela watched his every move, interpreting every gesture and expression. *It's over*, she told herself, steeling against the inevitable breakup.

"I really thought we had something," he began.

Wetting her lips, Gabriela began to speak. "I—" The words scraped her dry throat. She would not argue or plead with him; if he wanted out, she would not try to stop him. She had learned that the hard way with Jim, believing at first that they could work through their problems. In the end, Jim had left anyway, because that's what he'd wanted all along.

"Why didn't you tell me you had a meeting at the museum? Did you think I'd try to stop you? Am I that overbearing?" Daniel asked.

Gabriela studied the toes of the canvas slip-on shoes she wore. "I didn't want to upset you," she said. "I know how you feel about me helping out the people of Livery."

"I never tried to stop you from helping—" he interjected.

Gabriela held up her hand, and he stopped speaking. "You have made it very clear that you don't think I should be up there, that I'm just inserting myself where I don't belong. But there's someone who needs my help. A young woman—the one who owns the drawing I showed you. She's in danger, and if I can help her, I will."

When Daniel nodded, she felt the tension between them defuse.

"When I saw her husband drag her away . . . " Gabriela shook her head. "I would have given anything to take her away with me. I fear for her life, Daniel. I really do."

Daniel looked up, catching her eye. "And what about Lucinda?"

Accusation lurked between Daniel's words. *You didn't tell me the whole truth.*

"What if she's charged with murder, Gabriela? You going to try to save her too?"

"She didn't do it," Gabriela said. "If you knew her like I do, you'd see."

"But you don't know her—not really," Daniel blurted out. "You met her—what? Three weeks ago? That woman wants something from you, but you can't see it."

"No, she doesn't do anything unless she's asked," Gabriela shot back. "People judge her harshly because she's different. Because she's an herbalist who can feel the energy plants give off. And because of small-town prejudice against her relationship with Parnella."

"And now she's killed someone with all that 'plant energy.'" Daniel made air quotes with his fingers. "She poisoned someone who got in her way. What happens if you don't do something for her? Will she try to kill you too?"

Gabriela pulled herself inward, making her body smaller and increasing the distance between herself and Daniel.

180

"If I didn't know you better, Gabriela, I'd think you had a death wish. Three months ago, you were nearly murdered. But instead of taking yourself out of harm's way, you seem to run right toward trouble. No matter what I try, I can't protect you."

Gabriela wheeled on him, eyes wide and nostrils flared. "I don't want to be treated like some porcelain doll. I'm not broken and I'm not sick. I'm not—" Her top teeth pressed into her lower lip, preparing to make the "V" sound, but she stopped herself before it escaped her.

From the pain and anger that took turns contorting Daniel's face, she could tell he intuited the unspoken name. He got up, arms dangling limply, and left. Gabriela stayed in her chair, staring blankly into the darkness of her backyard.

CHAPTER
SIXTEEN

On Monday morning, while straightening a book display on the main floor of the library, Gabriela looked up to see Trooper Morrison walking in the front door. She nodded a greeting, which he did not return, and started walking toward the stairs, knowing he'd follow her. Entering the administration suite, Gabriela said nothing to Delmina as she passed, with Trooper Morrison behind her. She shut her office door and ushered him to the seat opposite her desk.

He removed the brimmed hat with the dimpled crown—a "Smokey Bear," she remembered them being called. Gabriela gathered her scattered thoughts, knowing her mind chased trivia when she was nervous.

"You want to tell me about your little road trip with Lucinda on Saturday?" he asked.

Knowing he would reach out to her, she had mentally rehearsed the answer to this question a dozen times. But now, seeing Trooper Morrison's impenetrable expression—eyes fixed on her, mouth firmly neutral—she could not recall the opening words.

"I did not plan it," she said. "My mother, my son, and I were the only ones going. To the museum. In Blue Mountain Lake." She blanked on the name of it and looked at Trooper Morrison as if he might mention it. He didn't.

He wanted her to be nervous, Gabriela knew, to wander verbally in contradictions that would incriminate Lucinda. Maybe even herself. Taking a deep breath, Gabriela closed her eyes for two seconds and pictured the welcome sign at the museum. "Adirondack Experience," she added.

The name centered her in what she knew to be true: She had gone to the museum to authenticate the Shumler drawing. She explained this in detail to Trooper Morrison—how she had met Wendy Haughton at Lucinda's a few weeks before and how she'd been asked to examine an old document that belonged to Wendy's family. When he didn't interrupt with a question, Gabriela went on to explain the theory of it being a schematic of a foldable sail, the possible connection to Robert Fulton.

"Why do you think Lucinda accompanied you to the museum?" he asked when she finished.

Gabriela raised her shoulders an inch. "It was an outing for a day—an adventure of sorts. Especially when Wendy said she could get away since her husband was out of town."

The state trooper rubbed his mouth and chin with his hand. "This isn't my investigation—the sheriff's department is handling it. But when I heard about the arrest for Todd Watson's murder—"

"Arrest?" Gabriela blurted out.

"—I remembered what you'd said about an argument you'd had with him. I called a sheriff's deputy I know, and he told me that Lucinda had been out when they searched her house. Then I find out Lucinda was with you."

"I had nothing to do with all that. Wendy wants to sell the Shumler drawing so she can get away from her husband."

184

"And you want to help her," Trooper Morrison interjected.

"Authentication is my background; I've told you that. I'm using my expertise to help a young woman in trouble."

Gabriela pressed her fingertips against the rim of her desk, pushing her upper body forward. "That drawing has been in Wendy's family for generations. J.J. cannot get it—it's not his. If you could have seen the way he grabbed Wendy's arm and shoved her into the cab of his truck."

"Has Wendy Haughton made a complaint against her husband? Accused him of violence or threats against her?"

Gabriela recognized the questions as rhetorical and didn't give him the satisfaction of answering them.

Trooper Morrison got up from the chair, holding his hat in his hands. He rotated the brim. "Be careful who you're protecting," he said. "Lucinda Nanz has pleaded guilty to accidental manslaughter in the death of Todd Watson."

Sweat spread from Gabriela's hairline to the back of her neck. Her mouth gaped open, but she couldn't form any words. "Why?" she breathed at last.

"Once again, I suggest that you remove yourself from this investigation. You're not a suspect, but if you keep involving yourself, you could be." He put his hat on and left her office.

Hands trembling, Gabriela mistyped three times as she searched the internet for the plants in Lucinda's most secluded garden: belladonna, hellebore, and monkshood. Websites, both scientific and fanciful, filled the screen with a mix of botany, legend, and lore—all pointing to the same conclusion. The three plants were not just toxic but decidedly poisonous. Their properties made arrowheads and daggers more deadly; added to teas and wine, they became their victim's last drink.

Lucinda, the herbalist, grew them; Parnella, the botanist, knew them just as well. How long, Gabriela wondered, before both women were jailed under suspicion of Todd's murder? Suddenly, she felt her body temperature drop as she considered another possibility: that Parnella's watchful eye on Still Waters Chasm had put her on a collision course with Keith and Sheena. Had they witnessed her in some act of sabotage and she needed to silence them?

Gabriela sank back in her chair, eyes closed, longing to go home and pull the covers over her head. A quiet tapping on her door refocused her attention. Delmina stood in the doorway, a stenographer's pad in her hand. "I need to talk with you," she said.

"Not now, Delmina. I have a splitting headache." Gabriela straightened some papers on her desk.

"I'm sorry, Gabriela, but this can't wait."

Turning, Gabriela tensed for the rundown of one of Delmina's infamous lists of everything going on in the library, right down to refilling the paper towel dispensers. Instead, the notebook stayed closed.

"You need to be careful," Delmina began, and it struck Gabriela as the second time in about twenty minutes that someone had delivered that message to her.

Delmina had always been a direct pipeline to the board of trustees and to City Hall, but she had also proven herself a loyal ally to Gabriela and her predecessor, Mary Jo. "The board is concerned about your involvement in Livery," she said. "I'll be honest with you, and it pains me to say this, some of the board members are questioning your judgment."

Gabriela sprang to her feet. "The outreach program was started by Mary Jo—I just expanded it. We had two successful programs until county politics shut them down."

Delmina clutched the notebook against her chest. "I know that, and I've told the board. But you have to see it from their perspective." Delmina dropped her hands and opened the notebook and rattled off the dates of events: the incident at Still Waters, the bodies being found, several meetings and phone conversations with the state police, the backpacks being mysteriously returned to the library, the

186

county refusing access to the Livery library building, Todd Watson's death, and Lucinda Nanz's arrest. "And that's just what I know," Delmina concluded.

Listening to that litany, Gabriela had to admit it seemed like a chain reaction of tragedies and missteps. Most lined up only coincidentally, but she couldn't deny one commonality: location. She had to stay away from Livery and Still Waters Chasm. Trooper Morrison and Daniel had both urged her to take these precautions; now her job depended on it.

Too distracted to work, Gabriela longed to go home, but she had optics to worry about—making sure her staff saw her and, likewise, that Delmina could report back to the board her full engagement in running the library. And, if nothing else, being around would keep a lid on the gossip. She stopped by the circulation desk to chat with Francine and Pearl, then spent forty-five minutes wheeling a cart around, shelving books. As she moved through the stacks, she conversed with patrons about their book selections and made recommendations from the meager array of new arrivals.

In the Children's Room, the program director introduced Gabriela to several parents who had brought their preschoolers for story hour. Sitting in the back, Gabriela beamed a smile while pretending to listen to the adventures of a tortoise and an angelfish in search of blue whales, while her mind reeled with Lucinda's guilty plea and her suspicions that Parnella could be an accomplice. Fear clawed at her gut, and Gabriela caught herself grimacing. Quickly, she rearranged her expression into a smile, but a pain shot from her stomach and caught her under the ribs. Getting up quietly, Gabriela moved farther back in the room, leaning against the brightly painted shelves.

As her thoughts churned, Gabriela considered the possibility that she could have been unintentionally complicit in Todd Watson's death. She had been so angry at him for denying access to the Livery library building, and even though she had calmed down considerably by the time she spoke with Lucinda, Gabriela knew she had conveyed some of that upset. Perhaps that added to Lucinda's justification for poisoning Todd. As she considered this possibility, Gabriela remembered what Parnella had told her after Todd's wake—with Todd dead, no one could stop the outreach programs in Livery.

When the program concluded, Gabriela moved slowly through the parents and children, asking if they had enjoyed the story. As she neared the door, she held her breath then exhaled in the privacy of the corridor, where she let loose her tears. She headed to the basement stairs her pace quickening to a run as she fled to the dark and quiet of the gloomy lower level of the dungeon. Slipping inside the workroom, lights off and door left open a crack, Gabriela sought refuge in shadows as soft and enveloping as a cocoon. She cried.

Footsteps outside silenced her. Gabriela held her breath again, hoping whoever paced outside would leave. The sliver of light from the hallway widened to an arc. In the open doorway she recognized the backlit form of Mike Driskie, his features cloaked in shadow.

"You okay?" he asked.

Gabriela stifled a groan; at the moment, she couldn't imagine ever being okay again. Every choice she had made had brought her into the line of fire and now suspicion.

"You've gotten yourself caught up in something, and it's hard to back away," Mike started. "I mean, when those backpacks showed up here, it's not like you could just ignore them."

Gabriela shifted her stance. "Well, it looks like that's exactly what I have to do. I'm not getting involved anymore."

Mike took another step closer. "Maybe somebody up there—" he pointed toward the ceiling "—is trying to get your attention. Maybe you're the only one who can do what needs to be done."

Gabriela wet her lips and swallowed, losing the knot in her throat. "But what is it? What am I supposed to do?"

Mike pushed the door open the rest of the way, and Gabriela squinted at the brightness. "Well," he told her, "I guess you're going to have to find out."

Mike's words stayed with her long after she had wiped her eyes, collected herself, and returned to the administration suite. Although she'd never thought of herself as fatalistic, Gabriela considered the possibility that she had been meant to be at Still Waters Chasm that day. If she and Daniel had not been there, no one would have known what happened to Keith and Sheena. As for Lucinda, their budding friendship was now complicated by Todd Watson's death. But Lucinda had also been the conduit for her meeting Wendy and agreeing to help authenticate the Shumler drawing. This remained the one job she could accomplish. But she couldn't do it alone, and she couldn't sacrifice her job.

Gabriela stopped by Delmina's unoccupied desk and waited for her to return. A moment later, Delmina bustled in, carrying a ream of paper. Gabriela helped her load the printer. "I wanted to thank you," Gabriela began, "for telling me about the board's concerns."

"That's my job. I've been here a million years, so everybody comes to me." Delmina set the rest of the ream aside, then raised her eyes. "But I work for you."

"I'm grateful. I'm going to call Charmaine and see if I can get a meeting with her this afternoon. And I'd like you to come with me. You should hear everything that's been happening, and how I think Charmaine can help me with a special project I've taken on."

Delmina smiled and scurried over to the phone. "I'll get her on the line right now."

Gabriela would have preferred to place the call herself but knew Delmina enjoyed the old protocols. As she waited, Gabriela wondered why she hadn't reached out to Charmaine before. She didn't need to search for the answer: authenticating the Shumler drawing on her own would be a thrill. She remembered that feeling from years ago, when a seemingly ordinary piece of paper revealed its historic significance. But now she needed allies, and Charmaine topped the list.

———

Charmaine Odele lived in one of Ohnita Harbor's old Victorians: a big, square house with a wide porch and three chimneys sprouting from the roof. Gabriela had been inside the home only once, for a holiday tea Charmaine had hosted last year. After they arrived, an hour after Gabriela had spoken to Charmaine by phone, Delmina led the way to the kitchen door in the back. Following her, Gabriela had to wonder just how many times Delmina had visited Charmaine and what kind of library business they discussed.

Two huge flowerpots brimming with multicolored coleus and feathery decorative grasses flanked the steps. As Delmina rapped on the door and called for Charmaine, Gabriela surveyed a small stone patio that held a wrought-iron table and six chairs and, beyond it, a generous backyard garden and a fence at the perimeter where grapevines draped their profuse foliage. As she admired the landscape, Gabriela thought of her own yard, neglected for the better part of the month—marigolds needing deadheading, leggy petunias that had stopped blossoming. Her mind wandered to Lucinda's gardens, which had appeared almost magical with their long rows of vegetables, herbs, and flowers; borage standing guard and snapdragons protecting from harm; bees dancing in the air. Yet what had charmed her had also fooled her, Gabriela admitted to herself. Healing hadn't come from Lucinda's gardens; harm had.

Charmaine swung the back door open and greeted them. "My kind of weather," she said over their heads toward the bright blue sky.

"Cool and crisp, and a steady wind bringing the smell of the lake. I must have been a sea captain in a former life."

They entered a kitchen streaming with sunlight, where stainless-steel appliances gleamed, offset by a black granite countertop and white cupboards. Charmaine offered coffee from an insulated carafe, explaining that she'd just brewed it. Gabriela smelled a hint of cinnamon and wrapped her hands around the mug as she followed Charmaine down the hallway, their footsteps muffled by patterned rugs in burgundy and deep blue that covered the hardwood floors. Charmaine ushered them into a room in the middle of the house. Recessed bookshelves covered two walls, crammed with volumes and several framed photos.

"All original from when the house was built in 1852," Charmaine said, pointing to the shelves.

Gabriela rang her fingertip along one of them, feeling the smoothed edges worn by use and time. The ceiling was wood too, giving the room a cave-like feeling. Along the far wall, a wrought-iron grate spanned the breadth of a stone fireplace. The thought of sitting in this cozy room on a dreary winter day elicited a soft hum in Gabriela's chest.

Gabriela and Delmina sat on a loveseat, while Charmaine took the armchair opposite them and arranged three coasters for their mugs on a coffee table. Each had a different sailing ship on it, Gabriela noticed; hers was a three-masted schooner.

Sitting back, one black trousered leg tucked under the other, Charmaine thanked them for coming. Gabriela recognized the opening and skipped the small talk preamble. "I know there have been some questions about my involvement in a few recent incidents."

Charmaine took a sip of coffee. "Start from the beginning; I want to hear everything."

Gabriela began with that Saturday afternoon hike at Still Waters, describing in detail the construction site, the thumper truck, and finding the two bodies on the beach. As she spoke, Delmina wrote quickly

191

in a stenographer's notebook. Gabriela drew her eyebrows together; it felt like a deposition. So be it, she told herself. She had nothing to hide from Charmaine or the board. She'd tell them everything.

It took nearly an hour, with questions from Charmaine, to tell the entire story. At the end, Gabriela took a long sip from her coffee, now lukewarm. "I assure you, I had no intention of involving myself in anything nefarious," Gabriela said.

Charmaine combed her short, thick hair with her fingers, mussing the white waves. "No, I'm sure you didn't." She unfolded her legs, planted both feet on the floor, and leaned forward toward Gabriela. "What can I do to help?"

Save my job, Gabriela thought. "I don't know what more there is to do. The state police are handling their investigation, and the sheriff's department arrested Lucinda in Todd Watson's death."

"Any chance they could be connected?" Charmaine asked.

Gabriela kept her suspicions that Lucinda and Parnella could be implicated in all the deaths. "I've been asked to stay as far away from the investigations as possible, so that's what I'm doing. But the Shumler drawing authentication is something I can do, and I'm hoping you might be able to help me. The biggest piece of the puzzle now is linking Shumler and his drawing to Robert Fulton."

"I could try. I'm not that familiar with Fulton's submarine, but I'll make some inquiries," Charmaine said as she got to her feet. She suggested they refresh their coffee, and Gabriela and Delmina followed her into the kitchen where they stayed, sitting around a table bathed in sunlight.

The jolt of extra caffeine revived Gabriela. When the conversation segued to library business, Gabriela felt the tightness ease between her shoulder blades. Job crisis averted, for now at least.

"I'm here for you anytime," Charmaine said when they left an hour later. "Whatever you need, just call."

Back in the car, Delmina let out a sigh and announced that the conversation could not have gone better. "The board will follow Charmaine's recommendation. You have nothing to worry about."

Gabriela grimaced. If the past few weeks were any indication, having nothing to worry about did not seem likely.

CHAPTER

SEVENTEEN

It was nearly four o'clock when they returned to the library. Gabriela did a quick round before retreating to her office. Fighting the urge to put her head down on her desk and close her eyes, she called up the latest report and started typing. As she worked, her thoughts returned to Daniel. She had not heard from him since their conversation late Saturday night. The silence on Sunday had not surprised her, knowing they both needed time to process all that had happened. But she had expected him to call or at least text her. Twice she picked up her phone, and both times she put it down. Maybe he just needed time and space; if so, she could give it to him, Gabriela thought. A nagging doubt triggered the other possibility: that their relationship had ended.

Ben arrived at the library after playing at the park following school dismissal. Gabriela packed up her things and left soon thereafter. At home, she busied herself with routine—making dinner, helping her son with his homework, doing laundry. Finally, she couldn't take it any longer. She punched Daniel's number into her cell phone. It rang four times then went to voicemail. Gabriela hung up. If Daniel wanted to screen his calls to avoid speaking with her, she'd gotten the message. She wouldn't reach out to him again.

When Ben went to bed shortly after nine, Gabriela tried clicking through a few channels on the television, but she felt too restless to sit still. Pulling on her jacket, she left by the back door, double-checking that it locked behind her. Reaching the sidewalk, she looked back at her small Cape Cod house—just big enough for her and Ben, and her mother when she came over to visit or to spend the night. Recalling Ben's question from a few weeks ago—would they move into Daniel's house one day?— Gabriela knew that never would be possible. Ben would have to change schools, for one thing, and she couldn't see herself living in Vicki's house, either. There was no way Daniel would want to leave his art gallery home. Better to end the relationship before it went any further. Ben would miss seeing Daniel, but he had his friends. Her mother, though, would hound her about the breakup and scheme about how to patch things up. Agnese had become tied to Daniel—too quickly, she could see now.

Gabriela tipped her head back and aimed a heavy sigh toward the night sky. It had felt so natural from the beginning, their first dates of long walks and even longer talks as their friendship transitioned to romance. They'd guarded their feelings, not saying too much too soon, but she never doubted they both cared for each other. Not enough, she told herself. Not for Daniel, still grieving the death of his wife. Not for her, either, suffering from trauma and trying to pretend her heart didn't race and her hands didn't shake. Maybe they'd never had a chance.

Her tears fell, leaving tracks down her cheeks and dampening the edge of the cotton turtleneck she wore. Of all the times she'd cried over the past few months—out of fear, shock, or sadness—these tears came from a different source.

She loved Daniel.

Gabriela squeezed her eyes shut to staunch the flow and the feelings that leaked out of her. This had not been the infatuation of a new romance, as she'd tried to convince herself. She had fallen in love with him. But never, not even in the tenderest moment between them, had she taken the risk of telling him. Playing it safe had cost her the relationship.

Her throat constricted and her breathing became labored. Gabriela steadied herself against the trunk of a tree and counted backward from twenty. At "eight," the sensation passed. Her life would go on, she reminded herself. She had Ben and her mother. She wouldn't be alone.

After the second loop around the block, Gabriela went in the house, peeked in on Ben, who was asleep upstairs, and did a sweep through the kitchen. She checked and rechecked the doors before heading out again, widening her route this time, down three blocks and over two. Cold penetrated her thin jacket, and she pulled the hood up to cover her ears.

She needed to plan. In two months it would be Thanksgiving, and Ben would have a long weekend—maybe they could go back to the Adirondacks for more zip-lining. In three months, at Christmas, Ben would have two weeks off. They could go somewhere, maybe drive to Vermont and stay at an inn for a few days. They'd go tobogganing, try some downhill skiing on a bunny slope. She pictured Ben, cheeks red from the cold, a ski hat pulled down over his curly dark hair.

California. Ben had told her that his father wanted him to come out to Santa Monica after Christmas to spend part of the holiday. Jim hadn't talked to her about it yet, so she hadn't put much stock in it, but if Ben wanted to go to California, he would go. She and Ben would have just a couple of days at Christmas, then Ben would be gone. Tears threatened again, but Gabriela brushed them away. She needed to keep herself busy. Go down to Binghamton for a day or two and visit Mary Jo. Or maybe she should go to that inn in Vermont, try skiing, have a spa treatment. But she'd never leave her mother behind at the holidays, and convincing Agnese to go would be impossible. The best thing would be to work and take care of her mother. Both those responsibilities could occupy her time.

Rounding the corner to her street, Gabriela saw a pickup truck at the curb. The brake lights glowed bright red, then extinguished. She heard the low rumble of the idling engine.

A pickup only meant one thing, and the realization quickened her pace. Breaking into a run, Gabriela kept her eyes on the sidewalk to avoid tripping on the cracks. Her thoughts surged with what to say to Daniel: how much she missed him; how she wanted them to start over. She glanced up to see if he had come out, but the cab doors stayed closed.

The truck had a trailer hitch.

As that detail registered, Gabriela stopped. In the dark she couldn't see the license plate, but she knew this was not Daniel's truck. Stepping off the sidewalk and into the shadows, she crept across her neighbor's lawn and ducked down beside a shrub at the corner of her house. The truck cab glistened in the glow from the corner, making it look black, but in this low light Gabriela could not be sure. She inched closer, took her phone from her pocket to photograph the truck, but first pressed the flashlight app for a moment to read the license plate.

The brake lights blared red, and the engine roared.

"Get away from my house!" Gabriela screamed and started running after the truck. She made it no more than ten feet before tripping over something in the gutter. Instinctively, her hands shot out to brace her fall. Pain seared her right arm.

Lying on the pavement, Gabriela rolled to her side, cradling her wrist. Cold sweat dampened her face and torso. Getting up slowly, Gabriela limped toward the house, feeling a burn on her left knee where she'd struck the pavement and an ache in her left shoulder. Her right wrist, though, had taken the brunt of it. Slowly, she made a fist, wincing as her fingers tightened, but at least she could move her hand.

In the house, Gabriela pulled a bag of frozen mixed vegetables out of the freezer and wrapped it around her wrist with a towel. Using only her left hand, she managed to take off the loose yoga pants she'd put on that evening and gasped at the abrasion on her knee. After stripping off the rest of her clothes with difficulty, she got in the bathtub and rinsed the blood and dirt from her wounds. She winced at the sting of soap and water on the fresh cuts and scrapes, and each time she moved her hand, a dozen tiny knife blades jabbed from inside her wrist and forearm.

She reached for her towel with her left hand and dried herself off as best she could. Gabriela lifted her bathrobe from the hook on the back of the door and slipped it on. The right cuff tucked inside itself, and when Gabriela tried to force her hand through, the pain made her feel faint. Sitting down on the closed toilet, she knew what would come next—the sensation of separating from her body, even losing consciousness.

She shivered as the cool air hit her bare, wet skin. The wounds stung and burned. But no tunnel effect, no lightheadedness.

Grinning despite the discomfort, Gabriela pulled her robe closed and went off in search of her pajamas and to retrieve the bag of frozen mixed vegetables from the counter. She had beaten the trauma with her own brand of exposure therapy. Of all the horrible things that had happened over the past month, at least she had this victory.

—

Wide awake from the throbbing in her wrist, Gabriela heard her cell phone buzz. She went downstairs to retrieve the text. "You up?" the message from Daniel read.

She made three typos while thumbing, "Yes, I am." She corrected the message, hit Send, and waited.

When the phone rang, she intercepted the call on the first ring and headed to the downstairs bedroom that doubled as both her guest room and her home office.

"I know it's late," he began.

"It's fine. I was awake." Gabriela shut the door and sat on the twin bed in the corner, tucking her bare feet underneath her. Her wrist twinged with pain as she held the phone in her right hand; she transferred it to her left.

"I should have called before now."

"Me, too. I tried once but didn't leave a message." Her heart hammered, and she struggled to take a deep breath.

"I was out all day at an industrial job, almost to Lakeside."

The mixed memories of that date—the flirty restaurant hostess, Colby's intrusion at their table, the romantic night at Daniel's, and finding the photo of him and Vicki in the drawer—took away Gabriela's response. "Oh," she said finally.

"I have something to tell you."

Gabriela shut her eyes. Nothing good, she knew, ever started off like this.

"I'm going away for a little while—four, five days, maybe a week. I just decided today."

"Oh, okay. Where?"

"Fishing, up on the St. Lawrence, near Plattsburgh. I've got a buddy up there who's been after me to come and, well, I think this would be good for me. Will you be okay?"

What did he mean by that? Gabriela wondered. Okay with him going, okay by herself? "Sure, it sounds good for you."

"So much has happened. I just need time to sort things out," he said.

Gabriela closed her eyes, recalling that Jim had said almost that exact thing to her at the end of their marriage. He'd gone away for a couple of days to the Berkshires—supposedly for cycling, running, hiking. Jim had made it sound like a pilgrimage to the woods. Only much later had she found out that Shelley had met him for that weekend, that the two of them had decided they wanted to be together.

"This isn't about you," Daniel added.

Gabriela pinched the bridge of her nose with her sore hand. "Please. Don't."

"I'll call you when I get back," Daniel said. "I'm leaving in the morning; that's why I worked so late tonight."

"Safe trave—" Gabriela said, unable to squeeze the second word out of her throat. She ended the call and slumped onto the mattress. She awoke four hours later and dragged herself upstairs to her own bed, but all sleep had been lost.

CHAPTER
EIGHTEEN

Dark circles ringed Gabriela's eyes on Tuesday morning, and she rubbed concealer over the purplish half-moons. Her wrist still hurt, and bruises covered the back of her hand, but if she could move her fingers, Gabriela felt assured nothing had broken. An old wrist brace from when she'd had tendonitis a few years ago helped ease the discomfort. She dressed in easy, pull-on clothes and got Ben up for breakfast.

On her way to the library, Gabriela stopped at A Better Bean for a large coffee, wearing sunglasses to hide her tired eyes and keeping her braced wrist hidden in her coat pocket. Behind the counter, Sharon Davis greeted Gabriela and held up a scone with a pair of tongs. "Fresh from the oven."

Gabriela noticed how Sharon's perfectly applied lipstick matched the flush in her cheeks from the warmth of the kitchen and the espresso machines. "Not today. Bit of a rush."

Sharon rang up her coffee, and Gabriela waved her change toward the tip jar. Sharon handed her a paper sack with something warm inside. "Just try the scone. New recipe. Let me know what you think."

Gabriela had to take her hand out of her pocket to hold both the coffee and the scone.

"Oh, what happened?" Sharon asked.

Gabriela raised her coffee in salute and said, "Thanks for the breakfast."

At the library, Gabriela greeted Mike downstairs and Delmina upstairs, then settled into the day's work. She took off her brace, but her wrist started throbbing. As she refastened the Velcro straps in place, Gabriela decided to tell anyone who asked that she had a sore wrist after raking leaves—a nice, boring, uncomplicated injury. But the more she thought about the black pickup truck idling at the curb with its lights off, the more certain she became that the incident had to be reported. She called Trooper Morrison, left a message for him to return to her call when he had time. When her cell phone rang five minutes later, Gabriela recognized the number. She related the facts to Trooper Morrison.

"There's not much we can do, you know," he said.

"Of course not," Gabriela replied. "I thought twice about even telling you, since this could be a coincidence."

"But you don't think it was," he said. "I'd trust your instincts on that. You okay?"

Gabriela looked down at her right wrist encircled by a brace, trying to find a more comfortable way to rest it against her desk. "Just fine," she said and ended the call.

That afternoon, Mayor Duncan Phillips convened the grant proposal committee for a planning session at City Hall. Just thirty-two years old, Duncan had gone from being a partner in his family's accounting business to being the unpaid mayor of his hometown. After many years of Mayor Iris Sanger-Jones, now in jail for corruption, Duncan had the fresh perspective and untiring optimism that Ohnita Harbor desperately needed.

"What happened to your wrist?" he asked Gabriela, interrupting a recap of the proposal plan.

"Nothing interesting," she said. "Sore from raking leaves."

"It's all the typing," one of the city planners said, fluttering his fingers in the air as if on an imaginary keyboard. "You do any stretches?" He proceeded to go through a series of finger and hand stretches, while Gabriela pretended to pay close attention.

"I'll try that later," she said, knowing she could never do such a routine with a sprained wrist.

Any other time, the bureaucracy of the grant meeting would have bored her, but today she found it soothing. The balm of normalcy, Gabriela decided, and dove into two hours of discussing beautification projects: new benches and planters for the downtown area; pavers and walkways at two city parks; landscaping around the library and a garden with interactive stations for young readers to follow storyboards along a serpentine path. Given all the structural work needed at the library, these superficial improvements seemed ridiculous, but perhaps they'd help attract patronage, which could help secure more funding in the future. At the end of the session, the grant committee agreed to review the draft and suggest any last edits by Friday, in time to submit the proposal the following Wednesday.

As she gathered up her notebook and folders, Gabriela smiled with satisfaction over the progress—her first grant committee project and, most likely, many more to follow. "Take care of that wrist," Duncan told her.

Gabriela waved her good hand. "I'll be good as new to type my edits and submit my report."

Back at the library, she stopped by the circulation desk and relieved Pearl, who wanted a quick break, which Gabriela suspected meant a late-day cigarette, even though Pearl had supposedly kicked the habit again. She kept up light chatter with Francine about her children and shared her own thoughts about having a fifth grader, just two years from middle school. "Honestly, Francine, I want to stop the clock," Gabriela said.

Francine gave her a warm smile. "I see you with Ben when he comes to the library every day. You're such a good mom."

The compliment caught Gabriela with a lump in her throat she found difficult to clear with a swallow.

When Pearl returned, smelling of tobacco and the damp leaves of a fall day, Gabriela gave her a sideways grin.

"I'm quitting—my way," said Pearl. "I figure if I smoke one cigarette less every week, I'll quit by this time next year. Or the year after." Pearl's laugh ended with a throaty cough.

At her desk again, Gabriela scratched off three items on her handwritten to-do list, reveling in the satisfaction. Her life had become simpler and less complicated, which meant she could make significant progress on her projects for the Ohnita Harbor Public Library, she told herself. Without the outreach programs in Livery to manage, she had more time to devote to programming with guest speakers, community book clubs, and monthly family movie nights for all ages.

Her cell phone rang, and the caller ID showed an unfamiliar number with a 315 area code, for central New York. Gabriela considered ignoring it, thinking it could be spam, but curiosity got the better of her. "Hello?" she said tentatively.

"Gabriela? It's Parnella Richards."

Hearing her voice, Gabriela didn't know what to say other than to ask, "How are you?"

Parnella scoffed. "Oh, just fine thanks—and you? Lovely weather we're having."

The sarcasm burned, but Gabriela kept her voice steady and neutral. "Just want to know how everyone is doing."

"It's horrific. Lucinda's being held in jail. She wants to change her plea. She says she was confused."

Gabriela's head pounded with fatigue. "So now she's pleading not guilty?"

"Of course, because she didn't do it!" Parnella snapped. "Do you really believe Lucinda murdered Todd Watson?"

Gabriela opened and closed her mouth a couple of times. She managed a loud exhale into the phone line as her only response.

"Well, she didn't. But she'd gotten scared during the questioning and tried to protect someone," Parnella said. "The police bullied her."

"I thought the police seized everything in her garden," Gabriela blurted out, then steeled herself for Parnella's reply.

"Yup, they dumped, sampled, and trampled, and somehow came up with contamination in Lucinda's teas. But guess what? She doesn't grow foxglove. And no foxglove, no digitalis."

So many thoughts fought for her attention, Gabriela felt dizzy and couldn't think straight. Being exhausted didn't help.

"Parnella, let me call you back," Gabriela said. "I need to tend to something here."

Parnella sputtered that she only needed a minute, but Gabriela insisted and ended the call.

Standing at the window, watching the clouds darken the surface of the lake in the distance, Gabriela pulled through the strands of thoughts tangled in her mind, weighing whether Lucinda's plea reversal indicated her innocence or merely a lack of evidence. Gabriela had always liked Lucinda, but something about Parnella put her on edge.

Stay away. Trooper Morrison's words echoed in her brain, as did Daniel's plea that she stop walking into trouble.

Gabriela called Parnella back, braced for whatever would be asked of her.

"Lucinda wanted me to ask you to stay in touch with Wendy and to keep track of the Shumler drawing," Parnella said. "That's so like her—facing the fight of her life but thinking about someone else."

"Of course," Gabriela promised. "I'm not sure if I can call Wendy directly. She always seemed so worried about J.J."

"What I wouldn't give to stage an intervention and pull her out of there," Parnella said. "Wendy has no idea how many people would swoop in to help if she'd just leave that idiot and stay away from him. You know she walked out on him last Christmas? Right out the front door, with his parents sitting at their table. Stayed away five or six days. Lucinda took her in, of course. Then she went back to him—why, I'll never understand."

"Shame, fear, wanting things to be different," Gabriela said. "She might even love him."

"J.J.? Not even his own mother could love that bastard! Although if you meet Esther Haughton, you'll see what Wendy will be like one day. Completely without any life or spark."

"I thought Jake wasn't as bad—"

Parnella sputtered. "The apple, as they say, doesn't fall far from the tree. Jake is mean, but J.J. raises it to cruelty."

Gabriela mulled over the twisted family portrait Parnella had painted in a few words. She couldn't turn her back on Wendy.

"Here's the house number. I don't have her cell." Parnella rattled it off quickly, and Gabriela had to ask her to repeat it. "Call during the day when J.J. is out at his shop." She huffed a disgusted laugh. "Which is where he sits and drinks."

"I promise I'll contact her," Gabriela pledged.

"Thanks. That will make Lucinda feel better. And that makes it a priority for me." Parnella's voice softened. "She's the love of my life. We only found each other a few years ago. I'd do anything for her—just as she would for me."

Including murder? Another thought flickered through Gabriela's mind. Maybe Todd's death had nothing to do with Still Waters Chasm, but everything to do with the fact that he detested Parnella. Passions, Gabriela remembered reading once, motivated most murders. Maybe in this case, those passions covered both love and hate.

———————

A half hour later, Gabriela dialed Wendy's number from the library's landline, not wanting her cell phone to be on Wendy's list of recent calls. The phone rang four times before J.J.'s recorded voice boomed over the line. Gabriela hung up. An hour later she called again. After three rings she nearly disconnected, then she heard a quiet voice on the other end of the line.

"Wendy? It's me—Gabriela."

"Not now," she whispered.

"Can you write down a phone number and keep it private?" Gabriela asked.

"Yes."

209

Gabriela gave Wendy her cell phone number, repeating it a second time to make sure she heard it, but the line went dead before she finished.

At least Wendy had answered the phone, Gabriela thought, and she had a way to reach out when she needed to. If she didn't hear from Wendy, she'd call again, Gabriela decided. She'd wait three days; that seemed long enough to keep from raising J.J.'s suspicions, but not too long.

Gabriela sagged in her chair and held her head in her hands. Then, summoning both her energy and courage, she dove back into her library duties.

CHAPTER
NINETEEN

The next day arrived under a thick veil of clouds and steady rain that lashed the tiny dormer windows at the roofline of Gabriela's house. Showered and dressed, she stood in her bedroom, watching rivulets run down the glass of one of those windows. A perfect day to lounge in bed, she thought. Just this once, she was tempted to keep Ben home from school; the two of them could play hooky, watching movies, baking cookies, and shutting out the rest of the world. Gabriela turned her attention to her unmade bed, the pillows askew, the comforter sliding off one corner. She could put her pajamas on right now and crawl back in for another hour before even thinking about getting up.

Ben's door opened. "I'm hungry," he announced before disappearing into the bathroom just off the landing, between their two bedrooms.

Gabriela smoothed the bottom sheet, fluffed the pillows, and pulled the top sheet back in place. She turned down the edges, tucked the corners, spread the comforter, and placed a decorative pillow embroidered with lilacs and violets against the bed's headboard. Then she headed downstairs to make breakfast and pack lunches. *Only Wednesday*, she groaned. This week would never end.

Without the sun streaming through the library's arcaded windows, the overhead light fixtures did little to cut the sepulchral gloom. Rain kept most of the patrons away, but the regulars who did show up stood in the foyer and let their coats and slickers drip for a minute or two before entering the main room. They left a trail of wet footprints and sodden leaves. Mike set up a yellow "Caution—Slippery floor" sign and mopped repeatedly.

Gabriela watched as the first two patrons headed straight to the upholstered chairs along the far wall. They settled in with their books and takeout coffee; in bad weather, she turned a blind eye to bringing in hot refreshments. If only they had a fireplace in that reading nook, she mused, thinking of the one in Charmaine Odele's library at home: a fire in the grate, the crackle and pop of hardwood burning. With a shake of her head, she walked away. Given the state of their financial affairs, they'd be lucky to afford two flashlights and a space heater.

Upstairs, the panes rattled in her office windows with each gust off the lake, and the draft lifted the corners of papers on her desk. Pulling her cardigan sweater up to her neck, Gabriela hunched over the keyboard and began inputting her final edits on the beautification grant document. *Flower boxes, planters, and gardens*, she griped quietly, wishing once again that she could apply for money to add staff, expand programming, or purchase a minibus to circulate books in the rural areas. She went back to typing the description of the interpretive garden, where storyboards could be erected to engage young readers in an outdoor learning experience.

Delmina tapped at her door. "You have a visitor downstairs."

Gabriela wheeled around. *Daniel.*

"Mr. Earl Buntley," Delmina continued. "Shall I send him up?"

Gabriela got up from her desk. "No, it's so cold here. I'll meet with him downstairs." She paused on her way out and turned back to Delmina. "You should come too. He's probably here about the Shumler drawing."

No secrets kept from the board, Gabriela told herself, as she waited for Delmina to grab her stenographer's notebook and a pen.

Earl Buntley stood in the middle of the floor, smiling, and pointing upward. "I'll bet there's a grand ceiling up there, behind all this acoustic tile."

"Yes, and if I had my way—" Gabriela stopped. Suddenly, she had an idea for the beautification grant proposal: restoring the old ceiling and putting in some better light fixtures. She'd update the grant and tell the committee as soon as possible. Restoring the structure of a historic building to its original design qualified as beautification. As for the flower boxes and planting a garden, the Friends of the Library could manage that on their own with volunteers and donations.

She turned her attention back to Earl. "It's great to see you again."

"I know I should have called first, but I'm on my way to Syracuse for a meeting this afternoon and dinner tonight. So I thought I'd come early and swing by," Earl explained.

Realizing that she hadn't introduced Delmina, Gabriela did so hurriedly, then suggested that the three of them sit at one of the tables in the Reference section where they would have the most privacy. "I'd invite you upstairs, but I'm afraid you'd get hypothermia in our offices."

Earl smiled. "It's okay. We'll need a big table. I brought some documents with me, including Wendy's drawing."

Opening a canvas tube with a leather shoulder strap, Earl slid out the Shumler drawing. He pointed out several features of the design that he found most noteworthy, especially the hinged mast that could be hauled upright or folded on its side. "But the real ingenuity is this." He pointed to a configuration of lines and pulleys. "This double rigging had me confused at first, until I considered another possibility."

Earl unfolded a photographic enlargement of the double rigging. He explained how basic foldable sails acted like kites; they moved only in the direction of the wind, not against it. To head into the wind, a sail had to be adjusted so that the wind hit it at an angle. "That creates a difference in air pressure. Now, instead of a kite, you've got an airplane wing, which splits the air. Air moves faster on one side than the other, and that creates lift."

Gabriela nodded, recalling the fragments of some high school science lesson.

"What creates lift for an airplane wing allows a sail to push against the wind." Earl tapped the photo enlargement. "When I look at this double rigging, I'm convinced that Shumler's design was meant to do the same thing."

"And Fulton's earlier designs couldn't do that?" Gabriela asked.

"All we know about Robert Fulton's first prototype is based on what we can see in his drawing at the British Museum. That drawing doesn't have the double rigging," Earl continued. "Shumler's drawing is a more advanced design, and it's just the kind of thing Fulton would have wanted to try."

Gabriela turned to Delmina. "I think we should contact Charmaine, see if she's free for a meeting." Delmina agreed and went off to make the phone call. Gabriela explained Charmaine's background to Earl, not only as library board president but also as a historian and history professor. "I've talked with her about the Shumler drawing. She's dying to see it."

Earl bit his lip, and his mouth curled downward. "She'll have plenty of time for that. Here's the other reason I showed up unannounced this morning. The Adirondack Experience's attorney called me last night and told me we absolutely could not keep this drawing. Not with what's been happening."

Gabriela clenched her hands in her lap, wincing when she twisted her right wrist. "I'm afraid to ask."

A sigh rounded Earl's shoulders. "The Ohnita County Sheriff's Department contacted Cynthia, asking about your visit to the museum."

Gabriela groaned. She should have called Cynthia Rahlberg out of professional courtesy and alerted her after Lucinda's arrest. She'd been so distracted, it never occurred to her.

"The sheriff's department didn't make much of a fuss. They asked a lot of questions about the Shumler drawing, which Cynthia answered thoroughly. A bit of inconvenience, though no harm done." Earl shook his head. "Hard to imagine Lucinda being in that kind of trouble—poisoning somebody."

As much as Gabriela tried to convince herself of some other possibility, all the signs pointed to Lucinda's guilt, no matter what Parnella claimed. Parnella's protest about Lucinda's arrest could be an attempt to evade suspicion, herself.

Earl touched a corner of the Shumler schematic. "Well, none of that has anything to do with Wendy and her wonderful drawing. But her husband suspects something. He called the museum, asking to speak to somebody who, and I quote, 'knows about treasures.' Wendy must have told him something about why she went to the museum, but given the questions he asked, it sounded like she made up some old antique."

That explained a lot, Gabriela thought, recalling how quickly Wendy got off the phone. She was lying low until J.J. lost interest. But if he smelled something valuable, J.J. would probably keep hounding Wendy.

"Giving the drawing back to Wendy seemed inappropriate, and frankly we don't have her contact information." Earl smiled with

215

one side of his mouth. "Thankfully, Wendy made it clear to us that she never wanted her husband to know about the drawing or take possession of it."

"We'll keep it for her," Gabriela said, though she had to wonder what Charmaine and the rest of the board would say about that.

Scanning the schematic, Gabriela took in the details once again: the windowpane pattern of the laid paper, the drawing done in ink, the name and date recorded with a flourish in the lower right-hand corner. Something struck her: Why had Shumler, an obscure nineteenth-century sailmaker, branded this drawing with his name and not Robert Fulton's, who by 1808 had achieved international acclaim? Her spirits sagged under the possibility that Shumler, alone, had created this sail.

"But I'm not the bearer of only bad news," Earl continued. "The British Museum is interested in seeing the Shumler drawing. They requested high-resolution photos of it, and we emailed them yesterday."

"Thank you for that," Gabriela said. "I guess they put some stock in the Fulton theory, because I was having second thoughts." She voiced her concern that, without Fulton's name on the document, Shumler could have acted on his own.

Earl's laugh seemed to fill the library, and Gabriela looked around, not wanting to attract too much attention, though the Reference section rarely had much foot traffic. She saw only Delmina approaching, a pink message slip in her hand.

"You never worked in advertising." Earl chuckled one more time and wiped his eyes with a meaty forefinger. "In my day, I knew guys who'd put their names on every page of an ad campaign and in a bigger font than the client's name. When I see Gerald Shumler's name and date, I see somebody who wanted to make sure he got his share of credit."

Delmina waited a few feet away until Earl finished speaking, then stepped up to the table. "I just got off the phone with Charmaine

Odele, our board chair." Delmina placed the message slip in front of Gabriela.

Don't agree to do anything until you speak with Charmaine. Rip this up as soon as you read it. Gabriela folded the message in two and slipped it into her pocket.

"Charmaine would like to invite you over to the Ohnita Harbor Maritime Museum, which is not far from here," Delmina told Earl. "She'd like to show you around the displays and take you to lunch. And see the drawing, of course."

"Sure. As long as I'm on the road by, say, two o'clock?" Earl looked at his watch, which struck Gabriela as almost a novelty, since almost everyone told time by their phones these days. "It's after eleven, so we should go."

"You're coming too," Gabriela told Delmina. "I always value your opinion."

When they left the library, the rain still fell in torrents, and the wind gusts made an umbrella a futility. Instead, they made a mad dash, all of them half-soaked by the time they reached Earl's car in the parking lot. Once inside, Earl drew the document tube out from under the tent of his rain gear. "Not a drop is going to get on this," he said, handing it to Gabriela while he drove.

Charmaine held open the front door of the Ohnita Harbor Maritime Museum as they raced inside. Thunderous crashes of waves brought them to the windows of the main room, which occupied what had once been the harbormaster's house. Gabriela watched the waves smash into the breakwater, spewing spray and foam into the air.

"My God, you don't see anything like this at Blue Mountain Lake," Earl commented.

"Ten-foot waves today—maybe some twelve-footers out there," Charmaine said. "When we get a nor'easter, they'll top sixteen feet."

Earl gave a low whistle. "I could sit at this window all day long."

Charmaine nodded. "You and me both."

When the others followed Charmaine toward the displays, Gabriela lingered just a little longer to watch one more wave roll in and then another.

Charmaine showed Earl the exhibits, explaining how Ohnita Harbor and its protected shoreline had been coveted by the Iroquois, the French, the British, and later the colonial Americans. She summarized Great Lakes shipping and the Erie Canal, which had expanded Ohnita Harbor into a commercial center, until the railroads crisscrossed the state further south and the town lost its stature and a good deal of its future. Opening a door, she escorted them out of the original structure, with its brick and stone walls, and into a modern annex that displayed canoes, skiffs, paddles, and pieces and parts of boats, barges, and ships.

"A modest collection, but it's a beginning," Charmaine said. "Five years ago, we didn't even have this museum."

Earl fingered a carved canoe paddle and read the inscription aloud: "Algonquin, circa 1730." He pulled his hand back. "Sorry, I must have missed the 'Don't touch' sign. I'm incorrigible that way."

Charmaine laughed and beckoned him to follow. "There's something you can touch. In fact, you can ring it."

In the center of the annex stood a brass bell held in a wooden mounting, bearing a plaque that identified it as belonging to "a fine Sloop, the *Lady Margaux*." Gabriela leaned closer to read how the ship broke up in a storm in 1887 and sank just beyond the safety of the harbor. It was recovered by salvagers in 1974.

"Go ahead," Charmaine said to Earl. "Give her a ring."

Earl wrapped his hand around a leather strap and gave a couple of firm tugs. *Clang, clang . . . clang, clang.* "What a sound," he said.

As Charmaine and Earl discussed the *Lady Margaux*, Gabriela sidled up to Delmina to ask if she thought Charmaine would keep the Shumler drawing at the museum. Delmina's slow smile told Gabriela what she had been thinking and orchestrating all along.

After their brief tour, Charmaine took them to the director's office, where Earl unsheathed the drawing and unrolled it across a table. He pointed out every feature to Charmaine, explaining how a foldable sail worked and how the double rigging would allow whatever vessel it propelled to sail both with and against the wind.

"A foldable sail that could tack into the wind would have been a breakthrough for Fulton," Earl said. "It would have answered the biggest criticism against his submarine design: a lack of maneuverability. When his tests failed, they did so miserably. Seeing this—" He stabbed at the paper."—I have to believe this was Fulton's work."

"But wasn't Fulton at work on the steamboat by this time? Wouldn't that have been vindication enough?" Charmaine asked.

"True," Earl replied. "The *Clermont* went into service in 1807, and that was Fulton's design. A success by all measures. But I can't believe that he gave up on his dream for the submarine. Maybe publicly, but not in his heart."

Gabriela scanned the schematic again, longing for some name, initial, marking, or detail to explain why this drawing had been executed and for whom. But she could see nothing other than Gerald Shumler's name and the date.

When the time came to head out for lunch, Earl and Delmina left to retrieve the coats while Gabriela called Charmaine aside. She quickly explained that the Adirondack Experience could not keep the Shumler drawing and told Charmaine why. "We can't give this back to Wendy because her husband will get his hands on it, and Wendy expressly asked us not to let that happen. But I'm not sure the library is the best place for it."

Charmaine's eyes narrowed. "Any suggestions?"

"*Hmm*, a museum with a thematic affinity?" Gabriela replied.

Laughing, Charmaine agreed. "We'll store it here. But—" Her expression sobered. "We do need to get a sign-off from Wendy."

219

Gabriela promised to reach out as soon as she could. Her decision to wait three days to call Wendy would have to be amended; she'd try again tomorrow.

———

The rain had eased to sprinkles, and the clouds began to lift. Delmina produced a compact travel umbrella from her coat pocket, and Gabriela ducked under its shelter as they left the museum and walked three blocks to a small restaurant. Up ahead, Charmaine strolled beside Earl under a large black umbrella with a bamboo handle.

"Is he married?" Delmina asked.

"Yes, and for a long time from what I gather." Gabriela elbowed her lightly. "Are you matchmaking?"

"Charmaine's been divorced a long time," Delmina said. "It's nice to have somebody. I've been married thirty-seven years. And you're with Daniel now."

Gabriela tightened her mouth into a pained smile.

"I've been thinking about making an amendment to the beautification grant proposal," she told Delmina, steering the conversation to less emotional ground. She asked Delmina her opinion about taking down the drop ceiling and restoring the original.

Delmina gasped, eyes wide. "Yes! And I don't think it will take much to restore—other than a little plaster and paint."

"Having a vaulted ceiling will add to the heating bill, which we don't need," Gabriela sighed. "But at least the library would look as impressive inside as it does outside."

For just a second her mind drifted to the Rose Main Reading Room in the New York Public Library, with its fifty-two-foot-tall ceiling painted with murals of blue skies and fluffy clouds, which made it look as if the roof had been lifted off the building. The Ohnita Harbor Public Library would never be that majestic, but she could restore its authentic beauty.

A black pickup truck rolled slowly past.

Gabriela stopped on the sidewalk, while Delmina and the umbrella moved ahead of her. Standing there, surveying the traffic, she reminded herself that black had to be the most common vehicle color out there. To prove the point to herself, she spotted three black SUVs and a black sedan. She started walking again, catching up to Delmina in four steps. But when the same black pickup came around again, Gabriela quickened her pace toward the restaurant. Grabbing the front door, she held it wide for the others, as if that's why she had run ahead of them. The black pickup pulled over, and the passenger window lowered partway. Gabriela couldn't make out anyone inside, but she knew the driver had gotten a good look at her.

CHAPTER
TWENTY

The next morning, Gabriela drove an hour to the hospital in Syracuse for her mother's follow-up appointment with her oncologist. The appointment had been set for 9:15, but they had to wait until nearly ten o'clock before a nurse called Agnese's name; then came another wait in a tiny examination room. When Dr. Granger finally came in, he seemed pleased at first glance by how quickly Agnese continued to recover from her chemotherapy and a mastectomy earlier in the year.

As the doctor pressed the stethoscope against Agnese's back and asked her to take a deep breath, Gabriela saw his eyebrows draw together. "What is it?" she asked.

"Her lungs sound a little congested," he replied.

Gabriela pelted the doctor with questions: What could it mean? What tests would be necessary? Could an inhaler help? Dr. Granger waited until she finished, and then answered her questions one by one. The two cancerous lesions on Agnese's lungs had been eradicated with chemo, but some damage may have resulted, he explained. Just to be sure, he'd order a scan.

Since they'd driven all the way from Ohnita Harbor, Dr. Granger's nurse called the imaging department at the hospital to see if a scan could be done that day. "They'll get your mother in," the nurse told Gabriela, "but probably not for three hours."

"No, we go home," Agnese said. "I come again. Maybe Cecelia takes me."

Gabriela thought of how much her aunt had done throughout her mother's treatment and recovery. Day after day, Aunt Cecelia had driven from outside Syracuse to Ohnita Harbor to spend the day with Agnese while Gabriela went to work. She couldn't ask her aunt to do something as routine as take her mother to the doctor. "We're here already. Might as well stay," Gabriela told the nurse.

Stepping out into the hallway, Gabriela used her cell phone to call Delmina and inform her that she wouldn't be back until late afternoon at the earliest.

"The library can run without you, Gabriela," Delmina said. "Take care of your mother, and we'll see you tomorrow."

Before returning to the waiting room, Gabriela decided to try Wendy's number. She hesitated to use her cell but didn't want to wait until later in the day to call, since J.J. could be home then. She dialed the number, which she'd memorized, and counted the rings. *One, two, three.*

"J.J.," a man answered.

Gabriela froze.

"This is J.J." he repeated.

She clicked off the phone and stared at the screen. Twenty seconds later, her cell phone rang. Gabriela disconnected the call before it hit her voicemail. The phone rang again, and she disconnected. After the third time, it stopped.

Her heart thundered, and the hallway lighting appeared to dim. *How could she have been so stupid!* Gabriela raged inwardly. With a deep breath, Gabriela tried to center herself, confronting her fears one by one before they inflated into panic. First of all, she told herself, J.J. always suspected something; nothing had changed there. Second, for all he knew, she only wanted to check on Wendy. He'd be mad and sputter, but what of it? J.J. exhibited all the signs of a classic bully; he liked to intimidate, but once confronted, he'd back down.

Putting the phone on vibrate, Gabriela returned to the waiting room, where she asked her mother if she wanted water or coffee from the courtesy cart. Agnese shook her head. "Nothing."

Gabriela watched as her mother took an oversized change purse with a metal clasp out of her purse. "Do you want some money, Mama? I think there's a vending machine downstairs. Or we could get something at the café in the lobby."

"I pray," Agnese replied as she opened the clasp and extracted her rosary with the pink beads.

While her mother closed her eyes and silently moved her lips, Gabriela sipped weak coffee with powdered creamer and picked up a ten-month-old magazine and distracted herself by reading a feature on how to brine a Thanksgiving turkey. After two and a half hours, Dr. Granger's office sent them to the third floor to check in with the imaging department. Seeing the sign to turn off all cellphones, Gabriela reached for hers to comply. It had been on silent the whole time, and she had four missed calls—all from the same number. The voicemail icon indicated a message, and Gabriela held onto the slim hope that Wendy had been the one to call. After telling her mother she would be right back, Gabriela stepped into the hallway and listened to the message.

"This is J.J. Haughton. You call my house again and I'll report you to the police for harassment. Wendy has nothing to say to you." The message ended with an expletive, then twenty seconds of silence from a call that had not completely disconnected.

Gabriela fumbled the phone as she tried to put it back in her pocket and dropped it to the carpet. Picking it up, she saw the phone had started to dial J.J.'s number on its own. Panicked, she ended the call. With shaking hands, she deleted the number from her recent calls so a misdial couldn't happen again.

Despite all the promises she'd made to contact Wendy—to Lucinda and now to Charmaine—Gabriela couldn't imagine when she'd ever be able to reach out to the young woman. At least the maritime museum had the Shumler drawing, safe and away from any damage or harm and protected from J.J. Gabriela hoped the same could be said for Wendy.

———

The imaging took only minutes, and the technician informed Gabriela that Dr. Granger had asked for results to be sent to him immediately. Gabriela escorted her mother downstairs to the café in the lobby, where they split a vegetable wrap of julienned carrots and celery slathered in a chalky sauce. Agnese took three small bites and pushed away the rest. Gabriela managed to eat half of hers solely out of hunger. Then she bought herself a latte and her mother a black espresso before they headed back up to Dr. Granger's office to wait for the results.

After twenty minutes, the nurse called Agnese's name and escorted them to Dr. Granger's office. Sitting down in the familiar surroundings, Gabriela recalled how she and her mother had sat there earlier in the year when Dr. Granger had delivered the dreaded diagnosis: a recurrence of breast cancer. Chemotherapy and surgery had gotten it all, Gabriela told herself. The cancer couldn't be back in the lungs, the lymph nodes, or anyplace else. The doctor only wanted to be sure. Her thoughts circled into a tight loop of worry.

His white coat flapping as he bustled into the room, Dr. Granger announced, "It's good news."

"Thank God." Agnese clasped her hands.

Gabriela exhaled and rounded her spine.

"No lesions," Dr. Granger continued. "But from the sound of Agnese's breathing, she seems to have bronchitis. We want to head that off before she starts coughing." He handed three prescription slips to Gabriela—an inhaler and a decongestant to use now; a cough suppressant if she needed it later.

Gabriela stood halfway, then sank back into her chair. Looking up, she met Dr. Granger's narrowed eyes. "You getting enough sleep?" he asked.

She nodded. "Just busy—a little stressful."

"*Bah!*" Agnese interjected. "She carry the whole world on her back. You got a pill for that?"

Dr. Granger curled his bottom lip and shook his head. "I wish I did. I could use it too." He walked them out, asking to see Agnese in six weeks. His hand rested on Gabriela's shoulder for a moment. "You can't give what you don't have. Take care of yourself."

As Gabriela nodded and thanked him for his kind words, her phone buzzed in her pocket. She tensed, trying to guess whether J.J. was calling again or it might be Delmina with a message. When they reached the elevator, Gabriela pulled out her phone and saw a missed call from J.J.'s number, but no voicemail.

In the late afternoon, they returned to Ohnita Harbor. Three times, Gabriela asked her mother to come for dinner and stay the night, but Agnese insisted that she needed to be in her own house and sleep in her own bed. Reluctantly, Gabriela acquiesced and promised to check in with Agnese later. Getting back in her car, she hurried to the park, where she had agreed to meet Ben after school.

Four boys threw a football and ran around, chasing one another and occasionally falling to the ground. She heard their laughter and discerned Ben's voice. Gabriela waited for him to look over, then waved her arm.

Two other parents sat on a bench, drinking coffee from insulated cups. Gabriela stood back to give the impression of not wanting to break into their conversation, although she just wanted the physical and emotional distance. Even the thought of making small talk exhausted her, let alone the possibility that someone would recognize her name from the newspaper articles about the two dead people at Still Waters Chasm.

Keith and Sheena. She said their names to herself, her own brand of vigil for the man whose body had washed up at the shore of the lake, brutalized by the elements, and for the woman who had never been found.

After a few minutes, Gabriela walked to the edge of where the boys played and held up one hand, fingers splayed, giving Ben the sign for five more minutes. He responded with an exaggeratedly disappointed facial expression, but Gabriela shook her head.

Her phone rang. Gabriela considered ignoring it, not even wanting to see the caller ID, then worried that it might be Wendy. She didn't recognize the number but answered anyway. Better to get it over with, no matter who might be on the line. The caller identified himself as Deputy Tom Garez from the Ohnita County Sheriff's Department. "We'd like to talk with you regarding Lucinda Nanz and Parnella Richards."

Gabriela told the deputy she had nothing to say other than what she had already told the state police about Todd Watson's death.

"We have our own questions," the deputy insisted. "It won't take long."

"This is not a good time," Gabriela pressed. "I'm at the park with my son."

"Just a few questions, although if you'd like a lawyer present . . ."

"What?" Gabriela glanced over at the two parents on the bench, hoping that they had not overheard her side of the conversation. Their stares in her direction told her otherwise.

Cupping her hand around the phone, she turned her back to the bench. "Fine. I'll meet you at my house in half an hour." When the call ended, she raised both arms over her head and flagged down Ben. This time he didn't protest, and they left right away.

At home, Gabriela made Ben peanut butter on crackers, knowing full well a heavy snack would kill his appetite, but she couldn't be sure when they would be having dinner. She let him eat in the living room while watching television, breaking yet another of her rules for him. Putting on her coat, she went outside and raked a few leaves, hoping Ben would be too absorbed in his TV program to notice the SUV with a reinforced grill and bumpers and "Sheriff" emblazoned on the doors pull up in front of the house. She imagined the neighbors staring out their windows, wondering what could be happening at her house. Or with her—again.

As Deputy Tom Garez introduced himself, Gabriela assessed him quickly: late twenties, short but athletically built, dark hair, and clean shaven. He looked good in his uniform, and probably knew it. "I want to ask you about Todd Watson," he said.

Gabriela kept raking. "Like I told you, I already made statements to State Trooper Morrison. He has all my information."

"And as I told you, the sheriff's department has its own investigation," Deputy Garez added. "May we go inside to speak?"

Gabriela shook her head. "My son is in there. If we're going to talk, it's out here." She looked at the vehicle parked at the curb and knew that sitting inside would spark speculation that she had been arrested. "We can go to my back deck."

She arranged the two canvas folding chairs she and Daniel had occupied just a few days before. Who knew when they would speak again?

Deputy Garez slid his chair over a few more inches and extracted a small recorder from his pocket. "You don't mind if I use this? It'll be a lot clearer than my handwriting." He grinned as if sharing a joke, but Gabriela didn't return the joviality.

The questions covered the same ground she'd already established with the state police: when she had met Lucinda Nanz, the nature of their relationship; when she had met Parnella Richards, and how she would describe that relationship. She answered the questions truthfully but offered no additional information. Gabriela checked her phone for the time; forty minutes had gone by.

"You have somewhere to be?" the deputy asked.

"No, but my son is inside, and you said just a few questions."

"We can continue this tomorrow at the sheriff's department."

Gabriela rolled her hand in the air, signaling for him to get on with it.

"Why do you think Lucinda Nanz would have wanted Todd Watson dead?"

Grabbing the arms of her chair, feeling the pinch in her right wrist, Gabriela straightened up. "*Whoa!* That's a pretty big assumption on many levels. First of all, I don't know what Lucinda has or has not done. And second, I have no idea if or why anyone would want something to happen to Todd Watson. He struck me as a decent person who was well known in his community and loved by his family."

"So, you didn't have an argument with him just before he died?" the deputy asked.

Gabriela drew her breath in slowly. "Todd called me and said the county would no longer allow use of the Livery library building for outreach programs. He was afraid of liability. I disagreed, saying the community needed those programs."

"You didn't threaten him?"

"With what? Reading a story to him?" Seeing the slight twitch in Deputy Garez's mouth, Gabriela closed her eyes and shook her head. "I apologize for my sarcasm. I'm tired and I've been at the hospital in Syracuse all day with my mother, who is recovering from cancer.

To be clear, for the record, Todd and I argued about the library out-reach program. Nothing else. I am deeply saddened by his death and expressed my condolences to his family at his wake."

"Did Lucinda go to the wake with you?" he asked.

"No, I attended by myself. Lucinda was there, and we spoke."

"And you left together," he added.

Someone had seen them together, she registered, but why would that matter to anyone? Everyone in town knew Lucinda, and any number of people had probably spoken with her that evening. "We did. Lucinda asked me if I wanted to come to her house for a cup of tea."

"And what did you discuss?"

Gabriela's mouth dried, and she longed to clear her throat but didn't. "I was not there long—maybe twenty-five minutes. Parnella and Lucinda had been discussing a fracking project at Still Waters Chasm, but I did not know much about it."

"What do you know about that project now?" Deputy Garez asked.

Pursing her lips, Gabriela averted her gaze as if formulating her answer, but instead parsed through what she now assumed: The county wanted to know about connections to the fracking project. That's why this junior deputy had been sent out, to sniff out what she might know. And that's why her answers were being recorded, so other people could listen to them.

"I saw seismic testing equipment in a large clearing at Still Waters Chasm. I believe it's called a thumper truck. And I am told that there may be two of them. That's all I know."

"Who told you?" the deputy replied.

Gabriela first thought of Trooper Morrison but recalled her promise not to repeat what he'd told her. "I believe Parnella explained most of it to me. I don't know much about fracking."

Behind them, the back door opened. "Mom?" Ben asked.

Gabriela turned and gave her son a smile. "Hey, are you hungry for dinner?"

231

Ben shrugged.

"Motherhood calls," Gabriela said, rising to her feet. "I have nothing more to add to your questions."

"We'll contact you again," Deputy Garez said, clicking off the recorder.

"No, you won't," Gabriela told him. "I have nothing more to say, and you know it." She left him on the back deck, went inside, and closed the door.

CHAPTER
TWENTY-ONE

That evening, exhausted mentally, emotionally, and physically, Gabriela went to bed ten minutes after Ben did. She fell asleep with the sensation of slipping underwater into a current that dragged her deeper, surrendering into nothingness.

A voice called to her from a distance. Gabriela fought her way to the surface.

"Mom!"

Her eyes snapped open.

Ben stood beside her bed. "Your phone. It keeps ringing."

Gabriela sat up and rubbed her eyes, pulling herself back to full consciousness. "Where's my phone?"

"Downstairs. I can hear it all the way up here. Can't you?"

Gabriela swung her legs over the side of the bed, staggered a step, and then turned on the light. The clock read 10:46. "Go back to bed, honey," she told Ben. "It's probably nothing."

"They called, like, six times," the boy protested and followed her down the stairs. "What if it's my dad?"

Or Daniel, she added silently. In her bare feet and a nightshirt, Gabriela wished she'd grabbed her robe but didn't have enough energy to go back upstairs. Her cell phone, left on the kitchen counter with almost no charge on the battery, showed seven missed calls from a number she didn't recognize. It rang again.

Answering the phone, Gabriela heard only silence on the line and then a sob. "Who's there?" she asked.

"Can you hear me?" a woman whispered.

"Who is this?" Gabriela spoke in a low tone, but firmly.

"Wendy. I'm on my cell. I need help. Please."

Gabriela pulled open kitchen drawers, looking for her phone charger. "What's wrong? Where are you?"

"It's J.J. He's drunk and he threatened me. I got out of the house, but I don't have anywhere to go."

Gabriela left the kitchen and searched the downstairs bedroom that also served as her office, where she found the charger in the top drawer of her desk. She plugged it into the wall socket and connected her phone.

"Are you safe? Does he know where you are?" Gabriela looked behind her at Ben, who stood with one bare foot over the other, chewing his lip. "Just a second," she said into the phone. Facing Ben, she explained that Wendy needed some help because she was feeling a little sick.

"Is she gonna be okay?" Ben asked.

"Absolutely," Gabriela promised, "but you need to go to bed. I'll talk to Wendy and then I'm going to sleep too."

"I can't talk long," Wendy whispered.

Gabriela switched back to the phone. "Sorry, but I don't want Ben to hear all this. He's going upstairs. So where are you?"

"I'm outside, behind the barn. I can walk through the woods to the main road, but I need to get out of here. I can't call Lucinda and

I don't know Parnella all that well. If J.J. ever found me with her, he'd have a fit."

"Call the police, Wendy. You'll be safe."

"No! That will only make things worse. J.J. and his father pull a lot of weight in this town. The police won't do anything, and then it will be worse for me. I need to get away from here."

Gabriela went through the planning mentally. It would take her at least forty-five minutes to get to Wendy's house. "I'll call you back in five minutes."

"No!" Wendy squeaked. "I'll call you."

Gabriela hated calling her mother at this hour but could think of no other option. Agnese answered the phone after two rings. "What's wrong?"

She gave her mother the minimal details. "I need you to stay with Ben while I go get Wendy."

"No, I come with you."

"I can't leave Ben alone." Gabriela racked her brain. If only Daniel were here. No, she told herself; he never would have allowed her to go to Livery to get Wendy.

"Ask the lady from the library, the nosy one," Agnese said.

"Delmina? I can't call her in the middle of the night."

"You make her day—you see. I get dressed, and you come get me."

Wendy called again, nearly hysterical with fear. Gabriela assured her she'd be on her way soon. "I'll call you in a half hour and let you know where I am," Wendy said. "I'm going through the woods to the main road. Don't worry. I know my way."

Gabriela scrolled through her contacts for Delmina's home phone number. Her husband answered and asked what the emergency was before Delmina hurried him off the phone. "What do you need, dear?"

"I hate to ask you this, but I have to go get Wendy, and I can't leave Ben alone." Gabriela then told her everything about Wendy's phone call.

"Of course I'll stay with Ben," Delmina said. "But don't you think you should call the police?"

Gabriela pressed the heel of her hand against her throbbing forehead. "Wendy is afraid of the police. Once I get her in my car, I'll convince her to call them."

"You're a good person, Gabriela. If this young woman needs help, we'll help her." Delmina promised to be there in ten minutes.

Upstairs, Gabriela threw on some clothes and went into Ben's room. He rolled over on his bed, his face visible in the light from the doorway. "Where are you going?"

"I have to go out for a little while. Wendy needs some help. Nonna is going with me. So Delmina from the library is coming over."

Ben pushed down the covers. "Why's she coming? Can't Daniel?"

Gabriela closed her eyes against a wave of fatigue and sadness. "He's out of town for a couple of days. But Delmina will be here." She smoothed his hair and kissed his forehead. After tonight and once she got Wendy to safety, Gabriela vowed, no more involvement—and no more upsetting her family.

When Delmina arrived, Gabriela grabbed her purse and her car keys and thanked her profusely.

"Don't worry about anything," Delmina assured her. "Just go and bring Wendy back here."

For a moment, Gabriela hesitated, wondering if she should call the state police and tell them about Wendy's call. Then she remembered the young woman's frightened plea—that her husband and father-in-law wielded enough influence to keep the police from doing anything. Gabriela hated to believe it. She'd only met Jake Haughton once, and he'd seemed more windbag than threat. But the tinier the pond, the more even a small fish could make a big wave.

Pulling up in front of Agnese's house, Gabriela saw her mother's silhouette at the front window. She ran up the sidewalk to intercept her mother. "I don't think you should come with me, Mama. It's late, and I don't know how long it will take."

"You not going alone," Agnese barked. "*Avanti*. We don't keep her waiting."

Gabriela felt the force of the tiny body as her mother brushed past her toward the car, sheer determination in motion. As she followed Agnese to the car, Gabriela noticed the roundness of her mother's shoulders, the slight limp from an arthritic hip that showed itself, she knew, only when her mother became overtired. All signs that Agnese should not be getting into her car at nearly 11:20 at night, nor driving forty-five minutes to an hour to intercept Wendy and return home in the small hours of the morning. She could protest, refuse to start the car until her mother returned to her house. Instead, Gabriela opened the passenger's side door and Agnese slowly got in.

She did not want to go alone, Gabriela admitted. She wanted comfort and company, and right now her mother, who would turn seventy-seven in four months, seemed up to the job.

Along dark country roads, Gabriela didn't dare speed. Once, rounding a curve, she'd spotted two luminous eyes in the middle of the road and then two more. Gabriela braked hard, flinging out her right arm to protect her mother and keep her from going toward the windshield. She clutched the steering wheel with her left hand, feeling the car shudder as the brakes grabbed the pavement. Shutting her eyes, she braced for the collision with the deer, knowing that kind of impact could damage the car and even send it into the ditch.

The car came to a stop. Gabriela maneuvered onto the shoulder. She looked out the windshield at the pavement within the range of her headlights. Behind her, in the glow of the brake lights, she couldn't see a deer's body. Unconvinced, she got out of the car and walked on shaky legs to the front of the car, which showed no sign of impact, and then to the rear, where she neither saw nor heard anything. The deer must have scattered at the last moment, disappearing into the woods.

Gabriela became aware of the odor of burning rubber in the air. Her brakes had taken the worst of it, and her tires had streaked the pavement.

Suddenly, she didn't want to drive anymore.

Getting back in her car, she put it in gear and cranked the wheel. If she pulled hard, she could turn around and head back to Ohnita Harbor. She paused, then steered the car back into the lane and continued toward Livery.

In the darkness, Gabriela felt her mother's hand pat her arm then settle on her leg, just above her knee. The touch reassured her that they would find Wendy. They'd convince the young woman to call the police, file a report chronicling J.J.'s abuse, and pursue an order of protection. Within an hour or so, Gabriela assured herself, Wendy would put in motion what she needed to do.

———

As Gabriela neared the turnoff to Lucinda's house, she tried to remember the series of left and right turns they'd taken to Wendy's house on their way to Blue Mountain Lake. That had been less than a week ago. She recalled one landmark: an old cemetery with the iron gate—the Town of Livery Cemetery. Pulling over, she thumbed the name into Google Maps then pushed the button for directions.

"Head east," the automated voice said, and Gabriela followed.

Once they reached the cemetery, Gabriela remembered that Wendy lived in a house just down the road from there. She slowed but did not stop in front of the darkened house. She kept driving but didn't want to go too far until she heard from Wendy.

Their headlights beamed through the darkness with no ambient light. A quarter moon did little to alleviate the gloom. The woods hemmed in the road, obliterating everything. A mile or so down the road, Gabriela pulled over and waited. Her car had only a quarter tank of gas, so she shut off the engine. As they waited, Gabriela asked her mother how she felt and received a curt reply.

When her cell phone rang, Gabriela jumped. "Hello!" she nearly yelled, then stifled her volume. "Wendy?"

"I'm here," she replied in a faint voice. "I need you to come get me."

"We're just down the road from the house. Where are you?"

Wendy went off the line for a few seconds, which puzzled Gabriela, but she remained absolutely silent. "Come back to the house. J.J. is out. I'll be in the back."

"You're sure? What if J.J. comes home?" Gabriela insisted.

"No, he's gone. It'll be fine. I'll be there. Come now."

239

Gabriela executed a three-point turn on the country road that lacked shoulders on either side, careful not to let the tires slip off the pavement. Within a couple of minutes, they came to the driveway between the barn and the old farmhouse. She cut the headlights and rolled slowly down the driveway, coming to a stop toward the rear of the house.

Her heart hammered at the thought of seeing a pickup pulling in the driveway behind her. She thought of the truck that had parked in front of her house and rolled slowly past her at the restaurant. Black pickups seemed to be everywhere, and Gabriela refused to blame her perception.

"She comes." Agnese pointed to a small outbuilding where a woman appeared, carrying a flashlight.

"Douse it," Gabriela insisted aloud, though Wendy couldn't hear her. She swiveled in the driver's seat and looked out the back windshield, praying that no one had seen her car pull up. The driveway was clear all the way to the road. The darkness remained unbroken, without even the distant glow of headlights.

"*Madonna santa!*" Agnese said.

Gabriela's head snapped around. At the front of the car stood Wendy, her arms limp. Behind her, holding the flashlight, stood J.J.

CHAPTER
TWENTY-TWO

As J.J. came around the driver's side door, Gabriela considered whether to start the engine and back out as fast as she could. But the fear in Wendy's eyes made her hesitate, knowing this young woman's life hung in the balance of what happened next. After the two people at Still Waters and Todd Watson, she would not let another person die.

"Lock the door, Mama," Gabriela shouted.

Her next breath came with a sharp intake, ending in a hiss, as Gabriela made out the gun J.J. held at the back of Wendy's head. "Get out of the car," J.J. demanded. "You try to leave, I'll shoot her."

Gabriela took her hands from the steering wheel. "Stay here, Mama. Whatever you do, just stay."

"No, I don't leave you."

"Use my phone, Mama," Gabriela whispered. "Call 9-1-1."

Just then, a man in a dark hooded sweatshirt appeared at the passenger side door. "Open it up and nothing bad happens."

Agnese complied but pulled away from the hands that offered to help her out of the car. The hood blocked the man's face, but seeing the logo of the tree, the axe, and the stump across the chest, Gabriela knew who stood there. *Colby.*

"*Vada via!*" Agnese shouted at him. "Go away!"

"Don't you dare hurt her," Gabriela screamed at Colby, stabbing the air with her forefinger.

"Shut up!" J.J. hissed. "Both of you get out of the car."

Gabriela reached for her phone, but J.J. yanked her back. "Oh, no. Leave the phone."

"Parnella's on her way. She'll be here any minute," Gabriela blurted out.

"That goddamn lesbian won't step foot on my property. She's jailbait just like Lucinda. It took both of them to kill Todd Watson. Lucinda mixed the potion, but Parnella did the rest."

Lucinda's words came back to Gabriela from the discussion the night of Todd's wake: They'd do whatever it took to stop the fracking project.

"You wait," J.J. went on. "They'll pin murder on both of them."

J.J. spoke with an assurance that made Gabriela wonder if he had heard that directly from the police. She thought of the young deputy who had come to her house and wondered just who had sent him—the sheriff or J.J.'s father, Jake Haughton.

"Parnella has called the police—the *state* police," she added.

He leaned closer, his face inches from Gabriela's. "Police ain't comin'. I had the scanner on all night. Not a cruiser within twenty miles of here."

Wheeling around, he trained the gun on Wendy as he told Colby to pull Gabriela's car behind the barn. Small stones flew as Colby hit the gas and spun the tires in the gravel driveway. The brake lights seemed to scream a warning, then dimmed.

In the silence, Gabriela heard Wendy's soft sniffle and her mother's murmured prayers. Her own thoughts quieted to an uncomfortable numbness. She had no power and no idea of what to do next.

Her mother reached out her hand as if for support, and Gabriela seized it. The fingers that squeezed hers felt warm and strong. "*Va bene*," Agnese said, and Gabriela smiled, even though things hardly were going well.

"Don't she speak English?" J.J. asked.

"She's—"

"*No parlo inglese*," Agnese said.

"Figures. Stupid foreigner."

"She's old, J.J. Leave her alone," Wendy said, and J.J. responded with a smack to the back of her head with the side of his hand that held the gun.

Gabriela heard the crack against Wendy's skull and watched as the young woman's stunned expression crumpled into a grimace, then a wail. She started toward Wendy, but Agnese's tightened grip stopped her. J.J. wanted their fear, Gabriela told herself. He thrived on it, believing that it showed how much power he had.

Her eyes now accustomed to the dark, Gabriela made out Colby approaching from the side. "You walk with me," Colby said to Agnese.

Gabriela clutched her mother's hand. "She's sick. She stays with me."

Colby stepped back, but J.J. pushed forward. "Shoulda thought about that before you brought her along," J.J. said. "You're coming with me." He grabbed Gabriela's arm.

"*Va bene*," Agnese repeated, then turned her eyes toward Colby. "*Malocchio!*" She forked her fingers in his face.

"You check to see if the old lady has a cell phone?" J.J. asked the other man.

Colby pushed back his hood and leaned down to Agnese's level. "Cell phone?" He spread his thumb and little finger and curled the rest of his fingers, then put his hand by his face as if talking on a phone.

J.J. spun Agnese around and patted her pockets.

"Don't touch her." Gabriela fisted her hands, thinking of her mother's birdlike bones and knowing that if she tried to snatch her away from J.J., Agnese could fall—perhaps break a hip.

J.J. pulled an oversized change purse with a metal clasp out of the pocket of Agnese's sweater.

"Rosary," Agnese said, reaching for it.

J.J. unclasped the closure and pulled out the string of pink beads.

Agnese let loose a stream of Italian, rapid and guttural. Gabriela understood only every third or fourth word, but enough to know that her mother cursed J.J., Colby, and their entire families with every malady and misfortune.

J.J. handed back the change purse. "Make her shut up," he said to Gabriela.

She ignored him, her eyes on Colby now as he offered his arm to Agnese as if to escort her. When her mother slapped his arm away, Gabriela let out a laugh.

J.J. grabbed Gabriela's sore arm just above the sprained wrist, and she recoiled. He held fast and twisted. Gabriela bit her lip until she tasted blood, then let out a groan.

With one hand holding a gun to Wendy's head and the other gripping Gabriela's arm, J.J. led the way down the driveway, around the back of an outbuilding, and into the woods. Gabriela stumbled several times, and J.J. seized her wrist to keep her on her feet, sending a sickening stab up Gabriela's arm and into her shoulder. She'd taken off the brace earlier that evening and had forgotten to put it back on.

Panic shortened Gabriela's breath, and her body heat dissipated in a cold sweat. A shiver shook her shoulders before she could stop it.

"Cold?" J.J. asked. "Shoulda thought about that too."

Don't engage, Gabriela told herself. J.J. would slip up, make a mistake, and when he did, she'd hit him with all her strength in the sequence she'd learned in a self-defense class years ago: in the groin, at the throat, in the eyes. She pictured the drill in her mind, how each person in the class had practiced on a man in a padded suit. The instructor had yelled for her to kick hard, and she had, causing the man in the padding to grunt a little. She'd do it the same way,

Gabriela told herself; hard and swift. J.J. wouldn't see it coming, then he'd double over in pain.

Emboldened by the image, Gabriela walked steadily. She listened for her mother behind her—the crackle of slow steps through fallen leaves, the sound of her breathing. Then she heard nothing and could only assume Agnese could not keep their pace. Finally, she heard a brief, familiar phrase. "*Ave Maria, piena di grazia...*" Gabriela didn't know the rest of the prayer in Italian but repeated that one phrase over and over in her mind.

Clouds snuffed out the light from the quarter moon, as if someone had switched off a lamp. J.J. turned on a flashlight and lowered the beam. Walking became easier, and Gabriela hoped her mother could avoid the branches strewing their path and the rocks that protruded from the ground. "Careful now," she heard Colby say, and as much as she despised him in this moment, she had to be grateful. He wouldn't let Agnese fall.

Gabriela found it hard to estimate how long they walked, their pace slowed by darkness and Agnese's halting step. After what she guessed to be twenty minutes, but could have been longer, Gabriela heard her mother's labored breath.

"We need to rest," Gabriela told the two men. "My mother is recovering from cancer. She gets winded."

J.J. pulled Gabriela sharply against him, her face knocking into the rough fabric of his jacket that smelled of cigarette smoke and alcohol. "You're not in charge here."

Gabriela gritted her teeth and pulled away from him, ignoring the sharp pain slicing through her. J.J. brought his hand back and let

245

loose a slap that knocked Gabriela to the ground. Wendy screamed, and Agnese cried out then began coughing.

"I'm okay, Mama!" As Gabriela got to her feet, she shifted her position so she could face her mother. Darkness obscured her mother's expression, but Gabriela had seen those dark eyes all her life, knowing both the anger and compassion that burned there. "*Va bene, Mama*," she said, repeating the phrase she hoped would calm them both.

Gabriela felt the tears streaming from her left eye, which started to close from where J.J. had slapped her. It gave her a focal point to channel all her energy. *Keep both eyes open*, she told herself; *don't miss anything.* "Where are you taking us?" Gabriela asked.

The thick soles of J.J.'s boots scraped along the ground. "Outta my hair," he said after a minute.

"You've made your point. We won't interfere with you and Wendy."

"As if," he said. "You trespassed on my land. You brought this on yourself."

Pressing her lips together, Gabriela checked a retort that he had no right and would bring on far bigger trouble by involving them. She needed to keep quiet and alert for the moment she could break free and attack him. But even if she could disable J.J. momentarily, that still left Agnese with Colby. She had to wait until she could free them both.

Ahead, a small building came into view. Making out the trunks of trees denuded of leaves already, Gabriela wondered if this might be a sugar shack in a maple grove. When J.J. let go of her arm, she clutched it to her chest, holding her right wrist in her left hand. She approached Agnese, touching her mother's shoulder.

"Get back now," Colby said.

Gabriela turned her attention to J.J. and the gun he pointed at Wendy. She imagined Wendy up against the windowless wall of the shack, then the crack of the gunshot and Wendy's body crumpling to the ground. Then J.J. would turn his gun on her and her mother.

246

Blinking rapidly, Gabriela scrubbed that image from her mind. *No!* They'd find a way out. J.J. wanted something from them. As long as she withheld it, he would keep them alive.

Gabriela heard a chain, heavy from the sound of it, a long length coiling onto the ground. Hinges creaked and old wood squealed as the door opened.

"I know what you want," she called out.

J.J. pushed Wendy inside, and Gabriela heard the young woman crash into something and wail. J.J. reached for Gabriela's arm, but she yanked it away just in time. "I know what you want," she repeated. "What Wendy brought to the museum."

He pulled her toward the shack, and Gabriela smelled the musty scent of rotting wood and mouse droppings.

"It's quite valuable," she added, "perhaps priceless."

J.J. shoved Gabriela against the doorjamb, clipping her shoulder. "What's hers is mine. It belongs to me."

"Well, it's not like we have it on us." Gabriela forced a laugh. "Pretty big to carry around."

"First she told me some bullshit about it being a piece of jewelry from her grandmother. Then she said it was an antique paper, like a map."

"That's part of it. An old map. But there's something bigger and more valuable." Gabriela's mind raced. She needed to keep J.J. engaged, telling him something to whet his appetite and his greed, but not so outrageous that he'd recognize it as a lie. The fine old sloop, the *Lady Margaux* came to mind. "A brass bell from a ship lost in Lake Ontario more than two hundred years ago."

J.J. sneered. "Who gives a crap about that?"

Gabriela gulped a breath. She needed to up the game on this story. "A lot of people, believe me. That old boat was loaded with gold from the British treasury, lost during the War of 1812. The map indicates where it went down, and only the old bell has been recovered."

247

J.J.'s laugh turned into a phlegmy cough, and he spat. "You think I got shit for brains? Why would Wendy own something like that?"

Thinking of Shumler made this part easier. "Her great-great-great-grandfather, or somebody like that," Gabriela replied. "You must have heard Wendy's father telling stories about the family history." She took a chance on that one, but figured at some point Wendy's father must have talked about their legacy.

J.J.'s feet scuffed the ground.

"You let us all go, you get the map and the gold. We'll even throw in the bell." She heard Colby snicker behind her.

When J.J. headed back toward the shack, Gabriela exhaled the breath she'd held, knowing that he would let Wendy go. Then she'd figure the next thing out.

The smack of wood against wood and the metallic rattle of the chain brought a strangled cry to Gabriela's throat. With the snap of a padlock, tears stung at her eyes.

"Don't be afraid," Gabriela called out to Wendy. "We'll be back for you."

She braced for J.J.'s slap, but instead he just laughed. "Go ahead, promise her a helicopter to get her and Air Force One to fly her home. Now you and me can talk some more about whatever the hell you really did bring to that museum and how I get it back."

"J.J., please," Wendy begged from inside the shack. "I'll be good. I will." Her words drowned in a torrent of sobs.

Gabriela stepped close to him, wishing that she stood a foot taller than she did, but aimed her words loud and high. "You've been bullying her for years. I've seen the bruises on her face."

"Bruises?" J.J. wagged his head. "My old man made beatings into an artform. Nothing I could do ever pleased him."

"Just like nothing Wendy could do would ever please you, so you took your anger and frustration out on her."

J.J. cleared his throat and spat again. "You don't know shit."

"You can tell it all to the police," Gabriela said. "They're on their way now!"

J.J. stepped back and raised his arms above his head. "Come on out! I surrender! I won't put up a fuss."

"What the hell?" Colby said.

"I mean it. I'll go quiet—be a model prisoner."

The woods answered with a flutter of wind through the branches and a distant hoot of an owl. J.J. bent over and laughed, beating his fists against his thighs. "You could set off a bomb back here and nobody'd hear it." He sobered and stepped closer to Gabriela. She held her ground, willing herself not to shut her eyes against the sight of his shadowed face. She felt his warm breath, smelled stale beer and onions that had probably topped a greasy burger. "Nobody is coming for you," he said, his voice a low growl. "Once you see where I'm taking you and your ma, you'll tell me the real story and everything else I need to know."

J.J. walked them back along the path they'd taken, his grip a vice on Gabriela's upper arm. Colby trailed them, walking with Agnese, whose breathing had become audible. *Gasp, wheeze. Gasp, wheeze.* Gabriela focused on it, her steps now synchronized to the rhythm of each breath her mother took.

"Shut her up," J.J. bellowed.

"She's old," Colby said. "She ain't faking this."

J.J. wheeled around and stuck his finger in Agnese's face. Gabriela screamed and grabbed his jacket, trying to yank him away. "Leave her alone!"

249

With one flick of his arm, J.J. sent Gabriela flying; she hit the ground hard, her ribs colliding with a tree root. The wind knocked out of her, Gabriela gasped for air. Her mouth moved, but no sound came out and no breath went in. Finally, she caught an inhalation.

"Don't hurt my daughter!" Agnese screamed. "I curse you—you devil!"

"Well, now, the foreign lady speaks," J.J. said.

Gabriela got as far as her knees and raised herself up. "Your argument is with me, not my mother."

J.J.'s boot found the center of Gabriela's back, and he shoved her to the ground. She landed with a low moan. *Better me than Mama*, she told herself. And when the end came for them, she would shield her mother as best she could.

———

When they finally returned to the farmhouse, J.J. disappeared inside, leaving Colby with the two women. Gabriela grabbed Agnese and held her close, whispering how sorry she was for involving her mother, how she should be home with Ben right now—not here.

"*Va bene*," Agnese rasped. "I say my prayers."

Gabriela loosened her embrace but kept her arms around her mother. Agnese seemed to give her a look, but Gabriela couldn't make it out in the darkness. "I say my prayers, *heh*?" she repeated.

Gabriela patted her mother's arm.

"He's coming," Colby said, and stepped between the women. He held Gabriela tightly by the arm. His other arm, she noticed, slipped around her mother's waist.

"You want me to get the truck?" Colby yelled.

J.J. swore and hollered back that he would do the driving. "You just bring them."

250

As they walked along, Colby pulled Gabriela so close, she felt his hip bone against her side. "Be careful," he breathed into her ear.

Gabriela turned her face away and pulled back, creating as much distance as possible between her body and his.

When J.J. forced them into the truck bed, Gabriela flattened her back against a carton in the corner, then held her mother against her body. Colby wrapped the rope around Gabriela's ankles, fastened a knot, and then bound her wrists. He passed the rope around Agnese, but Gabriela could tell from the way her mother settled herself that he hadn't tied her tightly. Gabriela closed her eyes as a tarp spread over them, blocking out the lights of the truck and the night sky.

CHAPTER
TWENTY-THREE

Riding in the truck bed, Gabriela could feel the vehicle back up, swing around, bounce along the driveway, then finally reach pitted pavement. With her hands tied behind her back and her feet bound with the same rope, Gabriela managed to use her head and shoulders to shift the tarpaulin. Finally, a corner flapped enough to let in the night air and a glimpse of woodland blurring past them. The temperature felt colder here; above them, stars studded the sky. Gabriela registered the beauty of it for just a blink of time before staring down the grim reality of their circumstances.

The truck engine revved as J.J. accelerated up a steepening grade. With no visible landmarks, Gabriela could only guess where they could be headed, but her sense of distance from the farmhouse and the altitude gave her a general idea. They seemed to be headed toward Still Waters Chasm. Her eyes burned at the recollection of the tiny oasis in the woods she and Daniel had found just before the horror that had triggered every tragedy since then. Unable to wipe away her tears, she let each drop roll down her face. Daniel would never know how she felt about him. She could never explain how her fear of getting hurt had made her keep a distance between them, or how she worried that his continuing feelings for Vicki left no room for their relationship to take root and grow. So much remained unsaid.

The cold penetrated her thin jacket, and her shivers became tremors. Her world narrowed to that truck bed and the primal need to survive. "Ben." She said the name aloud for the prayer and the plea of it. If anything happened to her and Agnese, her son would lose his mother and grandmother. She refused to consider it.

"They don't see?" Agnese asked.

Gabriela turned her attention to her mother, who had wrapped herself in the tarpaulin like a cloak. "As long as we stay below the back windshield." The frosty night air stiffened her jaw and made it hard to annunciate, slurring her words.

Agnese stretched out her hand, and something loomed in Gabriela's face. In the dark and at such close range, Gabriela had to pull her neck back to make it out: her mother's change purse. The loose ropes that bound Agnese allowed her freedom of movement, but she still struggled. Watching her mother try to open the clasp, Gabriela knew her mother's hands had to ache with the effort. When the little purse clicked and the hinged top yawned open, Agnese drew out her rosary beads. "I keep these in the front pocket."

"That's nice, Mama. I am glad you have them." Gabriela closed her eyes. Pulling her knees up into her chest, she rolled into a ball to conserve body heat.

"But in this side, I keep the phone."

Gabriela opened her eyes. "What?"

Agnese held up the tiny flip phone that Gabriela had bought her years ago and could never convince her to upgrade. Now her mother's repeated comment—*I say my prayers*—made sense, and Gabriela felt a gurgle of laughter deep in her chest.

Flipping open the phone, Agnese revealed a dimly lit keypad and two bars for the signal strength, but also a red line where the battery charge indicator should be. Gabriela's hope turned to stone and lodged in her solar plexus. Agnese never understood that she needed to plug her phone in to keep it charged. But it wasn't dead, Gabriela reminded herself. They'd get one brief call, maybe two.

She thought of dialing 9-1-1 but couldn't make a report without knowing their exact location, and the phone would die before they could track the signal. "Mama," Gabriela instructed. "I want you to dial my house, then hold the phone so I can talk."

Agnese pushed the buttons slowly, then pressed the phone against Gabriela's face. After four rings, Gabriela heard her own voice as the voicemail connected. "Hang up, Mama." Agnese clicked the off button. "Now dial again."

This went on two more times, until finally Gabriela heard Delmina's voice. "Oh thank God you picked up! Listen carefully—this phone is about to die, and we are in real trouble."

"Where are you? What's going on?"

Gabriela interrupted. "We went to get Wendy, and J.J. was there. He locked her in a shed somewhere on his property. I think it's a sugar shack in the woods. Mama and I are in the back of a truck being taken somewhere—maybe Still Waters Chasm. Call the police—the *state* police. Do you understand?"

Gabriela heard nothing. The phone screen was dark.

"She do this? She call the police?" Agnese asked.

Hearing the brightness of her mother's voice, Gabriela couldn't tell her what she feared—that soon after she began speaking to Delmina, the phone had died. "Absolutely. She's making the calls now."

Agnese slipped the little flip phone back into her change purse and pulled out her rosary. "I pray now. You see, they come faster."

The truck transitioned from pavement to dirt, the wheels spinning and the back fishtailing at the first curve. Clouds of dust drifted over them, and Gabriela tasted grit and felt it in her eyes. "Get under the tarpaulin, Mama," she said. "You shouldn't breathe this in."

Agnese stretched across Gabriela and grabbed an edge of the vinyl covering but couldn't hold on as the truck jostled her like a pinball. Gabriela managed to grasp it between her feet but couldn't maneuver it. Agnese lunged again and grabbed the tarpaulin, tenting them both inside.

Unable to see, Gabriela could only hear the roar of the engine and the squeak of the suspension and feel the pitch and roll over each bump and pothole. Then everything stopped. One door of the truck cab opened, then the other. Gabriela heard the men's voices, then only J.J.'s as he did all the talking. The pauses told her he spoke to someone on the phone.

"I told you I did," J.J. shouted. "Yes, I did, goddamn it."

Agnese started to say something, but Gabriela shushed her.

"I got 'em both here. What else could I do? They were taking Wendy—practically kidnapping her." Another long pause stretched, followed by a string of expletives. "If you'd listen, old man, you'd get it. I said she's at the farm." A short pause interrupted. "Yeah, where else? I gotta put them someplace, and it ain't gonna be with Wendy." J.J. swore again.

"He's coming?" This time Colby spoke. "Where's he now?"

"At home, sitting on his ass while I do all the work. But my old man put me in charge of this, and I'm handling it my way."

The tarpaulin rustled, and a rush of cold wind hit Gabriela's face, interrupting her thoughts. She coughed at the dust stirred up in the back of the truck. Colby climbed up over the side and untied Agnese, who cursed him in Italian, including being the son of a *puttana*.

The ropes chafed as Colby tugged at the knots at Gabriela's wrists then untied her feet. His face pressed close to hers, and Gabriela turned away. He moved with her, his mouth at her ear. "Be careful. Don't try nothing stupid."

"Speed it up. We ain't got all night," J.J. bellowed.

Colby reached for Agnese and brought her to her feet. Gabriela crawled along the truck bed, feeling every bruise and scrape. She flung one leg over the side of the truck and cried out at the burning pain in her thigh muscle. Colby's strong hands gripped her and lifted her down. She tried to extend her right arm to reach Agnese, but her shoulder seized up and her injured wrist throbbed from J.J. twisting it. Gabriela watched, immobile, as Colby climbed back in the truck bed and carried Agnese to the ground.

Standing beside Gabriela now, Agnese wheezed loudly. "*Polizia?*" she whispered.

"*Presto.*" The word soured in her mouth, knowing that the police would not be arriving soon or maybe ever. She had to find another way.

J.J. paced in front of the truck, raking his hair and emitting a low guttural noise that ended in an expletive. Gabriela took three steps toward him. "You made your point. You want Wendy's map. We'll have it sent over to you today. Just let us go. You know you can't—"

"Don't tell *me* what I can't do!" J.J. lunged at her, but Colby threw himself in the way.

"Whose side you on?" J.J. barked in his face.

Colby grabbed Gabriela by the injured arm, making her cry out in pain and pulled her back toward Agnese. She sat down hard, the end of her spine hitting the tree trunk. "Just stay there," he yelled, then leaned in. He seemed to mouth something, but Gabriela didn't hear it and couldn't be sure.

The two men conferred, their voices raised, then lowered. Colby gestured several times toward them, but J.J. just paced. Gabriela closed her eyes. Waves of fatigue washed over her, and nausea crawled up the back of her throat. Her eyes curtained, and her head nodded forward.

Gabriela startled. Her mother grabbed her arm. "I can't go," Agnese said. "My legs—no."

She helped her mother to her feet. "You can lean on me."

"Get her up. We're moving," J.J. yelled.

"Walk with J.J. Do as he says and don't piss him off," Colby mumbled to Gabriela. "I'll walk with your ma, and when J.J. ain't looking, I'll carry her."

A devil's bargain, Gabriela knew, as Colby wrapped one arm around Agnese and held her up with the other. Forcing herself forward, she walked beside J.J. She would stay quiet, she would comply—for now. Then she would get herself and her mother away from this maniac and his henchman.

J.J. carried a small flashlight, and Gabriela concentrated on the ground, watching where she walked. After what Gabriela guessed to be a half mile, they turned off the path. Branches snagged her hair and clothing. She walked behind J.J., making enough noise so that he knew she followed him closely without turning around. He pushed through a clump of trees, and the sharp slap of a bare branch caught Gabriela's cheek.

Ahead stood a building, newer than the old sugar shack from what Gabriela could discern in this light. J.J. took a ring of keys out of his pocket and turned one in a padlock. The door swung open, and J.J. aimed his flashlight inside. Gabriela caught glimpses of a cot, a folding camp chair, and unidentified mounds in the shadows. He gave her a shove inside, and Gabriela tried to aim in the direction of the cot. She felt the frame and sat down. Colby walked Agnese in and set her down beside Gabriela.

Gabriela gathered her mother in her arms as the door swung shut. The voices outside faded. Then silence.

Feeling her mother's face, Gabriela expected cold flesh and drew her hand back when she touched a hot forehead. Taking off her jacket, Gabriela covered her mother then sat on the ground beside her. Laying her hand on her mother's side, she felt the slight rise and fall of her ribcage and prayed that it wouldn't stop.

The glow of faint light seeping through a tiny window roused Gabriela, and she raised her head from where she had slept on the floor beside the cot where her mother lay. She had no idea how much time had passed, but guessed it had to be at least an hour. Thirst thickened her tongue, and she felt gravel in her throat. Agnese coughed but did not awaken; one touch confirmed that her fever had not broken.

Gabriela's finger retreated from her mother's face and found, instead, the scar along her own neck. The camp walls closed to a tunnel, squeezing her into an epicenter of sheer terror as she sat beside her mother's limp body. *No!* Gabriela yanked her hand away from her throat. She needed to take control of their situation. Able to make out a few shapes around her—a table, a camp stove—Gabriela surmised that J.J. used this place as a fishing camp, which meant a body of water couldn't be far. Perhaps Still Waters Lake, just as she had told Delmina—that is, if the phone hadn't died before then. The police would search for them. She only had to keep herself and her mother alive until help arrived.

Needing to relieve herself, Gabriela searched the cabin for a toilet, but had to settle for a bucket. She pulled it to the back of the building, which was longer and narrower than she'd imagined, and squatted behind a mound of junk. Steadying herself as she stood, Gabriela put her hand against something smooth and cool. Feeling her way along the length of it, she traced a long straight plane that ended with a downward curve. An overturned canoe.

Every camp probably had one, and once they found a way out of this building, they could use the canoe to get away, Gabriela thought. There must be cabins nearby. Maybe they'd come across a game warden. Getting the canoe to the water would not be easy by herself, and she'd have to help Agnese. It would take two trips, and she couldn't carry her mother the way Colby had. All that would be minor compared with getting out of this place.

Gabriela picked up the curved end of the canoe and shifted it, feeling the surprising lightness of it, and something clicked in her brain: Trooper Morrison's comment that the new Kevlar canoes weighed a fraction of what the old fiberglass ones did.

Grabbing the canoe with both hands, Gabriela pulled, and it slid forward. The length of the canoe reached all the way to a small window, where a feeble glow of light illuminated the shiny sides that appeared black but Gabriela bet were really dark green. Why else would the canoe be here, in the back with all the junk, instead of near the door for easy access. The canoe wasn't being stored, someone had hidden it here, and Gabriela could guess why: J.J. or Colby, probably both, had killed Keith and Sheena.

Agnese coughed, bringing Gabriela back to the urgency of the present moment. Brushing her palms against her thighs, she tried to clean her hands before touching her mother's face, still hot to the touch. She felt for the change purse and found it in her mother's pocket. Gabriela pulled out the cell phone, but the screen did not illuminate; she then reached for the rosary and wrapped it around her mother's hands.

260

A few moments later, metal on metal cracked the silence, and the building shook. "We're in here!" Gabriela yelled. Agnese's eyes fluttered open. "We're safe, Mama!" Gabriela cried. "The police came for us."

The door swung open, and Gabriela blinked at the glow of early morning light. A man stood in the doorway, backlit by the rising sun. He didn't appear to be in uniform.

Daniel.

Gabriela rose to her feet, ready to rush to him. But the voice that echoed in the room was Colby's: "Come on."

Gabriela stepped back, deeper into the room's shadows. "My mother is too sick to move."

Colby gave a backward glance and strode in. At the cot, he bent down and stretched his hand to touch Agnese's face. Gabriela slapped it away.

"I'm not going to hurt her." He withdrew his hand and stood up. "We gotta go."

"No! You're coming for us, just like you did Keith and Sheena." Gabriela sat down on the cot, putting herself between Colby and her mother.

"Who the hell is that?" Colby demanded.

"The people you killed at Still Waters Lake, the people whose canoe is still right back there."

"It wasn't me," Colby said. "You gotta believe me."

"When the police get here, you can tell them all about it." Gabriela crossed her arms against her chest, squeezing herself against a shiver of cold and fear.

Colby's hands gripped her upper arms and hauled her to her feet. "Stop it! You know the police ain't coming. But you gotta get out of here."

Gabriela pulled away. "You're not marching us off someplace else."

Colby looked toward the door again. "J.J.'s passed out drunk, and so's his old man. When they come around, they'll be back for you."

"Why should I believe you? You're J.J.'s right-hand man."

Colby stepped closer. "Let me ask you this. A couple of weeks ago, did somebody drop off two backpacks at your library? Inside the front pocket of yours was a note that said, 'Be careful.' That sound familiar?"

A chill ran from Gabriela's hairline, across her scalp, and along her spine. She didn't need to nod.

"I've been trying to warn you off. Saw you a few times from the truck. Black pickup truck. At your house, then on the street."

"At the restaurant," she replied, her mind spinning with this realization. "Why warn me? What do you want?"

Colby looked away without answering. "I'll carry Agnese. She doesn't weigh much. You can't stay here no more."

CHAPTER
TWENTY-FOUR

Agnese moaned when Colby scooped her up, and Gabriela rushed over to soothe her mother. "If you could carry that," Colby said, nodding to a rucksack he'd left by the door. "There's water in there." Gabriela opened the zipper, extracted a plastic bottle, broke the seal, and drank. Holding the bottle to her mother's lips, she managed to wet them, but the rest dribbled away.

"Don't waste it," Colby told her. "It's all we got."

They headed straight into the woods behind the building. Gabriela couldn't see a trail or a footpath, but Colby seemed to know the way. The farther they walked, the more pronounced their ascent, which told her they moved away from the lake; she wondered why, but had no choice except to trust Colby. "Why can't we just use your phone and call the police?" she asked.

"Can't get a signal up here," he said, panting a little. "Once you're out of here, you can call anybody you want."

Gabriela started to slip but grabbed onto a sapling to break her fall. Her hand ran the length of a spindly stem, scraping her palm.

263

It came away bloody, but she said nothing. After about a half hour, Colby stopped and set Agnese down. Gabriela took out the water bottle and gulped half of it before she could stop herself, slaking a thirst so acute that drinking seemed to only make it worse. She offered the rest to Colby, but he shook his head. "That's for you."

He reached in a pocket and pulled out a mashed protein bar. "It's all I could get."

Gabriela tore at the wrapper and took a bite. As she chewed, she pinched off a small portion and pressed it between her mother's lips, but the crumb fell away. Gabriela took another bite. "Why did you come to our table that night at the Lakeside?" she asked between chews.

Colby wiped his forehead with his sweatshirt sleeve, the same black hoodie with the logo of the tree and axe. "I recognized him—Red Deer."

"His name is Daniel," Gabriela snapped.

Colby held up both hands. "All I remembered was the Red Deer part. Unusual. I recognized him and remembered seeing his name in the newspaper. But I didn't know who you were that night." He got to his feet. "Let's keep moving."

They weaved through breaks in the trees and around thick clumps of shrubs and vegetation, in the general direction of a rising sun that split the woods.

"How much farther?" Gabriela asked at their next rest break. She took another sip from the water bottle then handed it to Colby, who accepted it this time.

"A couple of miles. There's a bait shack. Somebody will come by. You can get help there." He capped the bottle and returned it to Gabriela.

"And you?"

Colby bent down to lift Agnese. "I'm out of here. Canada, probably. I gotta put as much distance as possible between me and J.J. for a long time."

They followed a path now, wide enough for Gabriela to walk beside him. "Thank you. I don't know what would have happened to us if you hadn't come."

Colby gave her a steely look. "I know exactly what would have happened, and I ain't gonna be part of it."

A faint, mechanical sound echoed in the distance. Gabriela raised her eyes toward the treetops, trying to discern the source and direction. As it grew louder, she knew what headed their way. *Helicopter.*

"I did make one call," she told Colby. "From the back of the truck."

"Shit," he said, rounding on her. "I've been trying to help you."

"Well, I didn't know that, did I? We were tied up at the time."

The roar of the helicopter went over their heads but passed them. Gabriela waved her arms, but the chopper never stopped. Her arms fell weakly to her sides. The police hadn't seen them in the thick woods. The sound of the rotors grew fainter. As their rescue faded from view, Gabriela sank to the ground. "I can't do this."

"Come on. It's not far. Maybe a mile." Colby tapped at her foot with the toe of his hiking boots. Gabriela noticed the split leather and the gap where a gray sock showed through. Seeing Agnese's head loll to the side, Gabriela got to her feet. Her cramped muscles hindered her step, and she staggered. "Let's go."

Up a rise, down the other side, around a bend . . . Gabriela focused only on the next step, and the one after that. A steady descent pulled at her thigh muscles, but she just kept moving as daybreak turned to early morning. Raising her eyes from the muddy trail, she noticed that the trees thinned and woodsmoke scented the air. She heard a car pass but couldn't see it.

"Up there," Colby said.

Gabriela stopped. "Do you want us to go from here? I can probably carry my mother a little way. Maybe I can get her to walk."

When Colby glanced up at the sky, Gabriela knew he thought about that police helicopter. If he bolted now, she wouldn't blame him. "Your ma's unconscious," he said. "You gotta get her to a hospital. I'll take you the whole way."

Everything blurred as tears brimmed and fell, a constant stream of fatigue and fear, released at last. "Thank you," she said.

Hearing tires crunching on the gravel, Gabriela knew they'd reached the bait shop. She walked first out of the bushes that flanked the trail, holding back the branches for Colby and Agnese. They passed green metal dumpsters and a portable toilet and crossed the parking lot dotted with mud puddles. Ahead stood a squat, two-story building with dark green siding and a gray porch with an ice freezer and a vending machine. A sign along the road read "Bait 'N' Tackle—Propane, Beer, Nightcrawlers." An illuminated ring of red blazed "Open" by the front door.

In the parking area on the other side of the bait shop, a state police cruiser idled. Gabriela looked back at Colby, but he kept walking. "I'll tell them," she promised. "You rescued us. You put your life on the line."

Colby passed her, carrying Agnese, as Trooper Douglas Morrison came out of the bait shop. Gabriela rushed to him. "Call an ambulance. My mother is really sick." Sobs choked the rest of her words, and the ground came up to meet her.

———

Sirens wailed and blared from the distance. When the paramedics arrived, they immediately put Agnese on an IV. One of them insisted on checking Gabriela, but she refused any help other than the blanket they draped around her shoulders and hot coffee from the bait shop.

Colby sat in the back of the state police cruiser, but he wasn't handcuffed, Gabriela noticed. While the paramedics tended to her mother, Gabriela spoke with Trooper Morrison, giving him a fast overview of everything that had happened from Wendy's first phone call to Colby rescuing them from the building in the woods. "There's a canoe in there—I swear it's Keith and Sheena's," she told him.

When Gabriela finished speaking, the state trooper explained that they had found Wendy in the sugar shack, shaken up and a little dehydrated, but otherwise unharmed. They were still looking for J.J. and his father, Jake Haughton. Trooper Morrison said he intended to question Colby about where they might be.

"Please don't forget that Colby risked his life to rescue us. I didn't trust him at first, but he came back for us. He was the one who put the warning note in my backpack."

Trooper Morrison held up a hand. "I won't forget. But I also think Colby knows more than he's told you or me."

Gabriela looked around at the bait shop, noticing a few faces in the front window staring out at them. The front door opened and a man stepped out, observing them. "How did you know we would be here?"

Trooper Morrison shook his head. "I didn't. We've been out all night, looking for you. I knew this place opened early, and I wanted a cup of coffee."

"Are we at Still Waters Chasm?"

"Yes. The other side of the lake, opposite from where you and Daniel went hiking that day."

"When we were in the back of J.J.'s truck, I thought we might be headed here. I didn't know for sure when I called Delmina. I'm glad she got that part of the message before the phone died."

Trooper Morrison shook his head. "She must not have heard that part. Just that you were in danger and something about Wendy being locked in a sugar shack. We had to piece it together from there. That's what took us so long."

A question she had put out of her mind days before now resurfaced, "Why did the county sheriff question me? Do you know?"

267

Trooper Morrison took off his Smokey Bear hat, scratched his scalp, and put the hat back on. "If I tell you this is more complicated than you can possibly imagine, will that satisfy you?"

"No."

"Let's just say that it appears the interview that young deputy conducted with you wasn't part of any official investigation."

"I knew it! Jake Haughton sent him, trying to figure out what I knew about the fracking."

Trooper Morrison turned his head, then looked back at her. "After all this? In the middle of what is obviously a very active investigation, you can't let it go?"

One of the paramedics, a short, stout uniformed woman, interrupted their conversation. "We need to speak with you, Gabriela."

"Thank God," Trooper Morrison said, but Gabriela didn't miss his smile. "I'm getting more coffee. You want another one?"

"Always," Gabriela replied, her attention fixed on the paramedic.

"We're taking your mother to Upstate Medical. There's a trauma unit there."

"Trauma?" Gabriela repeated and rushed to the gurney where Agnese lay, awake now as the IV drip revived her.

"Her condition is more complicated because of her age and health history," the paramedic said. "But she's stable and somewhat alert, as you can see."

Behind the oxygen mask strapped to her face, Agnese gave a faint smile and nod. "*Va bene.* I say my prayers."

Gabriela turned to Trooper Morrison as he walked up to them. "I should ride . . ." Her words trailed off at the sight of a figure emerging from the trees ringing the parking lot. "J.J." she said, pointing in that direction. His arms hung limp at his sides; in one hand was a gun. He'd followed their trail, Gabriela surmised, and far more quickly than they had made the trek with Colby carrying Agnese.

Trooper Morrison pulled Gabriela behind the cruiser just before a gun fired. Its bullet struck the top of the patrol car with a metallic crash that reverberated inside Gabriela's skull.

"Active shooter," Trooper Morrison barked into his radio and gave his location. A voice crackled back.

"My mother?" Gabriela whispered.

"She's safe in the ambulance." Trooper Morrison motioned for Gabriela to stay put, and she crouched lower, pressing her head against the back bumper. "Put the gun down, J.J." Trooper Morrison yelled out.

"It's over, J.J.," Colby echoed from inside the squad car. "I told them everything—the canoe, the bodies in the lake." For a moment, Gabriela had forgotten he was sitting in the back seat.

J.J.'s string of expletives ended with another shot, and the bullet struck the state police cruiser with enough force to rock it.

Trooper Morrison rose up and peered around the edge of the car. "Stay here," he whispered. "I'm going to draw his fire. That'll give the ambulance a chance to get out of here."

Gabriela's widened eyes saw only the rear of the squad car as Trooper Morrison inched his way around. Then a car door opened, Colby shouted something, and J.J. answered.

Two shots fired in rapid succession, and Gabriela pressed her eyes closed.

A siren screamed and a car skidded into the bait shop parking lot.

One more gunshot fired.

Through her mouth, Gabriela panted short breaths. Her ears rang, and everything around her seemed overly bright. Slowly, her vision began to return to normal. She watched Trooper Morrison straighten and train his gun toward the front of the car. A female state police officer appeared beside Gabriela, extending a hand to help her to her feet just in time to see the ambulance take off. Gabriela watched it go, grateful that her mother had not been harmed and crestfallen that she wasn't riding with her to the hospital.

Only after the ambulance disappeared did Gabriela train her sight to where Trooper Morrison and another state police officer stood beside J.J.'s body on the ground. Colby stood with them. The back door of the cruiser angled ajar, she noticed now, and allowed images to form based on what she'd heard: Colby had flung open that door, attracting J.J.'s attention and giving Trooper Morrison cover. In that split-second pause in the action, the other state police cruiser had arrived, and one shot had put an end to J.J.'s siege.

Teeth chattering and knotted hands shaking, Gabriela allowed herself to be escorted by the female officer up the steps of the bait store toward a bench on the porch. The owner and two customers came outside now to get a closer look at what had just happened. Someone handed Gabriela a bottle of water.

Trooper Morrison climbed the steps slowly, talking on a cell phone. "How far away are you?" Gabriela heard him ask.

"Almost there," a familiar man's voice replied, on speaker.

Gabriela choked back a sob. "Daniel? You called him."

"No, actually Delmina did. She called everybody. State police, the mayor of Ohnita Harbor, your board of directors. If she had a number, she called it. And, yeah, she called Daniel too."

Gabriela looked away. "He's been up in Plattsburgh, fishing. He must have driven all night."

"Not exactly. Daniel left Plattsburgh before he knew you were in trouble. He's been out all night with us, looking for you."

He had already come back, Gabriela registered, just as Daniel's SUV bounced into the parking lot. The driver's side door swung open before it came to a complete stop. Gabriela got to her feet and ran down the bait shop steps and across the parking lot toward him, not knowing if he would be angry at her for not listening, for staying in involved, for putting Agnese and herself in danger. She'd deal with all that later. For now, she had only one thing to say to him.

"I love you," she blurted out. "I do. And I have for a while."

Wrapping her in a tight embrace, Daniel pressed his face into her hair and cried. "I thought I'd lost you."

She pulled back and wiped her tears with the blanket draping her shoulders. "When you left, I thought it was over. I never told you how I felt." The words poured out in a torrent. "I didn't even admit it to myself. I was afraid that I was too much—that you still loved Vicki and couldn't be with me. And then there's Ben and my mother. I can't just go off anytime and have fun. You're free—you need to get away, you just go."

"*Sh-sh*. It's okay. I went away for all those reasons. I needed to get my head straight." When Daniel took her hand, Gabriela began to worry what he would say next. "I love you too, but I felt conflicted." He exhaled loudly and blew out his cheeks. "And you can't stay out of trouble for more than a week at a time."

She snorted a laugh and had to wipe her nose on the edge of the blanket.

"But I love you, even though it's a little complicated," Daniel added. "We'll figure it out."

Trooper Morrison approached them. "Sorry to interrupt, but we've got Jake Haughton cornered up at Still Waters. And I gotta get Colby in for questioning."

Gabriela reached out and stopped the state trooper. "You'll remember what I said about Colby. And you know what he did here."

Trooper Morrison nodded. "I do, indeed. And if he cooperates with us now, it'll be okay for him."

"I'll testify on his behalf," Gabriela said. "You know I will."

Trooper Morrison shot a look at Daniel. "Oh, you expressing yourself is never in question." He tugged at the brim of his Smokey Bear hat and left.

"We have to go. Mama's at Upstate," Gabriela told Daniel. "Oh, and I need to call Delmina and speak with Ben." Out of habit, Gabriela patted her pockets for her phone, which she'd left in her car, which was back at J.J.'s farmhouse.

271

Daniel opened the door of the SUV and helped her inside. "We can do all that from the road."

———

The monitors beeped and an automatic blood pressure cuff inflated every few minutes. Sitting at her mother's bedside in the ICU, Gabriela processed what the doctors had told her. What had started as a mild case of bronchitis had quickly escalated to pneumonia. Exhaustion, dehydration, and Agnese's weakened immune system increased the seriousness of her condition, but she would recover.

Gabriela pummeled herself with accusations for putting her mother in this hospital bed. She should have insisted that Agnese stay with Ben instead of allowing her to go to Livery. But that one call from Agnese's flip phone had saved them. If her mother hadn't been there, who knows what would have happened? Sagging with exhaustion and depleted of emotion, she allowed her body to crumple into itself.

"I should have just contacted the state police and told them that Wendy was in danger. I shouldn't have gone on my own."

Daniel rubbed the palm of his hand over her back. "The police showing up might have escalated things. Or Wendy could have denied everything out of fear. You can't second-guess yourself. You did the brave thing. The right thing."

Daniel knelt beside her chair, his face now even with hers. "And you couldn't have stopped Agnese. She wanted to go with you to protect you. That's what mothers do. That's what you do for Ben."

Gabriela reached for his hand. "You know I'm always going to do what I think I should, even if that's not what everybody wants."

Daniel's mouth curved into a grin. "Yeah, I figured that part out."

An hour later, the cocktail of intravenous antibiotics and hydration brought Agnese around. Lucid and aware, she opened her eyes to a slit. Gabriela leaned closer, showing her mother a smile and not tears. "Look who came to see you," she said and reached for Daniel.

"Hello, Agnese," he said.

The old woman nodded. "I knew. I pray to St. Anne. *Va bene.*" She closed her eyes again and drifted off.

Gabriela stayed by her mother while Daniel went down to the cafeteria for more coffee and something to eat. He came back moments later, emptyhanded. "I just spoke with Trooper Morrison," he began.

"Is everybody okay? How's Wendy?"

Daniel reached for her hand. "Let's take a little walk. It will do you good. Agnese is okay. We won't go far."

With that assurance, Gabriela followed him out of the dimly lit ICU room and into the brighter hallway where two nurses in dark blue scrubs looked up from their station. "We'll be right back," she told them.

They exited the ICU, continued into the main hallway, and rode the elevator in silence to the first floor. Daniel took Gabriela's hand but did not say anything until they had reached a café, ordered coffee and a bite to eat, and sat down at a table in the corner.

"Trooper Morrison just filled me in," Daniel began, and explained that the state police found the camp in the woods where J.J. had locked up Gabriela and Agnese. When the police arrived to investigate the place, Jake Haughton was hiding inside. "The police had a standoff for three hours. Jake just surrendered."

"Did they find the canoe? Dark green—Kevlar? I told Trooper Morrison," Gabriela said.

Daniel nodded. "They have to confirm, but it's probably the one Keith and Sheena rented."

"So J.J. killed them? Why?"

Daniel shrugged. "Jake Haughton isn't saying anything, but Colby is cooperating. That's all I know."

Her muddled brain, deprived of sleep and overwhelmed by stress, couldn't process much more, but one realization penetrated. She and Agnese had been captured and held by not just an abusive man but one who had murdered before and probably had planned to again.

—

CHAPTER
TWENTY-FIVE

The next day, Gabriela and Daniel went to the state police station to hear the details and corroborate Colby's statement about what happened at Still Waters Chasm. They sat with Trooper Morrison at the same bare desk where, only weeks before, he had shown them the photographs of Keith Maldon's body. Now, noticing the smudges under the state trooper's eyes and the stubble on his cheeks, Gabriela wondered how many hours a day he'd devoted to this investigation. He took out a yellow legal pad, turned it horizontally, and sketched out a timeline that started a year before, with Jake Haughton's sale of a ten-acre parcel of land at Still Waters to a man from Syracuse, ostensibly to build a few cabins. That land, however, was later deeded to Still Waters Resources, which quietly began buying more land.

"By this time, Jake caught wind of the fracking project," Trooper Morrison said. "He had twelve more acres to sell, but with one stipulation: They had to hire J.J. for the project."

"To do what, be his spy?" Daniel asked.

"Maybe. Or Jake might have just smelled money and wanted his family to get in on it. From what Colby says, J.J. became obsessed with the project. He didn't just go to work clearing the site, he practically lived up there. He knew the state law had to change to allow fracking, and Jake vowed to make that happen. But this puts an end to Still Waters Resources. No change of law, and no chance of fracking at Still Waters."

"So who killed Keith and Sheena?" Daniel asked. "Keith worked for the DEC. Seems like Jake and J.J. would have wanted him out of the way."

Trooper Morrison toyed with a paper clip on the desk. "The autopsy showed that Keith had been poisoned. No evidence of a gunshot. As for any physical trauma that could have killed them, Keith's body was too damaged to reveal anything conclusive, and, as you know, we haven't found Sheena."

"But when we saw them, they weren't injured or bleeding. They had been vomiting," Gabriela insisted.

Trooper Morrison agreed. "It seems obvious they ingested poison. But the only one who is remotely connected with poisoning is Lucinda."

Gabriela pursed her lips. "But Lucinda and Parnella were against fracking. It doesn't make sense that they would want to kill a DEC fisheries expert and a geologist."

Trooper Morrison blew out his cheeks. "The poisoning complicates matters. That just doesn't seem to be J.J.'s MO. He threatened Wendy and you with a gun and fired on us. There doesn't seem to be any plausible way that J.J. could have poisoned someone."

Something triggered in Gabriela's memory. "Elderberry wine." Her excitement rose. "Parnella had a bottle of J.J.'s elderberry wine." Gabriela described the night she stopped at Lucinda's after Todd Watson's wake and Parnella's comment that Wendy had brought them a bottle of his homemade wine. "She said something like, 'J.J. is a son of a bitch, but he makes a helluva nice wine.' She offered me some, but I had tea instead because I was driving. I remember wondering what elderberry wine would taste like."

"So how could Keith and Sheena get the wine?" Daniel asked.

Gabriela raised her shoulders. "J.J. practically lived up there at the site, right? He sees Keith and Sheena, strikes up a conversation, finds out what they're up to, then comes back later with a nice bottle of elderberry wine. Backwoods hospitality."

Trooper Morrison leaned back in the desk chair. "There are about three dozen bottles in the cellar of that old farmhouse. Looks like we need to crack them open and start testing."

———

Over the next few days, the details became known, from both Trooper Morrison and the front-page stories in the *Ohnita Times-Herald*. A forensics team combed through the old farmhouse and the outbuildings, finding thirty-eight bottles of elderberry wine. Two more were stored separately in Jake Haughton's garage, both of which had been tainted with nightshade and implicated Jake in the murders of Keith Maldon and Sheena Dowley. A state police toxicologist estimated that, based on the concentration in the wine, consumption in the evening would likely result in death the following morning.

When Gabriela's phone buzzed with a now familiar number, she agreed to another meeting with the state police. She got there five minutes before Daniel and waited inside the station for him. Trooper Morrison inquired about Agnese and Ben, and asked Gabriela about her job and the latest on the Shumler drawing.

"*Ugh*, nothing." Gabriela covered her face and spoke through her fingers. "The last I heard, the British Museum wanted to see photos of the drawing, but I haven't even followed up."

"Well, you have been a little busy. Except for about six hours when you were locked inside an old building." Trooper Morrison smiled at her.

When Daniel arrived, the conversation pivoted to the investigation. Trooper Morrison related what Colby had told police the night before—how early one Saturday morning, J.J. had called Colby, saying they had to visit a campsite. J.J. drove them both to Still Waters, and they hid in the woods, waiting for Keith and Sheena to show up. After the couple brought their canoe to the shoreline, Keith and Sheena became violently ill. Colby said he had tried to help, but J.J. had knocked him to the ground and threatened him. Colby had watched Sheena stumble up the rocky shore then fall within a few yards of where he and J.J. hid. When she vomited, convulsed, and died, J.J. had laughed.

Swallowing hard, Gabriela wiped the dampness from her eyes.

"Colby said he told J.J. he didn't want any part of what was going on," Trooper Morrison explained. "But J.J. said it was too late because of what he'd witnessed. Then the two of you showed up. Colby said J.J. was furious when you tried to revive Keith. Then you ran back up the trail for help."

"And that's when they went into action," Daniel said.

The state trooper related Colby's account of loading up the campsite, putting the bodies in the canoe, and dumping them in the lake. "Colby swears they were dead already," he added. "Otherwise, he would face murder charges."

"I'm positive they were dead," Gabriela said. "Sheena had no pulse. Her flesh was cold. We tried to revive Keith, but he died right in front of us."

278

"If that's the case, Colby is guilty only of helping dispose of two bodies illegally and his involvement in kidnapping you and Agnese. But given all he's done, especially to protect you and Agnese—"

"And you," Gabriela interjected.

"Plus, his testimony against Jake Haughton will probably reduce any charges against him," Trooper Morrison added.

Gabriela thought again of Colby's willingness to put his life at risk for her and Agnese and renewed a vow to do whatever she could to help him. "My mother and I might still both be in that shed without Colby."

"That's true. But you don't think the state police would have swooped in and saved you?"

Gabriela noticed the twitch in his mouth and the hint of a smile. "Eventually, maybe. But I might have kicked the door down first."

Daniel piped up. "If you ask me, my money is on Agnese. I'd never want to be on the wrong side of that lady."

Agnese spent two days in ICU for observation and treatment for pneumonia then transferred to a regular unit for three more days. Daniel stayed at Gabriela's house, and they soon fell into an easy rhythm with each other's lives. When the hospital discharged Agnese, Gabriela prepared the downstairs bedroom for her mother to stay for a while. Daniel said he should go back to his house but would still come over every evening for dinner.

Gabriela kept a close eye on Ben, who clung to her for the first couple of days then resumed his routine of playing at the park after school. When Ben asked if someone had wanted to kill her, Gabriela told him that she hadn't really been in danger, but his grandmother

279

had gotten sick. While she always tried to tell her son the truth, she believed downplaying the facts in this case would be better. When she overheard her son declare on the phone to his father that "Mom helped catch a murderer," Gabriela knew Ben would spin the story his own way with a heroic outcome in which bad guys get punished and good guys win.

Returning to the library after a week's absence, Gabriela prepared to face a mountain of paperwork and apologies, especially for being unable to update the beautification grant application with the proposal to restore the ceiling. Delmina, she found out, had taken care of it all: the calls, the reports, the grant revision, and the updates for the board. Every time Gabriela tried to thank her—for staying with Ben, mobilizing the police, running the library, and even getting Wendy to sign the custodial documents for the Ohnita Harbor Maritime Museum—Delmina dismissed it as being part of her job description.

After being fully briefed by Delmina, the library's board of trustees never questioned Gabriela; instead, they expressed only kindness and concern. A bouquet of flowers delivered to her home bore a card that read, "Glad you're a woman who keeps her cool. See you soon. C—" and Gabriela knew Charmaine had no issues with her.

———

Two days later, Gabriela looked up from her desk and did a double take as Trooper Morrison entered the administration suite. Instead of his gray uniform, he wore jeans and a collared shirt. She watched as he greeted Delmina and the two of them talked like old friends.

"Got a minute?" he asked Gabriela.

"Official or unofficial business?" she asked.

"A little of both."

Gabriela did not want any questioning or briefing to go on at the library; the gossip mill had been running on high with her kidnapping, rescue, and the murder investigation. She reached for her purse. "I'll show you my favorite bench by the river."

Unseasonably warm for early October, the temperature flirted with 70 degrees as they left the library in the early afternoon and walked a few blocks toward the Ohnita River. Gabriela tipped her face back to feel the sun, one of a dozen small pleasures she savored more these days.

"So are you undercover today? A plainclothes stakeout, Trooper Morrison?" she teased.

"Call me Doug. Technically, this is my day off, but these days I'm always working."

Gabriela led the way along a linear park to a bench bathed in sunlight that faced the river. They sat at opposite ends, with a good two feet between them. Gabriela pointed to a group of anglers along the opposite bank and told Doug how she'd gone fishing there with her father a few times as a child. He replied with a fishing story of his own—with his grandfather and his older brother out on Oneida Lake outside Syracuse. "Biggest lake within New York State—almost eighty square miles. But only about twenty feet deep," he recited.

"The exact opposite of Still Waters Lake," she replied, steering the conversation to the topic at hand.

He planted his elbows on his knees and clasped his hands. "I want to test a theory out on you—get your reaction. But this is way off the record."

Gabriela nodded. "We'll keep this between you and me and the lamppost—that one right over there." She pointed to a wrought-iron light fixture, painted a glossy black, with a decorative glass globe.

The state trooper smirked, then sobered. "The forensics team did a thorough sweep. They found the tainted wine in Jake Haughton's garage, as you know, plus some dried nightshade berries and leaves.

281

But they also found foxglove plants at J.J.'s—a source of digitalis. Not a large amount, but enough, along with what appears to be an herbal tea mixture—stuff I never heard of, to tell you the truth."

"One of Lucinda's blends?" she asked.

He shrugged. "Hard to say, but she seems to be the source of all the fancy tea in the county."

"So what was J.J. doing with it? Mixing up his own special blend and slipping it to Todd?"

"That's the theory. Either Lucinda was complicit, which seems unlikely given how much she detested J.J., or J.J. tried to frame her."

Gabriela waited through a long stretch of silence, until Trooper Morrison finally spoke again. "Lucinda's confession came after fourteen hours of questioning, which is ridiculous. She's almost seventy-two. She claims she wasn't able to speak with a public defender, even though she asked repeatedly." He shook his head. "Let's just say the sheriff's department didn't handle this by the book, and I think her confession would be ruled inadmissible by the court. Plus, there is a lack of evidence against her."

A bubble of hope swelled inside Gabriela. "So Lucinda didn't kill Todd Watson."

"There's not enough evidence to charge her, let alone get a conviction. And from what we learned, J.J. had more motive than she did for wanting Todd out of the way."

Gabriela turned and rested her arm along the back of the bench, though careful not to invade his space. "Why?"

"Can't you just take my word for it?"

"No. You wouldn't even know these crimes had been committed without me."

"Without you right in the middle, where you didn't belong most of the time."

"Guilty," she admitted. "But I do want to know—and I give you my word that I won't tell anyone."

Trooper Morrison explained that three members of the county board of supervisors had held a secret meeting to discuss the fracking project and what they could do to force a change of law in Albany. Only one other person had attended: Jake Haughton. The supervisors from Newlan and Mandeville pressed for approval, but Todd Watson had been opposed over environmental concerns. He wanted to bring in the DEC and hold public hearings.

"But he shut down my children's story hour because Parnella Richards showed up!" Gabriela interrupted.

"Only you would have a subversive story hour." He shook his head. "Todd didn't want Parnella to stage a protest at the site. He was a by-the-book kind of guy."

Gabriela watched the sun dapple the current of the river, a shimmering blend of fire and water. Further downstream, everything the river carried would pour into Lake Ontario and eventually flow along the St. Lawrence River on its long journey to the Atlantic Ocean. That was how lakes held their secrets, she thought, not just in the mix but in their increasing depths.

"So if Lucinda didn't poison the tea, who did?" the state trooper asked. "Do you know anyone else who might be involved?"

Parnella came to mind, but Gabriela had nothing other than suspicion to implicate her. "You know as much as I do—more, in fact."

"Somehow I doubt that." He got to his feet. "Listen, I know I was hard on you about staying out of the investigation. Mostly, though, I just wanted to protect you."

"Thank you—and I did stick my nose in. Other than endangering my mother, which I will never forgive myself for doing, I don't have any regrets."

Trooper Morrison got up from the bench. "You really are something. Seriously. You're one of the most courageous people I know. Not many people would have charged off to rescue Wendy the way you did."

"And my mother, too. We have to give Agnese credit."

He gave her a long look. "You know, if you weren't with Daniel—"

The comment hung in the air, and Gabriela felt the flattery of unexpected admiration, but let the words dissipate in the warm autumn breeze.

"Thank you for everything," she told him, and remained at the bench as State Trooper Doug Morrison walked away from the river and up the hill, looking back once to wave to her before turning left and continuing out of sight.

CHAPTER
TWENTY-SIX

"I want to sue the sheriff's department for Lucinda's wrongful arrest," Parnella said, her voice rising with each word.

Gabriela lowered the volume on her cell phone. It had been two days since her meeting with Trooper Morrison at the bench on the river, and her life had just started to return to a normal routine of home, Daniel, and library business.

"But Lucinda says to just let it go. No more negativity—and all that." Parnella's sigh became a laugh. "I'm just glad to have her home. They released her yesterday. And we've got a garden to repair. But we need to do a sage smudge before we can plant anything."

The green witches, Gabriela smiled to herself, and thanked Parnella for the update.

A cheerful "thinking of you" card had arrived in the mail with a postmark of Blue Mountain Lake, New York. She should have reached out to Cynthia Rahlberg, the museum director, and Earl Buntley before this, Gabriela chided herself. When she sent them an

285

email, thanking them for the card, Cynthia replied a minute later to say that Charmaine Odele had kept Earl informed.

"We're just grateful you and your mother are okay," Cynthia's email read. "We hope to see you soon."

The next day, Earl Buntley called Gabriela at the library and relayed his extensive discussions with the British Museum, which had found several design similarities between Fulton's original drawing and the Shumler schematic. "Shumler clearly made improvements," Earl told her. "But it certainly seems that he had either seen Fulton's original drawings or worked directly with Fulton."

Gabriela thanked him profusely for all this work, but Earl ducked the compliment, saying repeatedly, "What else does an old man like me have to do all day?" She heard the softening in his voice when he added, "Besides, this is for Wendy. I'll do anything I can do to help that young woman."

One letter between Fulton and Shumler—that's all it would take to establish a connection between the two men and increase the probability that the Shumler schematic had been made for Fulton, Gabriela thought. She began reaching out to historical societies across the state, knowing from experience that these smaller organizations sometimes had documents in their possession that appeared ordinary on the surface, but later proved to be a missing link in an authentication. After two negative responses, Gabriela pressed on, knowing that someone, somewhere had to have known about a Fulton-Shumler collaboration—if one had ever existed.

Early that afternoon, Charmaine showed up at the library to discuss Shumler, which made Gabriela wonder about the coincidence until Charmaine mentioned that Earl had also called her that morning. The two women sat in Gabriela's office, positing theories, and following flights of fancy into internet searches that led to interesting trivia—Fulton married Harriet Livingston in 1808, the same year as the Shumler drawing—but nothing was helpful.

After an hour, when Charmaine suggested they go get coffee, Gabriela suspected a motive other than fresh air and caffeine but knew she would soon hear about it. They strolled through town, past City Hall, the police department, and the few retailers in the tiny downtown, where fall decorations and Halloween pumpkins dominated the window displays.

"I've been entertaining this thought—two thoughts, actually—for a while," Charmaine began. "Your background and mine are perfect complements, and both of us are steeped in research. What do you say to a collaboration?"

Charmaine outlined an elective course on authentication that Gabriela could teach for the history department at the community college. Intrigued, Gabriela asked a few questions about curriculum and when the course would be taught, but also expressed concern about having enough time to teach and run a short-staffed library. As they waited at the light to cross the intersection of Main and Harbor, Charmaine promised maximum flexibility on the time commitment, as well as her help on the course design and administrative matters.

The women paused their discussion when they walked into A Better Bean. As the bell rang on the door, Sharon Davis looked up from behind the counter; Gabriela gave her a small wave. "Well, stranger, haven't seen you in a while," Sharon said. "Of course, it seems you've been busy getting kidnapped and rescued."

Gabriela's smile tensed and faded. "It's all good, thanks for asking." She turned to Charmaine. "What would you like? My treat."

Charmaine, who towered a good six inches above Gabriela, leaned forward. "I'll have a latte—no, what the hell, a mocha. And yes, I want whole milk and whipped cream." Gabriela ordered a nonfat latte and handed Sharon a twenty-dollar bill.

As Sharon busied herself with brewing espresso shots and steaming milk, Charmaine turned away from the counter. "Before you say yes or no to teaching, consider this: It's just ten weeks of talking about what you love, assigning a final project, and having the students present their projects to the class for a grade."

Gabriela bit her lip. Teaching had always been on her wish list, something to explore once Ben entered high school or went away to college. Only in fifth grade, Ben still needed her help with homework and after-school activities. Plus, she had Daniel back in her life and her mother needed care. But one course—just ten weeks and immersion in her specialty.

They brought their coffees to a table in the corner. Charmaine took an appreciative sip and set the cup down. "I've seen how you come alive with every authentication project. First that medieval cross and chasing down the Catherine of Siena connection, and now the Shumler drawing. But I can't imagine these kinds of projects will just keep popping up."

Gabriela looked at the chocolate shavings atop the whipped cream on Charmaine's coffee and wished she had indulged. "I've always loved authentication."

"So do it!" Charmaine said. "Teaching this class will keep your expertise alive and, selfishly from my perspective, it will also help keep you in Ohnita Harbor."

As with everything Charmaine had said thus far, Gabriela felt the truth of it all, not only her love of authentication but also her fear that, no matter how busy her administration responsibilities made her, she could become bored intellectually. "Okay, I will." Then she remembered her promise to be more of a partner in her relationship with Daniel. "Actually, I will probably do it after I discuss it with someone."

"Good. Now this brings me to my second idea." Charmaine proposed a research article for an academic magazine that they would coauthor about the Shumler investigation—the possible Fulton connection and efforts to authenticate through primary resources found in historic, rural communities. "I've done a database search, and no one has written anything similar."

"Wouldn't we need to confirm the Shumler-Fulton connection first?" Gabriela asked.

"That would help, but it wouldn't be a deal breaker as long as we didn't overstate our conclusion."

Gabriela had dreamed of writing another research-based article, having done so only once before. She didn't hesitate to agree to this project. When Charmaine began discussing which publications to approach and the editors she knew, Gabriela interrupted. "We need a long lead time, okay?"

Charmaine gave her assurance, and their conversation pivoted to the library, the grant proposal, and the board's excitement over the idea of restoring the original ceiling. As they talked, Gabriela's phone buzzed in her pocket, but she ignored it. Thirty seconds later, it buzzed again, but she did not want to be rude. The third time, she excused herself and explained that someone obviously needed to reach her.

"What's up?" she answered. "I'm in a meeting." Her mouth slackened and her eyes widened, then Gabriela told Charmaine she had to leave immediately.

———

The speedometer of the DRD Roofing pickup truck crept well above sixty-five miles per hour. Gabriela hung onto the strap above the passenger door and looked repeatedly at the Google Maps display on her phone. The app projected that they would arrive in thirty-one minutes.

Daniel turned onto a secondary road, which soon narrowed, and the shoulder disappeared into clumps of dead grass and fallen leaves. The broken and pitted pavement forced Daniel to slow down, and Google Maps adjusted their arrival time to thirty-three minutes.

After a few more miles, the app's automated voice alerted them to a turn in a half mile.

"There's no name," Gabriela said. "It just says 'gravel road.'"

"I think it's Mel's Falls or something like that, but there's probably no sign," Daniel said.

Google Maps announced a right turn, and the pickup lurched off the pavement and onto loose cinders. "Maybe we should slow down a little." Gabriela's words vibrated in her chest.

"It's not like they're going to wait for us," Daniel replied. "You sure you want to do this?"

Gray tree trunks with rough, gnarled bark streamed past. "Yes. I think it's the right thing to do." Gabriela looked out the window at woods, believing this would be a kind of benediction, completing a promise she had made, though not in the way she had first hoped.

The road dead-ended in a parking area and a trailhead. Two state police cruisers, an SUV filled with gear, and a county medical examiner's vehicle took up most of the spaces, so Daniel maneuvered into the end with the driver's side tires in the grass. A state police officer emerged from one of the cruisers, and Gabriela and Daniel introduced themselves and explained that Trooper Morrison had notified them. The state trooper made a call, and a voice crackled back over a radio. After getting clearance, he instructed them to follow the trail for about a mile and then take a left fork, which would lead them another mile to the shore.

They started off at a quick pace, and soon both breathed through their mouths. Every time the path rolled downward, Gabriela broke into a jog, but she slowed to a fast walk on the way up the other side. The stony beach seemed narrower on this side of the lake, Gabriela noticed; in some places, the water lapped almost up to the woods. Daniel took Gabriela's hand, and she squeezed his; together, they walked toward the group of state police officers in uniform and diving gear.

Trooper Morrison broke off from the group and approached them. "We just brought in a new team of divers. The last group exceeded their limit. They're going down 180 feet, which means decompression stops on their way back up."

"Will you bring her up now?" Gabriela asked.

"First team got her free. The second team will do the retrieval." Trooper Morrison looked at both of them. "When the body comes up, I'd suggest you stand back. You won't want to be too close."

They watched as the team of divers headed out in a boat until they were about one-third of the way across the narrow lake. Gabriela fastened the top button of her winter coat, grateful that Daniel had suggested she wear it. Cold seeped through the mesh of her running shoes, and she wiggled her toes to keep them from becoming numb.

"They've got her," someone with a radio yelled.

Trooper Morrison handed Gabriela a pair of binoculars, and she took a quick look at the divers' heads bobbing at the surface near the boat. As the boat approached the shoreline, Gabriela and Daniel backed away from the water. When the divers unloaded the body, Gabriela had thought she would hide her eyes, but instead she wanted to witness this moment, to pay her respects to Sheena Dowley.

The ashen face of the young woman, staring up at the sky with unseeing eyes, returned to Gabriela's mind. Instead of recoiling at the memory, she embraced it, trying to remember more details: the braided hair, the freckles on her nose, the red quilted vest.

The county medical examiner closed the body bag and placed it on a gurney for removal. The state police remained at the scene.

"Do you want to stay?" Daniel asked.

Gabriela nodded. "Just for a little while."

Trooper Morrison approached and explained that he had just informed Sheena's family, who lived out of state. "They expressed their thanks to both of you."

"But we couldn't save her or Keith." Gabriela's voice broke. "We tried so hard, but we couldn't bring them back."

"At least now Sheena's family has closure," the state trooper said. "Her students and her community too. She was a popular teacher."

Daniel swiped at his eyes. "What gets me is how J.J. could think that killing two innocent people would change anything."

"An exaggerated sense of self-importance—trying to prove something to his father. Who knows?" Trooper Morrison suggested.

Their conversation stopped when someone down the beach yelled for Trooper Morrison. Gabriela and Daniel followed and watched as two other divers returned with a cylindrical piece of metal. Measuring about four feet long, that curved piece of metal could have been anything. Then one of the divers wiped it with a rag, and Gabriela saw an oval nameplate etched with scrollwork.

Nautilus III
Fulton &
Shumler
1808

Eight days later, on a bright, clear morning with the temperature just above freezing, a crowd gathered on the shoreline while a salvage crew prepared for their next dive. Gabriela tapped her toes together and wrapped her arm around Ben's shoulders for warmth. Her son stayed about five minutes in her embrace before heading over to stand with Daniel near a tarpaulin spread on the beach where old metal parts had been spread out and tagged.

Charmaine Odele looked like a duchess with her white mane of hair and a full-length fake fur coat and matching hat. She leaned down to Gabriela and whispered, "Forget the article—let's do a book!" Before Gabriela could respond, Charmaine strode over to where Earl Buntley and his wife stood with a young woman in a short jacket and jeans: Wendy Haughton. Earl bent to listen to Wendy, who seemed to be talking animatedly. Wendy's father had called the Shumler drawing their family treasure; this new authenticated link exceeded anyone's expectations.

Cynthia Rahlberg from the Adirondack Experience picked her way over the rocks to Gabriela. "If I haven't said it already about a dozen times, thank you for inviting us."

They watched together as the divers took the boat back to the diving site and submerged. The crowd waited and talked as the crew extracted more metal and loaded the boat, then returned to the shore for the haul to be tagged and photographed.

Cynthia and Gabriela made their way over to Earl, who spoke loudly into his cell phone. He ended the call with a smile and a shake of his head. "I heard every fourth word, but it sounds like the British Museum wants to make an offer," he said.

"For the *Nautilus III*? I don't think New York State should let that go," Charmaine said. "This is a vital piece of our state's history."

Earl beamed at Wendy. "No, for the Shumler drawing. They want to display Wendy's treasure along with Robert Fulton's first schematic."

Wendy twisted the fingers of her blue knit gloves. "I was thinking that maybe I should just give the drawing to the Adirondack Experience—or maybe your museum, Charmaine. You've all been so helpful."

Earl shook his head. "No, dear girl, you're not going to give anything away. We're going to make sure that your treasure finds the right home and that you benefit from it."

"But we will take a copy," Charmaine interjected.

"Make that two copies," Cynthia added.

They turned their attention back to the boat bringing back another piece of the *Nautilus III*. "I wonder how Robert Fulton would feel about the rediscovery. Maybe he scuttled it here because he didn't want anyone to know about this experiment," Gabriela said.

Earl raised his chin. "But he hid it in plain sight. One hundred and eighty feet is hardly inaccessible. I'd rather think that he wanted someone to find it one day. Or maybe Shumler did." He looked over at Wendy. "Your family held the key all these years."

"I feel so bad about the woman who died, though," Wendy said. "If her body hadn't got caught in the *Nautilus*, they would have found her sooner."

Gabriela saw Wendy's eyes glisten and felt the pang of empathy. Wendy had suffered far longer and more deeply than any of them, not only J.J.'s abuse but now knowing that he had been a murderer.

"Sheena Dowley was a teacher," Gabriela said. "And geology is closely linked to history. So I think Sheena would be proud to help discover something as significant as the *Nautilus III*."

"I hope so," Wendy said softly.

When the boat reached the shore, two divers carried splintered wood and a length of rope. "My God," Earl exclaimed, "the foldable sail!" He wrapped his arm around Wendy's shoulders. "That's your family's contribution to history, right there."

Gabriela imagined how brittle the mast and supports would be after more than two hundred years buried in mud in a very cold lake and thought of all the strange places the trail of authentication had led her thus far—from crumbling documents at the New York Public Library's Archives and Documents to a tiny medieval cross in a cardboard box on the steps of the Ohnita Harbor Public Library, and now to the depths of a lake at Still Waters Chasm. She couldn't help but wonder what might be next.

CHAPTER
TWENTY-SEVEN

The last of the leaves loosened from the trees and scattered in the prevailing northwest wind off Lake Ontario. Color leached from the landscape as the reds, yellows, and golds of October faded into November's stark gray. Not death, Gabriela mused as she drove through a stretch of woodlands, but dormancy—nature's long sleep and restoration to prepare for spring. Gabriela drew the parallel to her own life. After the hectic pace of summer and fall, the approaching wintry sleep would be a welcome shift to the slower rhythms of home-based life.

With her mother beside her and her son in the back seat, Gabriela navigated the rural roads without GPS or a glance at landmarks. Frequency had brought familiarity, even though she would never be regarded as a local here; the distance between Ohnita Harbor and Livery might as well be two hundred miles. She would always be an outsider; to some, the stranger who came to their town because she cared, to others the interloper who should have minded her own business.

Gabriela turned onto the road that led to Lucinda's house. She had not seen Lucinda since her release, though they had spoken twice by phone. Then, a few days ago, Lucinda had invited her to tea, and Gabriela had eagerly accepted, provided she could come on a Saturday afternoon, with her mother and her son—neither of whom she wanted to let out of her sight for a while.

The kitchen's cozy warmth welcomed Gabriela. She noticed that Lucinda's long hair had been trimmed to shoulder length and she seemed slightly stooped in the shoulders. Otherwise, Lucinda still exuded a vibrant and youthful energy. Parnella greeted Gabriela and chatted for a few minutes, then excused herself. Before leaving the room, Parnella gave Lucinda a light kiss and headed to the backyard, where Ben sat on the patio, playing with Corky the cat.

"I want to show Ben the beehives we're building," Parnella said.

"They're not full of bees yet, are they?" Gabriela asked.

"No, but don't worry. Lucinda's got the bees charmed and trained."

"I go too," Agnese said, getting up from the table and taking Parnella's arm. "You know, we keep bees back in Italy."

As her mother left the kitchen, Gabriela assessed Agnese's step, pleased to see her strength steadily returning. When the kettle whistled, Lucinda got up from the table to turn off the burner. Gabriela followed her to the counter and watched as Lucinda spooned a mixture of leaves and herbs into an infuser.

"They confiscated all my teas," she said. "But I managed to replenish my stock and even make some new blends."

Gabriela smelled peppermint and a hint of anise.

"When you first visited my garden, the petunias welcomed you and the snapdragons didn't turn you away. That tells me you can be trusted with a secret," Lucinda told her.

Feeling a rush of nervous energy, Gabriela took the mugs from the counter and carried them to the table. She stood, her back to Lucinda, until her heart slowed.

"Don't worry. I didn't kill anyone," Lucinda said. "But I'm afraid my tea did."

Gabriela closed her eyes. She really didn't want to hear how Lucinda had gotten away with murder on some technicality.

"The tea that killed Todd Watson had two special ingredients: catnip for calming, mugwort for regulation and to heal bruising." Lucinda put the teapot on the table, though Gabriela knew steeping would take at least twenty minutes.

"I made that blend for only one person," Lucinda said.

Gabriela could guess, but waited for what Lucinda would say next.

The older woman offered what she called "my theory." It started with the known facts: J.J.'s obsession over the fracking project and being intent on eliminating all opposition to it, and Todd Watson wanting public hearings and environmental studies and his love of tea. "We know J.J. put nightshade in the elderberry wine he gave to those two campers. How difficult would it have been for him to slip foxglove into my tea and give it to Todd? He could frame me in the process."

Gabriela nodded. "Did you tell that to the police?"

"To free myself? Absolutely not." Lucinda's mouth became a hard line. "It also occurred to me that J.J. would never have delivered that tea to Todd. He'd need someone else to do it—someone connected to me."

The air seemed to rush out of the room, and Gabriela fought to take a deep breath. "Wendy."

Lucinda's sigh creased her face and aged her five years. "That's why I confessed to killing Todd. Once I found out about the blend of the poisoned tea, I didn't want the police poking around and figuring out that it was Wendy's tea, and maybe that she delivered it to Todd. If she did, it was only because of J.J.'s coercion after suffering years of his abuse."

Gabriela watched a tiny curl of steam rise from the surface of her tea. "So, Wendy knows."

Lucinda nodded. "That's what happened the night Wendy called you. She confronted J.J. and accused him of poisoning the tea. He threatened to kill her if she said a word."

"But all this time you were being held on murder charges? Why didn't she speak up before then?" Gabriela asked.

"J.J. controlled Wendy's every thought and action. He'd brainwashed her. So when he told her I had murdered Todd, Wendy believed it. But she couldn't forget about the tea she had brought to Todd because J.J. had told her to do it."

"You have to tell the police," Gabriela insisted.

"Why? J.J. is dead. If they start to question Wendy, that young woman's life will be ruined. She's not an accomplice, she's a victim!"

They said little to each other for several minutes. Then Lucinda got up and poured the tea through a strainer into their cups.

The peppermint and anise filled Gabriela's mouth as she took a sip, engaging her senses of taste and smell. She wondered if the foxglove added to Todd's tea had altered the taste, or had he only experienced the calmness of the catnip. He must have savored it, because he drank enough of the tea to ingest a fatal dose of digitalis.

Her thoughts wandered to the gardens outside and the small circle in the deepest shadows where Lucinda cultivated monkshood, hellebore, and belladonna for reasons that she had never explained. Maybe knowing they grew there, with all their potency, was enough without Lucinda having to use them, or so Gabriela hoped.

Glancing up from her cup, still pondering these thoughts, Gabriela looked into Lucinda's eyes and saw her compassion for Wendy and something else she could not name at first. Then it revealed itself in Lucinda's strong brows, not pinched in worry but relaxed in assurance. Lucinda had been willing to put her own life on the line, even if that meant spending her last years in prison, to protect someone she cared about; to help, not harm.

"Okay," Gabriela said at last. "This is safe with me. For Wendy." She held up her cup and clinked it against Lucinda's, a toast and a bond to secrecy.

ACKNOWLEDGEMENTS

With gratitude, first and foremost, to my family: my husband and beloved life partner, Joe Tulacz; our son, Pat Commins, and daughter-in-law, Grace Vangel; and our niece, Stephanie Crisafulli. Dear sister, Jeannie Zastawny, for her loving heart, and brother-in-law Ben Zastawny, my gracious, patient, and faithful reader.

For my cousin, Melanie Stanfill, and her dark green canoe—the fiberglass kind that weighs a ton, and her husband, Alan Stanfill; thank you both for hospitality and great conversations.

To my aunts: Mary Helen Colloca and Margaret Crisafulli—matriarchs, role models, and all-around rockstars. To cousins near and far, especially Colette Robinson and Peter Regan.

To long-time friends, especially Janie Gabbett, JoAnn Locy, Margo Selby, and Susan Dolan. To new friends, Ella Indra and Len Seligman in Oregon, Malia Lazu in Boston, and Cecily Morrison in Oswego. A special thanks to my friend, cheerleader, and writer extraordinaire: Laura Roe Stevens. And to Cindy Jensen who read my pages with a sharp eye and an encouraging heart.

To my agent, Delia Berrigan Fakis, and to Sharlene Martin of Martin Literary Management, with more gratitude than I could ever squeeze into one sentence.

To my publisher, Woodhall Press, for enthusiasm and partnership, especially Colin Hosten, David LeGere, Miranda Heyman, Matt Winkler; and for Paulette Baker for a careful and thorough editing of this manuscript. And to Dana Isaacson, editorial advisor, for invaluable guidance.

To my publicist Lisa Munley of TLC Book Tours, and to Daniel Gefen and Gefen Media for my awesome podcast tour. To online arts magazine PersimmonTree.org for good words and great promotion.

And a special salute to the people of my hometown, Oswego, New York—an extraordinary community with a long history and incredible natural beauty. I am so fortunate to have grown up there and to draw on this place as the inspiration for my fictional Ohnita Harbor. Don't take my word for it—go visit: the Lake Ontario shoreline, Fort Ontario, the H. Lee White Marine Museum, River's End Bookstore—and, of course, the library that really does look like a castle.

ABOUT THE AUTHOR

Patricia Crisafulli is an award-winning *New York Times* best-selling author. She earned a Master of Fine Arts (MFA) degree (fiction concentration) from Northwestern University, where she received the Distinguished Thesis Award in Creative Writing. Patricia also studied in the prestigious Bread Loaf writers' program (in Sicily).

In summer 2019 Patricia received the grand prize for fiction from TallGrass Writers Guild/Outrider Press and was published in its anthology, *Loon Magic and Other Night Sounds*. She was also nominated for a Pushcart Prize. A collection of her short stories and essays, *Inspired Every Day*, was published by Hallmark.

The recipient of five Write Well Awards from the Silver Pen Association for her short stories, Patricia has been published in a series of anthologies featuring award winners. She is also the founder of FaithHopeandFiction.com, a popular e-literary magazine that features original fiction, essays, and poetry.

A former journalist, Patricia was a correspondent for *Reuters America* and has been published in *Forbes,* the *Wall Street Journal,* and the *Christian Science Monitor*. Today she is a communications consultant for a variety of companies, from tech start-ups to publicly traded firms.